INFINITE DIMENSIONS
POWERSHIFT

INFINITE DIMENSIONS

POWERSHIFT

CAITLIN DEMARIS MCKENNA

JENNIFER GRAHAM

MACKENZIE REIDE

PAUL SMITH

MICHELLE A. BELGRAVE

STEVEN L. ROSENHAUS

MICHAEL BEN-ZVI

JENNJETT MEDIA

Infinite Dimensions
Powershift

JennJett Media
New York, NY USA
www.jennjettmedia.net

ISBN 978-0-9994136-5-4

Table of Contents

Preface

The *Infinite Dimensions* anthologies have always strived to tell stories of hope and the promise of something better. But too often, how hope plays out depends significantly on who holds the reins of power. Power can make hope manifest, but it can also blunt its impact or stop change in its tracks.

Since the publication of our last anthology, the existential struggle we've faced was on who most deserved to wield power at the highest levels of government and whether or not that power was legitimate or not. Who has the power lies at the heart of any desire for change. Without power, you can achieve nothing. That said, the nature of what constitutes power can vary wildly. It needn't necessarily be political or military supremacy. Enough loud voices in the street, on social media, or even in a conference room can have power all their own to shape new outcomes.

These thoughts were what went into the stories that make up Infinite Dimensions: Powershift, our latest collective conversation, this time on the nature of power, what it changes, where it succeeds, where it fails, how we reach for it during difficult times, and what would we do with power if we were to achieve it.

Because, to quote Alice Walker, "the most common way people give up their power is by thinking they don't have any."

The Infinite Dimensions Team

Acknowledgments

As with our previous collection of stories, this collaboration would not have been possible without the many people who helped to support us and our writing along the way.

A special thanks to Valery Rodolico for her time and effort in proofreading our stories and ensuring consistency and quality throughout, and to our diligent beta readers: Shareen, Miranda, Brandy and Zoe. And thanks to friends and family, and all those who offered words of encouragement in this endeavor.

Queenright

Caitlin Demaris McKenna

"Queenright" refers to the state of a bee colony when it has a queen in the hive. I wanted to examine circumstances that might shake up traditional bee colony structure. What changes might drive bees to abandon that hierarchy? This story, set against a backdrop of ecological devastation and agricultural adaptation, is my effort to explore that question.

queenright — adj. (of a colony of bees)
    having a queen in the hive

The bees were dancing strangely. I noticed the change in their behavior as soon as my eyes adjusted to the glow of the lab's fluorescent lights. Normally, the bees' fuzzy yellow and black bodies flowed smoothly through the artificial hive's translucent tubes: here and there, clusters of workers would move in tandem as they danced the locations of fresh nectar to their fellows. The workers already endowed with tasks wouldn't pay them any attention. But today...

Rivers rather than rivulets of bees streamed from the peripheral channels of the hive and the meadows outside into the hive's heart. Little eddies marked where bees danced amid the stream, almost as if they were directing the others—not toward fresh fields, but deeper inside.

The experimental hive was a horizontal complex of translucent tubes and boxes, their sides filigreed with honeycomb and growing larvae. It filled most of the single lab we'd been allotted, with worktables and computer stations jammed against the sides of the room. A grotty prep counter and minifridge, the closest we had to a break area, took up one back corner.

At the moment, "we" meant me and my co-researcher, Julio. We'd had a couple post-doc assistants at the start of the project when resources were more flush, but we'd lost them to other, sexier projects, along with a chunk of our funding.

Julio hunched over a lab bench, fist curled around a paper cup of coffee and a printed report in his other hand. I tapped the table near his hand and he blinked owlishly.

"What's up with the colony?" I asked.

He brushed black bangs that were permanently too long out of his eyes. Julio looked more like an undergrad than the thirty-something junior scientist he really was—some combination of his laidback demeanor and the ever-present takeout coffee. "That's what I'm trying to figure out," he said.

"Does ART have any guesses about their behavior?"

ART was our shorthand for the Apical Research Translator, a boring name for a groundbreaking technology—a computer that interpreted the bees' dance language and rendered it into something like human speech.

Julio squinted at the printout. "Only that this new behavior is anomalous but within the project's parameters." He nodded toward the teeming bodies inside the hive. "It's organized behavior, whatever it is."

Neither of us wanted to voice what unorganized behavior would mean. The random, staggering throes of a colony succumbing to collapse, as so many unaugmented honeybee colonies had done in the last quarter century. Even with all the rigorous protocols the lab had in place to protect our bees from possible sources of contamination—mites, viruses, pesticides, other things we hadn't yet discovered—it was a constant shadow.

Organized or not, I didn't understand the bees' dancing, and that made me nervous. I left Julio to the printout and leaned over the large transparent box that was the center of the hive.

The vertical honeycombed chambers should have been filled with workers caring for larvae, or depositing nectar to be turned into honey or mixed with pollen into "bee bread." And it was filled—brimming, in fact—with workers. But not at their allotted tasks.

A dull gold and black ball of bees seethed in the hive's innermost chamber. Transparent, thinner-than-paper wings vibrated in their hundreds all over the living mass, which was adding to itself by the second as more bees poured in.

I recognized that behavior, although it shouldn't have been possible in this species. Then the question I hadn't asked struck me like a door slamming open. "Where's the queen?"

Before Julio could do more than turn at the panic in my voice, I was at the temperature controls for the hive. I turned down the interior thermostat carefully—too steep a drop in temperature would be as disastrous as doing nothing.

Julio was beside me by the time the first bees started to drop off the swarm, their limbs and wings made sluggish by the increasing cold. They plopped on their backs, legs pumping slowly, dazed but alive. The ones further in were dead, I was sure, not from cold but heat.

"What the hell, Jenna?" Julio said. Then his eyes widened at the disintegrating bee ball. "Are they swarming their queen?"

My throat felt tight enough to burst. I couldn't answer him, but the scene unfolding in the hive was answer enough. As the cold-blasted bees crawled away, a fan of dead ones emerged. Those would have been the first to envelop their queen, in a vibrating caul of wings that raised the ambient temperature inside the ball to lethal levels. It was the defense mechanism of a different bee species: the Japanese honeybee, *Apis cerana japonica.* A hornet foolish or hungry enough to invade a Japanese honeybee hive would find itself swarmed by bees that literally heated it to death.

Except our bees weren't Japanese honeybees. And the colony had just killed its queen.

The swollen yellow and black body that had been the hive's heart and brain was still except for a few clonic twitches running through her legs. A wave swept through her workers: more clusters of dancers formed, some still stumbling from cold. The rest of the colony seemed to listen before streaming away from the center of the hive.

Julio swore under his breath. "What just happened?"

The words I finally found were as bitter as bee venom. "The end of our research just happened."

#

Tell most people you research bugs, and they'll assume you find interesting ways to kill them. Agriculture does a good job of making it seem like most insect research is about pest control, and I went to school with more than a few people who went on to develop better natural insecticides or whatever. But I didn't get my entomology degree to kill insects; I was that weird kid who loved insects, who cried when she stepped on a bug by accident, who spent her summers studying the anthill in the backyard with a magnifying glass and a sample jar.

But in a weird backwards way, I did start studying bees because of dead insects.

My grandparents got the beehive when I was four. Watching them install it on the flat roof of their apartment complex is one of my earliest memories. The hive itself wasn't impressive, just a plain wooden box with slats of wood you could pull out from the top. But then my grandpa (kitted out in a canvas suit and netted hat) removed one of the slats to reveal an entire living world. The first sight of thousands of furry bee backs and vibrating wings milling over the precious honeycomb was one I'll never forget, for all that I watched him harvest honey dozens of times afterward.

I'll also never forget the day the hive died. My grandpa lifting out the wood slat like he had so many times before, only this time its surface seemed to dissolve. Bees dropped off in clumps, as if stunned, to fall to the concrete roof, legs shuddering in their last moments.

My grandparents tried to explain to me what happened—the weather had fluctuated for weeks that spring, a string of warm days plunging into cold snaps that probably made the colony susceptible to disease—but try to explain something to an inconsolable four-year old. I only knew that I'd watched a world die. And that I wanted to stop it from happening again.

So I went into apiculture research. The study of bees. Most people have fuzzier feelings toward bees relative to other insects.

They associate them with honey and with their role in pollinating so many of the world's food crops. That part's been pretty hard to ignore in the last couple decades.

Julio and I cancelled our planned tests for that shift. We spent the next eight hours going over our research notes trying to identify what could have caused the bees' murderousness toward their own queen. I was aware even as I did so that we weren't likely to find a single cause: a thousand factors could have fed in to the behavior. Although each bee was a fairly simple organism, together the colony approached a complexity that defied modeling, like a galaxy or a human brain.

We could rule some things out, though: the colony in our experimental pod was plain old *Apis mellifera*, the European honeybee. Other divisions of AgriCon, our parent company, worked with genetically modified bees—hybrids of several bee species who would (theoretically) be resistant to infection and pesticides through hybrid vigor. One of those hybrids incorporated genes from the Japanese honeybee, but our bees didn't have those genes.

Our experiments up until this morning had been decidedly less fancy. I don't have anything against GMOs—try working in agriculture and rising to a position of any influence if you do—but my proposal was based on KISS rules: Keep It Simple, Stupid. Instead of engineering hybrid bees, Julio and I had been inoculating their diet with fungi the bees already used to boost their immune systems.

I know—people who made it past the "so you study bugs" conversation starter usually wrinkled their noses once I mentioned it also involved fungus. But it had been working: the experimental groups we'd shocked with pathogens and mites had been able to shrug them off without the blight spreading through the colony. I'd been excited to test another vector. Hopeful, until I'd walked into the lab today.

Dusk was purpling the lab's plexiglass windows when Julio finally made me get off my bench. "We're not solving this tonight," he said. "Go home. Eat. *Sleep*."

There were dark rings under his own eyes. I nodded. "You too."

I didn't look at the colony as I exited the building. California's Central Valley opened up before me as I drove my secondhand Toyota out of the research campus. On either side of the road stretched wide fields that used to be home to acres of lettuce, tomatoes, cantaloupes, peaches, and other bee-dependent crops.

They were different now. The lumpy, spiky silhouettes of prickly pears marched away on one side, the darting shapes of the bats that pollinated them flickering overhead like a graphical glitch in the sky. The fields on the other side had been planted with more traditional fruit trees.

Even as night fell, those orchards were still lined with suited migrant workers, carefully hand-pollinating the flowers one at a time with pipettes. Tedious work, though less backbreaking and better paid than the pickers. You were lucky if you could get it, Julio had said once, with a heaviness in his voice I hadn't heard before or since. His family had immigrated a generation ago, before the current wave of refugees, but they'd come to California from the same places, for the same reasons.

The commute from campus to my apartment was close to an hour. Full dark had set in when I pulled up in front of the four-apartment complex. I dumped my work bag in the tiny foyer and thought about ordering food. But the effort seemed too much, and anyways I couldn't be reckless with money. I'd already spent as much on groceries this month as I dared. I ate a PB&J—the "J" part of the equation advertised strawberry, but was little more than sugar and artificial flavor—and slept on the couch.

#

The next morning, I arrived to a crude sign tacked up on the wall of the break area. On 8x11 paper, Julio had written with a black marker "Worker Bees of the World Unite!" Underneath it was a doodle of a flower crossed with a sickle. I stared at it for a full inhale-exhale cycle, aware of him hunched over his microscope in my peripheral vision, ostentatiously pretending not to watch me.

"This isn't funny," I said.

"You don't like it?" he asked.

"If this project goes south, so does our funding." What little there was left of it. "Our jobs." My apartment with its kitchen cabinets full of ramen noodles. I guessed I could live out of my car, plug a hot plate into the dash.

But I saw something other than black humor behind his smile. "Yesterday was bad," he said, "but the colony seems to be doing fine, Jenna. All of ART's readings on their behavior have been normal since last night."

"That's not possible." I found myself checking the activity logs on ART's screen. The system hadn't detected any disordered behavior of the kind that could presage a collapse. The colony had been running as smoothly as ever after cutting off its own head.

Julio waved me to his workbench. "I think I might have a hypothesis. Look here." I took his seat and peered into the micro-scope. It wasn't especially powerful, only 10X or so; we didn't need huge magnification to work with insects.

A bee corpse lay on the sample dish. Julio had carefully cut the head capsule away from the thorax, and opened up the thorax and abdomen dorsally. Lining the exposed body cavity and inside its head were tiny, glistening white threads. Fungal mycelia.

"I sacrificed one to see if I could detect any physiological changes, and I found this," he said in a low voice. "I sequenced the mycelia. It's our inoculation."

I blinked as though the fungal threads were something I had to clear from my vision. "Our fungus infected the bees?"

"*This* bee, anyway. I haven't dissected any others." There was a reluctance I didn't understand in Julio's voice. "Anyway, I'm not sure I'd call this an infection."

I pulled my eye away from the microscope. "You said you had a hypothesis?"

"We wanted to give our bees an immune boost, right? But what if it propagated through their bodies? We know trees communicate through fungal mycelia in their roots; maybe something like that's happening here."

Though my first instinct was to dismiss the idea, I stayed quiet. Bees normally communicate through a combination of pheromones and dancing, and their coordination is ultimately controlled by the queen. But mycelial networks are decentralized, with no one part being more important than the others. Julio hadn't said as much, but if a mycelial network had developed in and was transmitting messages between the bees, that network wouldn't need to be hierarchical. It could operate without a leader.

We didn't have evidence of a mycelial network yet. Julio had just sacrificed one bee. "I'll take more samples." I started toward the hive's sample box where I could coax in a few bees for testing.

"Wait." Julio put a hand on my shoulder. "I don't know if we should."

I shrugged him off. "It's just a few bees. It shouldn't hurt the colony."

"If I'm right—if the mycelia are acting like a neural network for the hive, it could be bad to disrupt it."

"You think the colony cares if we harvest a few bees?" It sounded ridiculous when I said it aloud; then again, so was the idea of the colony killing its queen.

Julio's shoulders slumped, but he didn't relent. "We're in uncharted territory here. I'm just saying it might be smarter to learn what we can through noninvasive methods first."

Which was how I found myself using ART's computer program to talk to bees.

#

Directly under ART's console and monitor was the box where we stored our robot worker bees. All the little robots were currently at full charge; we hadn't used them since the early days of the project, when we were testing and refining ART's understanding of the colony's dances. Often the best way to do so had been to use the robots to test dance sequences and see if the bees followed their directions to the correct experimental meadows outside.

I deployed the robots and directed them to one of the hive's major arteries where many workers were passing by. A handful of workers detached from the stream and formed a little eddy of their own nearby.

"Okay." I rubbed my hands over the keyboard. "Um. What should I say?"

"Greetings, comrades," Julio said under his breath. The amusement in his eyes was back.

I cleared my throat.

"How about 'hello'?" he said.

"It's a start." I typed it in. Our dictionary of bee language was pretty limited. We had dance patterns and pheromonal signals figured out for *honey, nectar, flower, field, predator, larva, queen,* and a few verbs like *harvest, feed,* and so on, but "hello" doesn't exist if you're a bee. Instead, ART translated the phrase into the closest equivalent, a simple dance meant to draw the workers' attention. The human equivalent would be someone waving their arms on a crowded sidewalk and shouting, "Look at me!"

The cluster of workers who had stopped to watch took it in with beady black eyes. Their antennae twitched. Then one of them scuttled forward into the circle our robots' dance had cleared and weaved a dance of its own.

ART processed it for at least thirty seconds. Its translation appeared one letter at a time onscreen, with a slowness that felt like hesitation even though a computer program isn't capable of doubt.

+Hello

+Not bee

+Not colony

+Honey taker

+Bee killer

"Whoa," Julio said.

I stared at the electronic words, those little accusatory jabs of white on black, and the first thing I felt was indignation. I know, it's absurd given what those words signified. But my first thought was they were being unfair.

I'd turned down projects with twice the funding, taken the

crappy salary and accepted the lack of research assistants. I'd bitten my tongue through funding meetings with our supervisor as he explained how AgriCon was shrinking its R&D budget despite turning record profits. All because I wanted to save bees from the ecological dangers they were facing without turning them into something they weren't—without creating Frankenbees through gengineering or robotic augmentation.

And now they were accusing us of killing them.

My stomach sank as I remembered the little corpse under Julio's microscope. "Okay," I said. "I think we got off on the wrong foot—tarsus, whatever." That's an insect foot, for you non bug nerds.

Trying not to feel ridiculous, I typed, "I'm sorry for harvesting one of your colony." I wasn't sure what ART would make of "sorry"—another word without a cognate—but its vocabulary included terms for bad and danger and illness and other things bees cared about. I hoped it would find something workable.

After our robots finished putting the message across, the single worker—their spokesbee?—vibrated its tiny body and wings again.

+One bee =/= us

Meaning? I replied.

+One bee / colony

+Is as

+One cell / honey taker

Julio drummed his fingers on the edge of the hive, lightly as to not disturb the colony. "It's saying one bee to them is like one cell to a human."

I tapped the last line. "I gathered that. So, 'honey takers' is their name for humans? That's not too flattering."

He shrugged. "It's accurate."

True—the entire practice of apiculture relied on a give-and-take mutualism between humans and bees: we provided them a readymade hive, and in exchange took the extra honey the colony produced. But it wasn't an agreement the way the contract between me and AgriCon was. The bees hadn't had a say before now. Should I be surprised they had their own ideas about how humans exploited their colony's resources, given how we'd screwed up that balance?

Julio made a motion toward the keyboard. "Can I…"

"Sure."

I watched over his shoulder as he typed, *Why did the colony kill its queen?*

The answer was almost instant: *+Sick*

That was news to me. AgriCon had acquired new starter colonies for this project; the queen should have been less than two years old, and they lived five to ten years. Although there had been a disturbing trend of seemingly healthy queens dying young. Researchers weren't sure if it was malnutrition, infection or some other vector. Had our bees picked up on something like that?

I bit my lip and typed, *Your queen was sick?*

+No fungus

+Not part of colony

Julio breathed in sharply.

"Looks like you may be onto something," I said, and typed another line: *How will the colony reproduce itself?*

+New queen growing

I seized on that claim. If the colony was growing a new larval queen, that was something we could verify. A single queen larva would be another anomaly, further proof the colony was changing its fundamental structure: normally, multiple queens were induced to grow either when the old queen died or the colony grew beyond its hive and had to split into daughter colonies. The strongest of the new young queens stung her competition to death before taking the old queen's place.

Normal bees wouldn't be capable of disobeying the queen's pheromonal signals preventing them from turning regular larva into queens. But it was clear we weren't dealing with normal bees.

I diverted three of our robot workers to circulate among the hive and do a visual and olfactory scan for any new cells that might house the infant queen. While I waited, I typed another question into the console.

A researcher isn't supposed to factor the interests and desires of her subjects into her experiments. Sure, ethics govern what kind of experiments we can run. But beyond ethical considerations, the person or rat or bee experimented on is an ontological black box. For purposes of the experiment, their desires are assumed not to exist.

Yet I found myself asking, *What does the colony want?*

The little bee that had danced its side of the conversation seemed to watch me, though I couldn't have been more than a mountainous shape to it. Then it began.

+Honey taker use bad water on fields

+Make bees sick

+Make colony sick

My heart juddered in recognition. "Pesticides," I said. "It's talking about pesticides."

Before Julio could reply, more text scrolled across ART's

screen:

+No more bad water

"Amen to that," Julio whispered. I didn't ask him why he was whispering; this was an exchange as momentous as it was absurd. I still had no idea how we were going to write it up in our notes, let alone our report for the quarterly review coming up way too soon.

The bee was still going:

+Honey taker bring fungus to other colonies

+Make colonies stronger

+Fungus = no more colonies sick

The bee seemed to face us as it halted its dance. Its wings fluttered and it started one last string, shorter than the previous one.

+No more honey

#

The colony carried out its threat—or kept its promise—over the next few weeks. Our robot workers recorded a decrease in honey production within the hive: it wasn't enough to cut into the reserves the colony made for its own use, but we couldn't justify harvesting any off the top.

There were other changes, too. Our robots confirmed the colony was growing a single new queen; though I obviously couldn't sacrifice her for testing, visual scans confirmed the fungus was growing on the larval queen. She would be part of the mycelial network.

And while the workers used to harvest nectar from all of our experimental meadows, now they refused to pollinate any fields we'd treated with pesticides. It didn't stop there. There were certain crops they refused to touch, even though they were untreated. The almond trees, for example.

I asked the colony about that one evening. For once Julio had gone home before me; I couldn't concentrate on writing at my apartment (maybe because my "desk" at home was a card table and kitchen chair), so I'd stayed into the evening to work on our report for the quarterly review. But I found myself staring at the screen. It wasn't that I didn't know what to write; I had reams I could have written, all of which I imagined would result in either the company's disbelief or the termination of our project.

So I shut the laptop screen and fired up ART.

Why did you stop pollinating the almond trees?

A worker—I'd long given up trying to determine if any of them were the one that had danced on the first day—spun and fluttered. *+Humans use pesticide on almond trees.*

We'd expanded our working vocabulary since that day. I'd made sure they learned the word "human", for one. Maybe I was still nettled by the bees' name, "honey taker", accurate or not.

Not these almond trees, I typed. *This grove is clean.*

My interlocutor wasn't impressed. *+Other almond groves and other humans use pesticide. Not like Jenna-human.*

I chewed that over. At least the colony had made an exception for me. *So you won't pollinate the almonds as long as some humans use pesticides on them?*

+Correct. The colony chooses not to harvest plants that hurt it.

I didn't argue with it. There was nothing in the colony's logic I wanted to argue with. Every living being is driven to seek things that benefit it—food, shelter, opportunities to reproduce—and avoid things that hurt it. But what I couldn't tell the colony was that it was part of an agricultural system that hadn't been designed with its benefit in mind.

Humans had imported honeybees to North America as useful

tools, ones that often supplanted or competed with the region's native bees. Our research had been in service of improving that tool, making it stronger and more resilient. But we hadn't been prepared for that tool to talk back, to start choosing what it would and wouldn't do.

And I knew the company funding us wouldn't be either.

#

"Do you think we're going to become victims of our own success?" I asked.

Julio looked up from his sopa de tortilla. "What do you mean?"

We were in a corner booth of his favorite Mexican restaurant. Green and red bunting decorated the walls, alternating with small photographs from the owner's hometown of Nogales. I liked the food—Nogales cuisine-flavored street food that was both tasty and affordable, a justifiable monthly luxury for me—but tonight I'd been too preoccupied to do more than pick at my chili relleno.

I set down my forkful of poblano pepper. "We created something amazing, right? Or at least facilitated its creation." The mycelial network we'd used on the bees had done most of the work. "But I don't know if the world is ready for an intelligent bee colony."

He sipped his soup, studying the printed vinyl tablecloth with a furrowed brow. "Maybe it's not ready for them, but I think it needs them. Relying on bats and human labor to pollinate major crops isn't a tenable position."

"I agree." I twisted the edge of the plasticky cloth in my fist. I hadn't said anything about the colony's demonstrations of resistance to Julio, but I realized that was where this conversation had been going all along. "AgriCon wanted us to make bees resistant to colony collapse, not ones that can decide not to pollinate a major crop because they don't like the way it's cultivated."

"You know, maybe they have a point." The edge in his voice made me sit up. "Agriculture does a lot of bad shit to make their profits. Spraying pesticides, sure, but it's also a terrible industry to work in for everyone except those at the top."

"And researchers like us," I said.

Julio gave me a wry smile I wasn't sure I'd seen on him before. "Don't want to be lumped in with the pickers?"

My face grew warm. "That's not it—"

He shrugged away my denial. "It's okay. That's part of the con—the execs make us think we're doing more important work than the people at the bottom. Make it so we don't have to put up with the shittiest parts of the industry—fifteen-hour shifts with no benefits or even a guarantee we'll have a job next week. And maybe there are a couple extra zeroes on our paychecks, but it doesn't mean any of us can save up month to month. Or see any of the profits our work generates."

I ate some chili relleno to cover my embarrassment. It was more acute because Julio had a point. I'd gotten used to seeing the workers picking and pollinating in the Central Valley as part of the landscape; figures from a pastoral painting who were vaguely connected to the produce I bought at the grocery store and the food I ordered at restaurants. The pepper on my plate had been hand pollinated and handpicked by people I might never meet, but who worked meters from our research campus.

"I guess I've had blinders on," I said. "Project tunnel vision."

Julio waved this aside. "Sure. Thing is, our colony is part of the same industry. Bees always have been, but these ones have a voice now. And they're doing what more of us should do—refusing bad work."

The words came out too smoothly for him not to have thought this through. I made an encouraging noise.

"I'm worried about AgriCon's response too," Julio said. "If they shut us down it'd mean more than our jobs. They'd probably destroy the colony."

I closed my eyes. That thought had been with me often over the past few weeks. "I don't know how to save them."

"They're in a stronger position than you think," Julio said. "They already have leverage; without them, certain crops won't get pollinated unless humans do it." He lowered his voice, even though there were only a few other patrons in the restaurant. "That's the other piece. They need people in their corner. People who have a stake in how crops are getting pollinated."

It clicked. "The fieldworkers."

His smile this time was pure Julio, the optimistic lab partner I'd met years ago. "A lot of fieldworkers are going to lose their jobs if the bees come back. But maybe we can get ahead of that, show them they're on the same side."

He was right about the first part: the big commercial concerns would fire the pollinators, or bust them back to worse-paid picking jobs, as soon as they were no longer needed. But I wasn't sure how I felt about the second part.

"Introduce the colony to the fieldworkers?"

Julio nodded. "I know a lot of the people out there. Their grandparents picked with my grandparents. That's the kind of community you hang on to."

I started to consider it. I trusted Julio to invite the right people, the kind who wouldn't laugh us off or blab to AgriCon about our project. Still, my ingrained impulse toward confidentiality made me shrink at the idea. "We're not supposed to share our research…"

Julio met my eyes and held them long enough until I started to fidget. "If we don't," he said, "our research might end before it can help anyone. Humans or bees."

I'd gone into agricultural science because I wanted to fix the industry's crises, but so many of those crises were self-imposed. Solutions suppressed because they threatened to upend the status quo. I'd wanted our research to change things for the better, and the key word was change. There were interests that wouldn't allow that unless they were forced.

I took a long inhale-exhale. "Tell me what you need me to do."

#

The sun-beaten men and women arrived at our lab in ones and twos. They wore light flannel shirts and worn T-shirts and jeans, baseball caps and bandanas. I recognized the pollinators by the yellow-spattered gloves tucked in their shirt or pants pockets. There were about eight or nine people altogether. I knew none of them, but Julio hugged one, a lean woman in a red kerchief, and shook the hands of two more men. He led the woman over to me.

"Jenna, this is Maria Mendez. She oversees one of the pollination crews."

I shook her hand. "Jenna Sykes. Julio and I are co-researchers on this project."

Maria's handshake was firm and dry. She looked around the small lab, her gaze lingering on the transparent boxes and tubes of the hive. "Julio said you work on honeybee colonies?"

"Yes." I looked at the fieldworkers who'd come. Julio had made the calls to the tight-knit Central Valley immigrant community to set this up; I could only hope what we showed them was worth the time they were sacrificing after their fifteen-hour shifts. I moved in front of the largest, central chamber of the hive, and the field-workers' attention gravitated toward me.

"Thank you all for coming," I said. "I know you're probably tired and want to get home to your families, so I'll try not to take too much of your time."

A man in a 49ers baseball cap cleared his throat. "Julio said your lab is working on something that could affect our jobs?"

I nodded. "Positively, I hope. But it's important you know what we're doing." I activated ART's console and primed the robot workers in their box below it. "We've been exploring ways to make bees immune to colony collapse. In the process, we created a colony that functions like a single brain."

Some of the gathered people's brows creased in confusion. Julio stepped in. "We created intelligent bees," he said. "Individually, each one is like a brain cell—not that smart, but together the colony is as smart as you or me."

"How can you tell?" asked a girl from the back of the room. She looked about fifteen.

I tapped the top of ART's console. "We can talk to them."

We invited people to take turns typing messages into the console and reading the colony's responses. Before the meeting, I'd told the colony to expect visitors. *Other pollinators*, as I'd put it. *Human pollinators.* That had drawn the colony's interest.

The other nut was harder to crack: how to convince the humans that the bees were actually talking to them. Sure enough, a few people, including Maria, thought Julio and I were pulling their legs.

"How do I know you two didn't just program the computer to talk to us?" she asked when it was her turn.

A man who'd introduced himself as Luis nodded. "It's kind of late for April Fool's."

I'd thought of that. It was a demonstration I'd originally planned for the company rep's upcoming visit, but it should work now. "Ask the colony to do something."

Maria started with simple commands: *Go left. Go right. Turn in a circle.* Once the workers completed those, she moved on to a more complex order: *Fly to field B-1 and bring back nectar from the apple trees.*

As a group, we followed the workers through their translucent tubes to field B-1 and watched them dutifully flit among the apple blossoms under their protective dome. "Dios mio," Maria said softly. Several of the others caught their breaths.

She ran the colony through a few more requests, sending them to different fields, even trying to trip them up by deliberately mixing up the field name with the crop planted there. But the colony never faltered, and even gently corrected her "mistakes."

"Okay." Maria sat on a lab stool and crossed her arms. "I'm convinced this is real. Why are you showing us this?"

Luis shrugged and snorted. "It's obvious, isn't it? They're showing us we need to start packing. Once these smart buggers get out we can kiss our jobs goodbye."

Julio took a stool across from Maria, but looked up at Luis. "That's exactly what we don't want to happen."

"There are things the colony told us it won't do," I said. "It refuses to pollinate any crops pesticides are used on, or produce extra honey for human consumption until we fix the system."

"Does that mean the bees are on strike?" the teen girl quipped.

I didn't laugh. "That's exactly what it means. They're vulnerable right now. AgriCon could decide to pull the plug, exterminate them and start over. But not if they have key workers supporting them."

"You're talking about a union," Maria said. "Between the human pollinators who do handle those crops and the colony."

I nodded. Worker bees of the world unite, indeed.

#

The next two weeks were a blur of activity. Julio and I alternated work on our report for the quarterly review with drafting our manifesto of demands over multiple meetings between us, the fieldworkers, and the colony. Neither of us saw much beyond the lab for those weeks, but when the day of the review came, we had a document we could be proud of. One that, I hoped, would open the door to a better future for all the workers in the industry, human and bee.

"So how does the colony survive without a queen?" Jeff Guthrie, the director of the apiculture research division, studied the bustling colony going about its work. I'd already briefed him on the fungal mechanism of the bee's enhanced intelligence and demonstrated their ability to communicate with us through ART's computer. He seemed duly impressed—a little dazed, actually—but was still stuck on the colony's lack of hierarchy.

On ART's screen, I zoomed in on a view of the former queen's chamber. The new queen hadn't yet had her nuptial flight, so she had no store of fertilized eggs, but I guessed that would happen soon. I was curious to see how the colony handled it.

"They still have a queen—a fertile female," I said. "But she's not releasing control pheromones. She lays for the colony, but she's not in charge."

Jeff blinked. "Who is, then?"

"None of them, by themselves. And all of them. It's a distributed, nonhierarchical organization. Kind of like a worker's collective." I paused in case he had questions; when none came, I said, "Let's tour the fields."

We walked together through the rows of apple and almond trees, melon and cucumber and squash fields. I'd given Jeff my tablet so he could review the results of our pollination tests, and he was head-down in the numbers, paying more attention to the screen than the rows of crops. I used the lull to text Julio:

Everyone ready?

Yeah, we're here, he texted. *Bring Jeff back whenever.*

Showtime. My heart turned over in my chest as Jeff cleared his throat. "I'm noticing some gaps in these test records. Looks like you couldn't get the colony to pollinate some crops, like the almonds?"

I took the tablet back from him, hoping he didn't notice how slick my hands were. "Yup, we're working on that. If you come back to the lab I can show you the progress we've made."

I opened the back door leading from the fields to the lab to reveal a room filled with people. Maria and Julio were in front, closest to the central chamber of the hive. The screen mounted to ART's console, currently blank, was turned toward us. Maria held a printed copy of our manifesto in both hands.

Jeff's eyebrows flew upward. "What's this?" He spotted Julio. "Who are all these people? This is a secure research facility."

Julio's throat bobbed as he swallowed, but his voice was steady.

"I know that. And 'all these people' are affected by that research." He nodded to Maria, who stepped forward.

"Maria Mendez. I lead the pollinator crews for AgriCon." She held out her hand and Jeff automatically shook it, though his grip looked a little weak.

"And about those almond trees." I left Jeff's side and typed the question I'd asked the bees weeks ago into the console, then stepped back from the screen.

+Humans use pesticide on crops = no pollination

"This colony is smart," I said in answer to Jeff's silence. "Smart enough it won't just do what we want unless changes are made." Maria handed me the printout and I flipped to the first page.

"We are the first human-bee agricultural workers' collective," I said. "And we have some demands."

Counter and Act
Jennifer Graham

What will someone do for a seat at the table or an invitation to join the club? These were questions I asked myself when writing Counter and Act. *I wondered how such goals were attainable when traditional avenues are blocked.*

"Happy Centennial Incorporation Day!
May your demand grow
And your profits overflow!"

Morgan rolled her eyes at the overly enthusiastic newscaster. "One hundred years since corps took over, no wait, saved the planet. Blah, blah, blah..." As usual Morgan was the first one in, so no one heard the sarcasm in her voice.

The newscaster continued to exalt the day corporations saved the world from economic ruin and environmental disaster. Seven corporations banded together to form a consortium that policed the other corps and kept the world safe from engineering disasters, global malpractice and anything else that might lead to a worldwide catastrophe. She tapped her mini and the holo disappeared from her desk. They policed the others so well that smaller companies were swallowed up and only the seven remained across the globe and moon.

She leaned back in her black leather swivel chair and tugged her turquoise jacket down. Her matching blouse, pants and shoes were the only things that broke the dullness of the office. Everything else was either black or clear glass. Even her desk was clear glass except for the dark cast iron legs.

Morgan steepled her fingers and sighed. So far, this job was a bore. It was healthy boredom though, since everything was going as planned. Her boss Ablington spent most days sequestered in his office with no visitors and few phone calls. She had time to explore the layout of the building through physical or virtual jaunts. The most exciting part of the whole enterprise was the trip from New York to London two months ago. Things were about to pick up though, since Jared Ramsingh's recent retirement initiated the election of a new CEO.

We'll make our way together.

The words echoed in her memory. A promise made months ago on a cold frosty road was about to commence. The man that found her that day expected her to want the same things he wanted — money and power—, and maybe she did, but for different reasons. She wanted stability and maybe a little payback. But power? Power came with more responsibility and constant paranoia because someone always laid in wait to take it from you.

The sound of elevator doors opening drew her from her reverie. Voices drifted in from the hallway outside the office, followed by a woman's uproarious laughter. Arm in arm her boss, Norman Ablington, walked into the reception area with Weimei Li, his latest conquest. Ablington preferred to wine and dine his potential acquisitions. If he was into men as well, he might own half the planet.

Morgan sat up straighter while Ablington paused near the doorway to whisper in Weimei's ear. The other woman laughed when he finished talking, her full attention on Ablington. Morgan twirled a finger around one of her kinky black curls as she waited for them to acknowledge her presence.

Then the hairs on the back of her neck stood up.

Something waited in her periphery to her left and she snapped her head in that direction; the swivel chair creaked at the sudden movement. A gray metal thing sat there silent, unmoving.

Morgan never heard its approach. Some black rubbery polymer covered the bottom of its four spindly legs that cushioned its footsteps on the gray marble floors. All its legs bent at angles normal for a canine, while it sat on its hind legs. Its head was a pentagonal pyramid with two isosceles-shaped darkened screens for eyes on either side. There was a five centimeter metal tail that currently helped the metal animal balance while it sat on the floor. The main body, like the rest of it, was a matte gray metal.

"Ah, I see you've met SCAT!"

"What?" Morgan swiveled to find Ablington and Weimei in front of her desk. She wrinkled her nose. "But scat is –"

"Well yes, the word scat can have a negative connotation, but the naming's a work in progress. I'll have a marketing team come up with something more snappy soon enough." He clapped his hands and rubbed them with fervent enthusiasm. "For now, that's what I'm calling our new supersensory canine android technology for the moment!"

Morgan put her elbows on the desk and rested her chin on her fists. She heaved an inward sigh. He always wanted her full attention when he was in pitch mode.

Ablington stood in the center of the room and waved his hand across imaginary words, as if they appeared in the air above him when he spoke. "It will see in visible, UV and infrared, day or night. Hear five times as many frequencies as a human. Detect smells of any substance. And though it doesn't have a tongue, per say, there's a sensor that juts out of its snout that will do analysis on a variety of substances. As soon as I get R&D to iron out a few power issues."

He lowered his hand and leveled his smug grin at Weimei. "We'll market them to airports, college campuses, hell, with the right AI program they can be every child's personal babysitter. And it's all thanks to this little roboticist right here."

Weimei shook her head, feigning modesty. "I merely did the groundwork. You have the vision."

He grabbed Weimei's shoulders. "Quite right, I do. Once I'm CEO I'll set up production and start the marketing campaign."

"Robotics is sort of a new area for a media company like GMN, isn't it?" Morgan asked.

"I already have a few ideas on how to tie it in to our industry. Don't you worry." He gave Weimei a nod and headed for his office. "We're putting the finishing touches on things for a few hours, and we're not to be disturbed."

Weimei followed him in. When the door closed, the glass wall and door turned from clear to shaded dark brown. Alone again and all was quiet, the soundproofing around Ablington's office preventing any noise from escaping.

A pang of concern for the other woman touched Morgan the moment they went through the door. Would she be alright alone with a man of his reputation? Morgan shook her head. Everyone knew his reputation. The woman knew what she was getting into.

Besides, Ablington would never do anything to jeopardize his chance at CEO. An office scandal was a risk Ablington would avoid at all costs. Of course, rumors circulated about how he became president of GMN, Global Media Network, in the first place.

The last GMN president, Clarke, went on an Antarctic vacation with his wife and a few of his closest employees and their partners. In the middle of the trip, Clarke vanished on the surface. Authorities said he decided to go on a solo walk on the ice but never returned. His wife had claimed to anyone that listened that he would never be so reckless, but no one took her seriously, or at least no one looked into it. Clarke's right-hand man retired from GMN and relocated to the Moon, also a bit suspicious.

Then Ablington became president. A few more of Clarke's people left the company, or disappeared. Disappearing acts in this day and age were no small feat. They involved major identity changes across all major networks or living off the grid. Morgan knew from experience. Despite the missing employees, Ablington had access to all of Clarke's confidential projects—very convenient—and work continued without a hitch anyway.

Now, according to Ablington, CEO was in the bag. He said he was the obvious choice. He had finished three of Clarke's projects and acquired Libre Multimedia covering all of South America in five years. On screen, his family was perfect. His doting wife ran the appropriate charities, his three children worked at GMN and managed to stay out of public trouble. He even owned a real dog and a real cat, appealing to either type of pet owner. Everyone was sure there was no way he could lose.

But Morgan needed him to lose.

Morgan got up, stretched and walked over to the window. Across the Thames, the London Eye was a diminutive structure in front of several towering buildings under construction. It was a bright sunny morning, but the shaded windows let in a small amount of natural light.

She folded her arms as she looked out into the city. Ablington was a narcissist and a sociopath. Unchecked by a CEO, he would reign havoc, not only in the corporation but any locale where GMN operated.

Morgan grew up in one such locale. Ablington worked for a different corp back then in the medical division. Her mother was dead because of his devious nature.

Her office ringtone chimed on her mini and she moved to stand over her desk.

"Answer! Voice only!" Morgan heard the connection. "President Ablington's office."

"Morgan, is it?" asked the haughty voice of Desmond Chesterfield, Director of Research. "Is Ablington there? I'd like to wish him good luck before the board votes."

"Mr. Ablington will be unavailable for the rest of the day, but I'll be sure to give him the message." She clicked the mini off.

Morgan knew the last thing Chesterfield wanted to do was wish anyone good luck. Chesterfield was also in the running for CEO, although he was the least likely candidate to get elected by the board. Young bachelors who visited the *Bake and Shark Shop* on the wrong side of town and rose through the ranks without old family money were unlikely to make CEO.

Still, he made GMN enough money that he had a chance at CEO, along with two other candidates. John Worth, Chief Operating Officer, was the oldest man at the firm, but his twenty-something fourth wife came with her own money and business connections. Kang Danbury, Chief Financial Officer, was perfect on screen with the right family and connections, but if certain proclivities ever came to light, they would keep him out of the running.

They all had perfect lives on screen, but for whatever reason Ablington was the board's favorite. He would become CEO if she did not find something they could use to discredit him in public. He had to be stopped not just for the truth behind the rumors surrounding him, but for the one act she knew made him a monster.

More memories flooded through her, memories of a time before she had a job or a place to live. Tough times ruled her teenage life for a while and she gave herself a little shake before the past made her lose focus.

Morgan sat down at her desk to do some work. Several of the VPs had sent presumptive congratulations to Ablington for his pending promotion. She returned the appropriate responses to each message.

Later she ordered lunch, but not for herself. She would never eat from the same place Ablington's lunch came from, not when so many despised him. It was delivered by a courier bot that resembled a small rectangular tank. She alerted Ablington to its presence and it rolled into his office after he opened the door. Grabbing an energy bar and bottled water from her bag she settled in to work.

An hour later Weimei exited, not that Morgan looked up. The way the other woman's heels clip-clopped along the floor told Morgan she was leaving. Morgan's mini vibrated. She left it two dimensional and stared at the image of the pic she received. An hour later Ablington left alongside the courier bot that led the way as it returned to the restaurant.

Everyone left early the day before a vote and the top two floors of the building, the executive floors, would be as silent as a tomb.

Morgan pulled up a display that listed any active minis or screens on the executive-level floors to check the offices for signs that someone was still at work. One screen was active on the floor below. Fifteen minutes later that shut down. The silence encroached on her surroundings, but yet she waited. She liked the quiet, it gave her focus.

Satisfied the executive floors were empty, she glanced at the door to Ablington's office. After one last look at the pic, the clue she needed, she disconnected her mini from the office link and tucked it in her bag. Now her real work would begin. She walked over, opened the door and froze. The robodog, SCAT, was still in the office.

It sat with its back to her, on its hind legs, a motionless statue. Morgan waited a full minute and it never moved. It must be powered down, she thought. She made slow, careful steps as she crept in front of it, never taking her eyes away. Recalling the basic specs, she looked for a sign SCAT was about to awaken. Its isosceles eyes were dark triangles. She had no idea what Ablington had added to it, if anything. Ablington was a trained roboticist after all and he tinkered with new tech on occasion.

Satisfied that nothing would happen, Morgan turned around to face the picture that was sent to her mini. Dogs Playing Poker. An original Ablington had said one day in one of his usual bragging moods. She felt around the edge of the frame, glancing back on occasion to make sure the robodog stayed still. Part of the lower left frame gave way and she pushed it, releasing a side of the picture from the wall. She swung the framed pic forward to reveal a safe embedded in the wall.

She took out the mini and called up the app that unlocked the safe. It opened with a click. Several data storage devices rested inside. She brought up another app and her mini turned into a data transfer device. It would upload every speck of data in the safe to her private server. Something had to discredit Ablington. While the data uploaded, Morgan turned to check on SCAT. Its eyes were lit electric green. SCAT was waking up. Morgan dove into her bag, while the green pulsed three times on and off. The green turned to two horizontal slits and its hind legs jumped up so it no longer sat. Morgan leveled her EMP gun at SCAT and fired. SCAT made a sputtering sound as the electromagnetic pulse shut down its power. The eyes went blank.

Morgan let out a sigh of relief. She checked her device. A minute left to upload. SCAT was still a motionless object.

#

Memory sparked of another dog in another time and place. After the death of her mother, she had lost the apartment they shared. On the last day of her residence, she packed a bag with her meager belongings and exited the building. The coffee shop across the street had the news playing on a wall and she stopped to peer through the window, not really focused on the images. Morgan retrieved her mini and pulled up her father's number. She stared at it for a long time. A call to him might get her the help she needed. The money he had been sending stopped a year ago, so she was not sure the call would help. Not that her mother had told her about him. She found things out the usual way, by snooping through her accounts.

She sighed, then put the mini away and turned from the coffee shop. Deep in thought, she had walked a block intending to spend the night in a nearby park, when a small brown dog in the middle of the sidewalk halted her advance. It stared at her quizzically, head tilted to the side. She wondered if the animal had a home, or if it was destitute like she was.

Brown Dog cocked his head to one side again and then jumped up to stand next to a man a few feet further down the sidewalk. He wore a gunmetal gray sweatsuit. Shoulder-length hair poked from under his hood about his head, while the edge cast a shadow across his eyes. A blur-tech suit, she thought, kept him anonymous.

"Morgan, right? Or should I say Lazerqueen?" He clasped his hands in front of him and waited.

"Do I know you?" Morgan swallowed, nervous about what might happen next. Was this about her snooping? She thought she had covered her tracks. Except for one time, she never took anything or changed anything, just looked around. It was simply about the challenge to get into a system.

"I doubt you know me, but we know of you." His stance never changed. She barely saw his lips move.

"We?" She looked around again, but no one seemed interested in their conversation.

"Yes, we saw what you did with Aspiron and thought you might like to come work for us." He gestured with his head. "All you have to do is follow me."

"Wait, this does not make any sense." What she did with Aspiron was hack into their system to dig up information on her mother's chip and send it to the newsfeeds. They had modified their one-way signal chips, turning the device into medical receivers that accept signals as well. In secret they tested remote control of somatic functions with limited success, until a few fatal seizures occurred. Her mother had been part of the unlucky few. One person in particular was in charge of the whole operation. Ablington.

She had found the data on the project and sent it out into the virtual ether for all to see. The project was stopped, but Aspiron had put out their own spin that blamed the deaths on the poor health of the patients. No one at Aspiron faced any repercussions.

Morgan had covered her tracks or at least believed no one cared, until this guy appeared in a stealth-tech sweatsuit with his hood up.

"You're not in trouble. Like I said, we have work for someone like you. Just follow me, if you're interested. The corporations are big but sometimes we thwart their plans. Work for us and you'll see." He turned and walked away. Brown Dog barked once and did the same.

The idea of thwarting corps got her attention, plus she had nothing better to do. Morgan followed the pair to an awaiting taxi.

"Is this really about a tech job?" she asked as she hesitated at the open door.

"Of course." Man and dog waited patiently in the backseat for her to get in.

Brown Dog looked pleasant enough panting happily as it eyed her from the floor of the car. Blur-tech made the man anonymous, but once she sat down next to him his face would come into view. She was desperate, she thought, but a ride in a cab beat spending the night in the park. Morgan took a deep breath and hopped in, holding on to a stylus in her pocket, just in case. She would take a swipe at his eye if he tried anything.

Instead of a psychotic kidnapper, he offered her a rare opportunity. A chance to use her skills and hack into Big 7 corps. She settled into her new home, an apartment building, in the city, but off the grid. They had their own power source, a water tower and servers. They only needed to leave the building for food. Quietly, she kept track of Ablington and prepared to send details of any transgressions to authorities if she found them, but he learned to cover his misdeeds after Aspiron. Darkstar became her new family, even the dog that she learned was named Brownie.

Seven years spent with the Darkstar cybergang. Three years in, the disillusionment started. The more she worked for Darkstar, the more information she gleaned about their clients, most of which were corps trying to beat the competition. It was like a zero-sum game. Darkstar sold her skills to the highest bidder. She would never make a difference if she stayed in the cybergang. Morgan plotted her own exit from Darkstar until her current employer found her and changed her life once again.

#

At the moment this new metal dog was her only threat. It sat unmoving, a lifeless thing mimicking life when it was powered up. An AI brain, more powerful than the normal canine cerebrum in the hands of a sociopath like Ablington.

Morgan glanced around the room. The only item on Ablington's desk was a holo of his family. A miniature cadre of children and siblings stared back at her from his desk, surrounding Ablington. Their expressions were blank while their stances exuded confidence. He would seed them throughout the company, placed in key positions, to do his bidding.

Staticky noise drew her attention to SCAT. Green lights flashed.

"Shit!" Morgan checked the upload. 98%!

Her EMP was offline. It needed fifteen minutes to recharge. 99%!

The flashing green had ceased, replaced by two horizontal slits. Pincers protruded in slow motion from what would be a normal dog's mouth. 100%!

Morgan snatched her mini, closed the safe and latched the picture back into place. A spark twinkled at its pincers. Morgan flew past intent on reaching the elevators down the hall. She smacked the down part of the call pad, but nothing happened. The down arrow never lit up and the rest of the pad remained dark. The elevators were offline.

SCAT poked its head out of the office. Morgan dashed for the corner stairwell with SCAT in hot pursuit. It must have turned off power to the elevators, her little EMP gun did not have that kind of range. Plus, the lights were still on.

Morgan crashed through the door to the stairs, the faint pat-pat of SCAT's feet close behind as it chased her. She pushed the door, straining against the resistance of its pneumatic hinges. SCAT appeared in view and rose on its hind legs, in preparation to leap. She shut the door, the robodog hit with a low thud.

After an exhale, Morgan took a moment to think. She could sprint fifteen floors down and hope robodog didn't alert anyone she was coming. Ablington was unlikely to connect SCAT to the network when he wanted his toy's new features to be secret. Otherwise, she could exit on the next floor and try taking the elevator straight to the garage.

Halfway down the steps her musings ceased. A glance back and the door handle rose and fell a few times before the door inched open. Morgan bounded down the stairs; decision made.

What would it do when it reached her? Tase her and wait patiently for Ablington to show up while she lay unconscious? She could end up on the street or would her employer bail her out once again? The specs on the prototype suggested SCAT ran at speeds she had no hope to outrun, at least not for fifteen flights. Anything Ablington worked on had to be faster than the prototype.

Morgan reached the fourteenth floor and exited the stairwell. The hall was similar to the top floor hall, with gold carpet sporting a white border and light tan walls. Bright recessed lighting traveled down the ceiling. While the walls on the upper floor were bare, these walls were lined every few feet with photos of past CEOs, there to remind the lower execs of a position most could never reach. The frames were solid gold and inlaid into the walls. Gold-plated nameplates underneath each picture carried each individual's name, some with the same last names since CEO positions were frequently inherited.

She tapped the call pad for the elevators as she ran, even though she knew the unlit pad meant they were shut down. Just as well, she thought. While the exec floors had no cameras since the higher-ups never liked to be watched, the elevators carried surveillance. She needed to keep her intentions secret until after the board meeting. If Ablington had time to cover his tracks, all efforts would be for naught.

Morgan heard the stairwell door close. A regretful glance back, made her stumble and reach out for the wall. SCAT stood in the center of the hall, just outside the door, its padded feet on the carpeted floor kept its arrival practically silent. It paused, performing a scan she realized. It needed to reassess its new environment.

It stretched its back and suddenly Morgan felt like a matador's red cape in a stadium with a raging bull. She turned before it leapt into a run, her own feet flying. Meanwhile, the inkling of a plan formed in her mind. She turned a corner passing through cubicles assigned to general personnel and executive assistants. Without a look back, at the end of the cubicles she turned right. A memo tacked to a board scratched her cheek as the wind shear she generated lifted it away from the wall.

Morgan slipped into a conference room and closed the door. She pulled out her mini and used her lock app to seal the door. The latch clicked the minute SCAT hit the door. The wall and the door to the conference was frosted glass, and the shadow of SCAT was visible on the other side. The robodog scrabbled at the door for a few seconds, then sat down.

If it found a way in too soon, her plan was foiled. Morgan scanned the room. A black oblong conference table surrounded by twelve black leather swivel chairs occupied most of the space. A walnut brown credenza rested next to the closest wall. It held a water cooler on one end and cups stacked in the center.

There was no window, but the wall adjacent to outside was blank and white. It projected the outside view if the conference room attendees desired it. At least no prying eyes from the outside spied on her at the moment. She shoved the cups to one side and climbed on top of the credenza. Removing the ceiling tile, she hoisted herself into the crawlspace between floors.

The crawlspace was barren. Not the worst place I've been, she thought. Not like Alaska. Then she had been freezing cold and tucked under a space while unknown critters flitted back and forth in the surrounding darkness. That job started simple enough, her crew contracted by climatactivists to shut down a corps secret drilling operation in Denali National Park. The corp was paranoid due to previous attacks and their firewalls were top-notch. She had to connect to their network onsite to get in. Darkstar had found a crawlspace in the site's plans where she could work for a while unseen. It took almost an hour, but she shut down the drill site's systems.

Then an emergency alert set off panic at the site. Not only were the drilling systems offline, but also the fail-safe systems. She shook her head. The resulting explosion threatened the lives of over one hundred people at the site, so she hacked in again and worked until she turned the fail-safes back on. The climatactivists wanted the deaths to promote their cause she realized. They wouldn't be happy with only a shutdown. Darkstar would be angry as well. She packed up, exited the crawlspace and snuck away from the site. No one was at the rendezvous point. She continued to walk, leaving the drill site behind. The nearest town was a mile and a half, while sundown was approaching. Her feet started to hurt from the cold when a man drove towards her in a black jeep. She ignored the vehicle until it swerved and stopped, blocking her path.

The driver poked his head out of the window. "Need a lift?"

He looked oddly familiar. That made her stop. He wasn't an exec checking on the operation or a lackey sent to investigate, not the way he was dressed all in black with no company logo in sight.

"Who are you?"

"I'm someone who wants to help." He paused. "Well…maybe we can help each other."

Morgan looked down the road. She had another hour to walk before she reached the bus depot, then she had to wait until morning for an actual bus.

He smiled. "Look, maybe you could step inside my car and we could talk about this. I promise I'll take you wherever you want to go."

And just like that she remembered where she had seen him or someone like him—in pictures with her mother.

"Devereaux?" she asked.

His smile grew. "Well Morgan, John Devereaux was our father's name. You can call me Desmond. I use my mother's last name, Chesterfield. Father was a bit of a rolling stone."

"How did you know my name?"

"I've been trying to keep track of all my family." He opened the car door. "Sorry I didn't contact you sooner. You seemed alright at Darkstar until recently. Why don't I program this thing to take us back to civilization while we talk?"

Morgan nodded and for the second time in her life she entered a stranger's car. At least she was reasonably sure this man with his red kinky hair and his features like a younger version of her father's, was a relative.

They sped past rugged Alaskan terrain in silence. After a few minutes Desmond said, "I would like you to come work for my company. You'd be working under this man." He pulled up a holo of Ablington.

Bile rose in her throat. "Why would you think I'd work for him?"

"I know what he did to your mother and the others in that medical trial. He's done so much worse since then and if he takes over GMN— that's where I work— he'll have even more power and do so much worse. Help me take him down."

Morgan considered it. Another chance to ruin the man responsible for so many deaths. Still, she wanted caution. "What's your angle?"

"Honestly, when I takeover GMN I believe I can do a better job. And I'm not a tyrant. I just need more people I can trust by my side."

Morgan was not sure he could be trusted, but as soon as she found a link, she would research Desmond Chesterfield. They arrived at a tiny inn where she promised to give him her decision in the morning. She spent the night investigating Desmond and GMN. Satisfied that his interest was legitimate, she agreed to join him.

They detailed a plan and she had flown back to New York to grab her few possessions and then on to London. Here she was, in another crawlspace with dust particles that floated in the dim light. Morgan replaced the tile and the space returned to darkness. Feeling in her bag for her mini, she found it and selected a flashlight app. The small light gave her some illumination in the empty crawlspace. She had to bend her head as she knelt, then slid away from the conference room, careful to stay on the support beams. When she thought she was over the next room she removed the tile and dropped into the darkness below.

Jordana had landed in between two stacked shelves in the supply room, just as she wanted. Silence enveloped the narrow room. The door to the room was solid and no light from the hall ventured in. She made sure the door was locked. Shadows bounced off items as she searched for what she needed. She plugged her EMP device into an outlet at the back of the room and searched the shelves.

A huge empty shredder bin. Twine. Tape. A few other items.

Morgan gathered the supplies, quickly yet quietly, and piled them on the floor. She assembled what she needed—an oversized rabbit trap. After a final check of her setup, she pushed the trap against the door and retrieved her EMP. Standing against the shelves to one side of the trap, Morgan held onto the string that would release the trap. She turned off the light on her mini and stored it away in her bag. Grasping her EMP in her other hand, she took a deep breath. Morgan unlocked the door and slid it open, just enough for a robodog to fit through and enter the trap.

Nothing happened for a few beats of a second, so Morgan yelled, "Hey! C'mon little doggie! Hey!"

She repeated the cry, yet nothing happened. *What if it returned to Ablington's office?* She needed to erase the thing's memory before Ablington found it.

Her efforts were met with more silence. Morgan opened the door wider and peeked out into the hall. The hallway was empty.

Morgan sighed. She quickly retraced her steps along the route she had taken. She paused at the corner by the assistant cubicles and peeked at the empty hallway before moving forward. Crouched low. She wanted a clear shot when she found it, she moved to the other end and peered around the corner. SCAT was now at the door to the stairway, a grappling hook protruded from what passed for its mouth, turning the door handle.

"Hey, you!"

SCAT released the door handle and swiveled its head towards her. Visual contact established, SCAT backed away from the door while its grappling appendage retracted. It leapt forward and Morgan sprinted.

She raced back, diving into the supply room. In seconds, she had the sliding door repositioned so the room opened to only the trap. Again, she held the twine in one hand and the EMP device in the other.

"C'mon! C'mon!" SCAT ran straight to her voice and right into the trap. Morgan pulled on the snare and the former shredder basket covered most of SCAT. Its back legs stuck outside of the basket. Morgan leaned on the basket to keep the robodog from escape. It floundered and jumped in an effort to get out, but Morgan held her grip on the basket. She aimed her EMP device at the basket and fired.

The floundering turned to an erratic twitch. Within seconds SCAT's movements stopped. Morgan leaned against the basket and sighed with relief. She put the EMP device in her bag and slowly lifted the basket. A hind leg twitched and she froze, prepared to use the basket as a weapon. SCAT remained motionless for a few heartbeats and Morgan put the basket aside.

Morgan used the light from the hallway to inspect the robodog and found a seam at its underbelly. She rummaged in her bag for a tool she used to pry the thing open. The CPU stood out, a shiny rectangle against the black inner workings of the thing. She retrieved her mini and uploaded the contents of the hard drive. Then she pulled up a holoscreen and located the records of SCAT's activities since she woke it up in Ablington's office, rewriting them so it looked as if she never disturbed the robodog.

She picked SCAT up and retraced her steps, depositing it in Ablington's office in roughly the same position she found it. Its power, backup and main, was knocked out. With any luck, Ablington, busy preparing for the vote, would assume his prototype had a glitch and not look into the problem too closely. One last check and she made her way down the stairwell to the underground parking garage before she slipped out into the night.

#

Election day arrived and the thirteen board members sat around the large conference room table, twelve in person while one holoed in. At a smaller square table near the entrance to the room, Morgan stood behind Ablington, a smug smirk cemented on his face. The other assistants stood behind their bosses as well. Chesterfield sat across from Ablington with a look of complete neutrality. Kang Danbury sat next to Ablington, intermittently readjusting his collar while he checked notices on his mini. Worth looked around the room, occasionally rapping the table, a movement that betrayed his impatience. The current CEO, seated next to the Chair, was also present via holo.

SCAT sat stationary in the office where Morgan left it. Ablington, so excited about his potential election to CEO, had not given the robodog a second look when he came in. Coming in a few minutes before the vote, her boss had made a call to his wife and checked his emails. "Let's go," he had announced, rapping lightly on SCAT's head as he walked past and made his way to the conference room. He had never even paused to see if Morgan followed.

Chairperson Kendra Willem brought Morgan's mind to the present. "Good morning, ladies and gentlemen. I call to order this GMN meeting for the purpose of electing a new chief executive officer. All members of the board are present, either live or virtually. As usual this meeting will be recorded for posterity." The chairperson steepled her fingers as she continued. "Let's get down to business. Boardmember Smith, what say you?"

Smith tugged on his collar for a moment, then took a deep

breath then said, "I...I elect Director Desmond Chesterfield to the position."

Ablington stopped the absentminded study of his manicure and glared at Smith. "What the..." he mumbled.

"Boardmember Ravisundar," the chairperson continued, "what say you?"

"Chesterfield." A smiling Ravisundar turned to Ablington and mimed a gunshot.

Ablington's manicured hands turned to fists as one by one each board member voted for Chesterfield.

The vote ended with the chairperson who also voted for Chesterfield. "If there is no objection..."

"I object!" Ablington pounded a fist on the table.

"Come now, Norman. Don't be a sore loser." Weimei waltzed in and stood next to Chesterfield's personal assistant. Morgan took the queue and stood on the other side of the assistant.

"What is this?" Ablington pounded a fist on the table.

"This is an election," Willem said. "I hereby declare Chesterfield CEO of the Global Media Networks. This meeting is adjourned."

"No." Ablington shook his head. "You know what will come out if you do this."

Willem sat back and folded her arms. "What Norman? You'll expose all my secrets? But who would believe you without any proof?"

"I have proof!"

Morgan placed both palms on the table and leaned forward. "No, I believe Mr. Chesterfield has all the proof in his new office."

Morgan saw the moment the light went on his head. He knew what she had done. He knew she was a danger to his orchestrated life, his power and his position. His fists curled in even tighter. "You..."

"As head of security, Ms. Gossett, the first order of business I'd like you to perform is to escort Mr. Ablington off the premises."

Morgan stood straight. "With pleasure, sir."

"You? You're just a receptionist. I don't need an escort."

"Oh, no, I'll escort you out. And so will they." Morgan nodded towards the entrance and pressed the special button on her new company mini.

The door opened and a pair of robodogs marched in, their movements synchronous. Members of the board gasped.

"Heel!" Morgan commanded.

The pair sat. Their heads angled towards Ablington; they were already programmed to guard him once they saw his face.

"As you can see, my dogs are ready to become GMN's security force," Weimei said. "No longer will GMN have to rely on assistance from other corps with investigations or security actions. Not with my babies around." She turned to Ablington and said, "They will not be marketed to children."

Ablington stood abruptly, anger seething across his face. He opened his mouth as if to speak, but closed it again. There was no doubt, plots of revenge danced in his mind. Morgan only hoped she could thwart any devious plans he threw their way.

Morgan got what she wanted. Ablington was a ruined man. Oh, he'd use his underworld connections to try to insert himself back into the mainstream, but Morgan had the full backing of GMN behind her. She'd counteract any move he'd make and ensure he never had enough power to hurt anyone again. In fact, after the twenty-four-hour grace period afforded certain former employees, she intended to file charges with anything she could prove Ablington was involved in. Aspiron just finished a new supermax orbital station and she intended to make Ablington a permanent guest there, poetic justice that the corp where the scene of his first major crime occurred would provide his ultimate prison.

Throughout the meeting, Chesterfield remained staid and professional. Meanwhile, a cool tension drained from the room. Several boardmembers smiled. Smith managed a fist pump before he regained his composure.

Boardmember Willem turned to Chesterfield. "Mr. Chester-field, I hope you will keep our secrets as well as the secrets of this corporation safe."

"Of course, I'll do," he paused, "what's best for the firm."

"What's best for the firm," murmured other board members like parishioners parroting their new cult leader.

"What's best for the firm!" Willem nodded agreement. "This meeting is adjourned."

Ablington turned and left the room. The robodogs got up and followed him in unison. Morgan trailed behind. They all climbed in the elevator and descended to the ground floor. For a moment she thought Ablington would pounce and she placed a hand on the new taser strapped to her side. Not that he would get a chance to strike her when her two four- legged friends would drop him when they saw him as a threat. Ablington called a car and entered the vehicle when it arrived. The two robodogs raced after the car and kept track of his whereabouts just as she programmed.

#

Back in Desmond's new office, Morgan looked out at sweeping views of the city. The new office was twice the size of Ablington's.

It had the same color scheme and style as her old office. Morgan watched Desmond for a minute, seated behind his desk as if he were born there.

"I do think we need to redecorate this place," he said.

"Well, you made me head of cybersecurity not interior design."

He smiled for the first time since the election. She turned to Weimei, who leaned against the desk drinking a flute of champagne. "And you could have given me a better warning about that dog of yours."

Weimei shrugged. "I had no idea what he'd done to it. You know he likes to tinker."

When Desmond found her in Alaska and explained who he was, she thought of it as a job and a chance to avenge her mother's death. Play the long-lost half-sister, get even and then move on, but he convinced her that once justice came for her mother's demise and that she had a future at GMN. Once she met Weimei, her wandering father's stepdaughter for all of four years, she knew the plan would work. No one at GMN had suspected their relation. His kinky red hair mirrored the image of their father. Their paths never crossed and even if they had as a receptionist with darker skin no one gave her a second look. Desmond also said there was another half-brother that lived off the grid. She hoped to meet him one day.

So, she would keep an eye on Ablington and make sure he'd stay ruined. If he stepped out of line, well, people were sent to the Moon every day. Other execs needed monitoring too. Morgan intended to watch them as well and squash any malfeasance when possible. This company was her family now, nothing traditional like most of the execs, but they were family just the same.

Transfer
Mackenzie Reide

We live in a world where technology is changing every day. Pushing the limits moves us forward and can even be life changing. But is there a limit to how far we should go? And to whom are we developing these wonders for?

It was a muggy September morning as Edita ran out to catch the hoverbus. Rain drizzled on top of her umbrella, which of course broke upon the first blast of wind. She shoved the useless pile of metal sticks in her bag and scrunched her coat up against her face.

The rain began to beat down harder. She was going to be drenched before she even got on the bus. Not a great way to make an impression on the first day of her internship.

The internship. She had longed for this since she was five years old. That's when her adopted parents first told her the story of her special heart.

Her birth parents had been driving back from a convention, when their hovercar was hit head on by a garbage scow. The AI system on the scow failed to "see" their car as its cameras were obscured by the torrential downpour that was happening. They were both killed instantly, but her car seat was pinned between the floor and the ceiling. They used the jaws of life—big giant metal teeth—to extract her from the wreck. When the ambulance got to the hospital they realized she had been hit in the chest by a piece of scrap metal. So, she was given the first 3D printed heart from the public health care printer.

It was groundbreaking work by the renowned bio-mechanical engineer, Dr. Helena Mason. Edita had been fascinated with Dr. Mason's work ever since. She excelled at mathematics in school, and took programming and robotics at summer camp. Her adopted parents had been delighted at her interest in mechanics—they were both dentists—so they hoped she would grow up to build better robotics to help them with their work.

While mechanical arms and sonic drills were all fine for fixing teeth, Edita was more interested in the device that created her little heart. It was the Unico 3D Printer. That same printer led to breakthroughs of larger adult-sized organs that were now regular procedures in hospitals all over the world.

When you could get the parts, that is.

There was a huge waiting list for printed organs. The need was far greater than the public health care printer could manage. Edita's internship was to assist in creating a program that could increase the printer's speed and efficiency. She felt she was up for the challenge. And the need was there.

The only other printer in existence that could create viable organs was owned by the big tech company, Sloutech. But only the rich and famous could afford the price tag.

Edita's parents had encouraged her to apply for an internship at Sloutech, but Edita wanted to work with her idol. Especially when, much to her delight, Dr. Mason sent a personal invitation for Edita to be part of her team! Her parents couldn't argue with that, not when the leading researcher, the one who designed her very own heart, accepted her intern application.

The hoverbus swerved sharply as it careened around a corner. Edita mumbled an apology to the young man beside her. He shrugged and continued what looked like an attempt at dozing. She looked out the window at the gray clouds that hung low over the city. So much for the dry season. She huddled more into her jacket. She was just going to have to hope her hair didn't frizz out too much.

The hoverbus wobbled as it pulled up to the door of a large glass building that towered over the other buildings in downtown Macapa. This was a very special building, as it wasn't really a building at all, but a giant space elevator that swept people up to the research lab that was located on a space station in a permanent orbit around the Earth.

Macapa had been chosen to host the elevator, as it was located right on the Equator. The city slogan was "The Capital of the Middle of the World." As a kid, Edita used to love to stand on the dividing line with one foot in each hemisphere.

Now, she was going to step into a whole new hemisphere—space. And the home of the largest research facility in the world.

A thrill shot up Edita's spine as she poured out of the bus with the other passengers who took off in various directions, all in a hurry to get the day over with. But not Edita; she was excited and terrified at the same time. She paused for a second at the entrance and swallowed hard. What if she blew it on her first day? What if Dr. Mason took one look at her and decided Edita wasn't the right candidate for the job? She had just turned fifteen, the bare minimum to be an intern. What would she tell her parents? They were so excited for her. Someone pushed on her back—she stumbled forward through the doors.

The lobby was nearly empty except for two security guards standing one on each side of a large white door at the far end of the lobby. In front of them were two tables with transparent screens.

"Er…" It dawned on Edita that she didn't know how to enter the building properly. How was she supposed to check in? No one had actually told her the procedure for her first day. Just to take the space elevator to Level One and walk down the hall to the lab at the end.

"You're new, aren't you?" said a voice behind her.

Edita turned and recognized the young man from the hoverbus. He stood at her height with dark hair and brown eyes that seemed to bore into her. She thought of her own unruly brown hair and felt her face grow warm. Tomorrow she would put it in braids.

"Oh, er, yes. It's my first day," she stammered.

He raised his eyebrows. "That much is obvious. Where are you headed?"

"To Lab One."

He looked taken aback. "You're going to Lab One?"

"Yes. I'm starting my internship with Dr. Mason."

Now he looked shocked. "Really? She's taking an intern? That's news. I don't think Dr. Mason has had an intern, in like, forever."

Edita's heart pounded in her chest, as if reminding her why she was there. "Well, I guess she was impressed with my robotics studies."

"Indeed." The boy's eyes narrowed. His handsome face looked skeptical. Then he relaxed and gave her a smile. "Well, since you're a newbie I should warn you, the elevator is a bit temperamental."

"The elevator?"

He nodded. "Yes. One of Dr. Mason's creations. Early AI

model. Anyway, you'll find out soon enough. All you need to do is a hand and eye scan at one of the kiosks." He pointed to a line of three people standing in front of one of the tables. Each time a turn came up, the individual would put both hands on the flat surface and lean forward, then a blue light scanned each eye, then the screen lit up in green.

"You are free to proceed," said a calm Peruvian female voice.

"You can always tell Dr. Mason's work as she likes to utilize different accents. Anything that sounds bland and tinny is Sloutech engineering." He gestured with his hand. "After you."

Edita felt her heart begin to race as she stepped up to the monitor.

"Please place your hands on the table and look at the center of the screen," instructed the Peruvian voice.

Edita did as she was told. It struck her in that moment that she might not be in the system. After all, this was her first day. The blue light scanned both her eyes. *What if I get arrested?* What a terrible way to start her internship! How would she explain to her mentor that she couldn't follow the procedures to get into the building on the first day?

"Scan accepted. Please proceed to the elevator."

Edita breathed a sigh of relief. At least someone had the where-withal to put her in the system. She walked over to the elevator. It was scheduled to arrive in the next few minutes.

She turned to her new friend. "I didn't catch your name."

"Oh, I'm Douglas. My friends call me Dougy."

"Hi, Dougy, I'm Edita. Have you been working here long?"

He shrugged. "I started my internship four months ago. I'm hoping to get a full scholarship to University through Sloutech."

"What do you want to study?"

"Robotics and programming."

"Me too!"

He crossed his arms. "I can't believe you got an internship with Dr. Mason. I tried and was refused. I was told she doesn't like people in her lab. Disturbs her creativity."

Edita frowned. "That's odd. She's the leader in 3D printing of human organs. She's an advocate for public health care."

Dougy nodded. "True. I heard she did have an intern once, but he stole her work and gave it to Sloutech. They monetized it for their own gain."

Just then the elevator door opened. Edita stepped in and the door swooshed shut immediately behind her.

"Hey!"

Edita caught a glimpse of Dougy jumping back with his hands pulled against his chest.

"That's better," a cheery voice with an English accent said. "He's Sloutech. He can wait for the next round."

"Ahhh..." Edita said.

"Hi! I'm Eddy. I'm your Space Elevator Unico 5000 model. Welcome aboard, Edita!"

"Ah ... hi, Eddy." Edita remembered Dougy's comment about the elevator. "You know my name?"

"Of course! I know everyone who comes and goes. I'm linked to the security system as part of the scanning process. Can't have bad people coming up, now can we?" Eddy seemed to take his job very seriously.

"How come you wouldn't let Dougy join us?" Edita asked. "There's lots of room."

"Oh, I wanted to welcome you on your first day," Eddy said cheerfully. "Dr. Mason was too busy to meet you in the lobby so she asked me to give you the orientation."

"Oh! Okay, thanks, Eddy." Edita smiled. She liked Eddy.

"The space station is in a Geostationary Orbit at 41,700 kilometers above the planet's surface," Eddy began, as Edita had the sensation of rising very fast. "We are traveling at 695 kilometers per minute. I am the first and only fully functioning space elevator. My cable is made from a high-grade aluminum-titanium alloy and carbon nanotubes. The elevator car can be used as an emergency space pod should a malfunction occur. Though, that's very unlikely," Eddy stated with pride. "I monitor all my systems constantly and I'm in top repair."

"That's impressive."

"Thank you! Now, you will be working in Lab One with Dr. Mason and her team."

"Her team? I thought she worked alone."

"Just because she works with non-humans doesn't mean she's alone," Eddy sniffed. "And you won't be alone, either."

"Oh, I didn't mean to offend," Edita said hastily.

"None taken," Eddy quipped. "Now, the space station has five levels, but you only need Level One for the lab and there is a cafeteria on Level Two. Though," Eddy lowered his voice, "I recommend bringing your own lunches. I hear the food is not so great."

"Why did you lower your voice?"

"Because you never know when the walls might be listening," Eddy said conspiratorially.

"Ahh... Thanks for the heads up."

"Good. You get it." Eddy sounded pleased. "The space elevator ride is sixty minutes one way. So we'll have lots of time to catch up on how your day went. Can't wait to hear!"

Edita smiled as Eddy chatted merrily away explaining the tensile strength of the elevator cable and the pressurization process that he used to keep beings like her comfortable during the ascent.

It didn't feel like sixty minutes when the elevator slowed and came to a stop. As the door opened, Eddy said, "Just walk down the hall to the end. Lab One is behind the hatch. You might feel a little weird getting used to the artificial gravity."

"Thanks, Eddy!" Edita gave the elevator a wave as it closed its door and swooshed away.

Edita stood in the corridor. All was silent except for a slight hum coming from the walls. She imagined it was the station's life support; otherwise everything was still. Edita ran her fingers along the curved wall. She could almost feel the vacuum of space, cold and deadly, on the other side. Even with artificial gravity, it felt weird. She was acutely aware that she was a little being inside a large aluminum can, high above the planet. The gravity felt artificial. This wasn't Earth.

She took a deep breath and let it out slowly. Her heart began to pound, but this time with excitement. She was about to meet her idol, the great Dr. Helena Mason. Leading bio-mechanical engineer and founder of the public health care printer. Edita walked faster. Eddy was right about the wobbliness of the station's gravity, but she would get used to it. She stomped awkwardly down the corridor to a large circular wheel mounted on an aluminum hatch.

Edita frowned. *I guess I spin it?* She grabbed the wheel with two hands and spun it counter-clockwise. The wheel turned slowly and a loud click sounded. The hatch swung open.

Edita held her breath in anticipation. The hatch opened to reveal a short barrel-shaped bot that spun in a circle and let out a series of musical notes.

"Hello," Edita said shyly. "I'm Edita. I start my internship today."

A side panel opened on the bot and a metal rod with a clamp at the end reached out and tugged at her shirt.

"Do you want me to follow you?" Edita asked.

The bot let out two C notes.

Edita nodded. "That's a yes, I take it."

The bot turned and rolled away on its three wheels.

Edita stepped through the opening. The lab looked like the rooms she used at summer camp except that it was smaller and cramped. The equipment looked—well, old. The monitors were at least ten years old and they had keyboards! Her camp programs had used the latest touch screen technology and voice commands.

This wasn't the lab she had imagined Dr. Mason working in.

The bot led her all the way to the back to a small cluttered room with a desk covered in computer hardwire. Edita frowned. *This is an office?* She had expected something a little more grandiose.

There was a commotion, then a short, chubby figure with shoulder-length blue hair burst out from behind a cabinet, holding a stack of papers in her arms.

"Edita!" the figure exclaimed. "How nice to finally meet you." She held out her hand, dropping half the stack.

"How nice to meet you, too." Edita shook the proffered hand.

"I'm Dr. Mason." The woman pushed her glasses farther up her nose and took a step back to give Edita the once over.

"Not bad." She nodded to herself.

"Er..."

"There was doubt as to whether or not you would grow properly with your 3D heart. But look at you—175 centimeters?"

"Ah..." Edita stammered. "Yes."

"Excellent. Those doubters! But what does height really have to do with it. Look at me, I'm only 152 centimeters. Maybe I should give myself an upgrade one day, eh?" She laughed at her own joke.

The bot let out a short blast of Mozart's Requiem.

"Yes, yes, Binder, you are correct. Where are my manners? Let me introduce you to the team." Dr. Mason dropped the remaining papers. "This is Binder who is my assistant. Binder was a power station bot at one of the first electrical storm catching stations in Macapa. This bot can store up to three lightning strikes of power at once."

"That's quite a feat!" Edita was impressed.

"When they upgraded their systems, the power company put the bots up for scrap, but I saw potential in Binder so I negotiated the purchase, and now Binder handles my calendar and runs the lab when I'm away."

"It's a pleasure to meet you, Binder." Edita gave the bot a friendly pat.

Binder chimed a happy tone.

"Binder likes you. Excellent!" Dr. Mason sounded pleased. "Now, you must meet Angus. My right hand, if you pardon the pun."

Dr. Mason walked over to a mechanical arm that was mounted on a square metal frame with four wheels on the bottom. It was writing a poem on a whiteboard with very fancy penmanship.

It's cold in space, but warm inside,

The station's our home, and now you reside,

Welcome, Edita!

Dr. Mason smiled. "Angus does my calculations and is an excellent programmer! He's also a poet."

"He?"

"Yes, the other engineers accused me of anthropomorphizing my bots." Dr. Mason tilted her head. "But I let them decide, though Binder chooses to be non-binary."

Binder played a C scale.

"All my bots have AI programming. I coded them myself." Dr. Mason laughed. "Angus prefers cursive writing while Binder likes music."

Edita realized her jaw was hanging open.

Angus continued writing, *How do you like being in space?*

"It feels funny," Edita answered honestly.

Angus moved his arm up and down, then wrote, *Yes, it does feel weird, but you will get used to it. Soon this will be normal and you will walk funny on Earth!*

Edita laughed.

"Very good!" Dr. Mason was pleased. "I see you will get along great with the team. Did you know that Angus monitored the printer that made your heart? Ran seventy-two hours straight keeping an eye on it."

Edita was floored. "Really? I had no idea." She smiled at Angus. "Thank you."

You're welcome!

"You can chat more later. But let's get you set up at your desk," Dr. Mason said.

"Yes, please." Edita nodded eagerly.

Dr. Mason stepped over to a desk that was across from Angus.

"This is where you will work." She grabbed a pile of papers and plopped them onto a nearby cabinet. The papers slid a bit to the side so the stack looked skewed. "We'll deal with that later," she mused.

She turned back to the desk. "This computer is for you." Dr. Mason pointed at an antique monitor and hard drive. "I know it looks clunky, but I've given it some upgrades. This lab is funded by the public sector, so we rely on refurbished equipment."

"My summer camps have the latest equipment from Sloutech donated to them. Wouldn't they do that for this lab?" Edita asked. "Your work is revolutionary."

Binder let out a loud B flat. Dr. Mason's eyes narrowed. "We don't use anything from Sloutech here."

"Oh, I'm sorry." Edita cringed inwardly remembering what Dougy had explained about the doctor's intern.

"I know it's not fancy," Dr. Mason continued. "But I think you'll find everything you need." She gave Edita a warm smile. "The project for your internship is to help me catch up with my programming so we can move forward with creating a more efficient printer. I need you to transcribe the work from my papers to the drive on your desktop computer. Each night, please download a copy into Binder for storage."

Edita eyed the stacks of paper piled throughout the room. "All of them?"

Dr. Mason laughed. "Yes. I like to compose with a pen. But it's gotten out of hand as you can see. I need to get it under control and Binder and Angus can't type."

Edita felt her heart sink at the sight of all that paper. This was going to be her internship?

"Do you think you're up for the challenge?" Dr. Mason asked. "It's a great way to learn coding. I think you will find it very interesting, and you'll be working with the code that created your heart."

There was something in Dr. Mason's expression that Edita couldn't quite put her finger on, but she felt the doctor was being genuine.

She took a deep breath. "I've wanted to work with you ever since I found out about the 3D printer. I'd be honored to help out."

Binder played a friendly flute composition as Dr. Mason nodded.

Welcome to the Team! Angus drew a smiley face.

#

The first week went by with Edita buried in paper. She set up her work station as best she could with her antique computer. It had to be turned on and off manually each day and took forever to start up in the morning. While the computer was doing its start up sequence, she would collect more papers from throughout the room. She found papers in drawers, on tables, all over Dr. Mason's office, and even under the file cabinet.

Finally, she had what she thought was the entire pile. She sat at her desk squinting her eyes trying to read the doctor's writing. It was odd that Dr. Mason elected to code by hand. Even stranger, she only stored one copy in Binder.

Not the best backup system, Edita thought, but she didn't say anything. After all, this was her mentor. But she still couldn't help but wonder if she'd made the best choice for her internship.

#

Despite her misgivings on her first day, Edita began to really enjoy her work. It was challenging to decipher the code that Dr. Mason was pouring out of her brain. But Edita soon found she was following the logic.

The 3D printer was complex. It was no ordinary procedure to print a new heart and the program was beyond anything Edita had ever seen. There was code upon code—and something that she couldn't quite get. There was a program embedded in the coding that seemed to store an enormous amount of data. But what for?

She heard a whirring and trilling behind her and glanced back. Binder and Angus appeared to be in deep conversation as she sat at her desk and munched on a peanut butter and jam sandwich. Her internship did seem a bit odd. She only saw Angus and Binder as Dr. Mason spent more time in meetings than in the lab.

It was a bit lonely. But Edita was glad to have Binder and Angus to chat with and of course, Eddy.

Everyday Eddy would take great delight in hearing about her day even though not a lot happened other than transcribing. He took her work very seriously and asked lots of questions about what she was learning.

Soon Edita fell into a routine. In the morning, she chatted with Eddy who always made sure she was the only one on the elevator. He would share a factoid or two about space, then she worked all day transcribing the code.

Thanks to Eddy's tendency to slam his door in Dougy's face, Edita only saw him on the bus, though he was half-asleep most of the time. One Monday morning, he perked up enough to ask if she had tried the cafeteria yet.

"I usually bring my lunch. Can't afford to eat out everyday," she had answered.

"Oh, it's free for anyone who works on the station." He gave her a hopeful look.

"Maybe I'll check it out."

She mulled this over while pouring over Dr. Mason's code. Should she go for lunch? What if Dougy wasn't there? She would feel silly. Then she admonished herself. It was just a cafeteria.

She decided to give it a try.

"I'm heading out for lunch today," Edita said as she grabbed her coat.

Where are you going? Angus asked.

"I'm going to try the cafeteria."

Don't eat the pea soup, Angus wrote.

Binder played *In the Hall of the Mountain King*.

Edita laughed. "I'll steer clear of the soup." She closed the hatch behind her. As she walked down the corridor it dawned on her she didn't know where the stairs were. As she was on Level One, she figured there were no stairs to descend.

She waited impatiently for Eddy. He seemed to take his time. When he finally arrived, Edita stepped in. "Cafeteria, please."

"You really want to go there?" Eddy asked, not moving.

"I'd like to try it."

Eddy paused. "I could take you down to the surface. There are some good eating places near the entrance."

"Oh, is there?"

"Yes, there's a great ramen place right next door. Why don't you try that? I hear people talk about it all the time."

"That's good to know, but I'll try the cafeteria."

"You're absolutely sure?"

"Yes, I am."

Eddy grunted. "Fine. But if you get heartburn, don't say I didn't warn you."

Edita smiled. "I'll be careful."

"Good." Eddy zipped up to the second floor and opened his door. "Don't eat the pea soup."

"Don't worry, I hate pea soup." Edita laughed.

She stepped out into a corridor that was brightly lit with a colorful rainbow painted along the walls. *We don't have that on Level One*, she noted. She heard chatter and followed the sound. She emerged into what looked like her high school cafeteria. Long tables had people huddled together in conversation.

When she stepped into the room, every conversation stopped and all the patrons looked at her. Suddenly, Edita felt like a fish in a glass bowl.

"Er, hello," she said awkwardly.

The others continued to stare.

"This is Dr. Mason's intern." Dougy walked up beside her. "She's okay. She talks to humans."

The entire cafeteria seemed to give a collective grunt, then went back to their meals and conversation. Though Edita could feel eyes on her back as she walked up to the counter.

"Pea soup?" asked a burley woman wearing an apron spattered in yellow stains and holding a giant ladle.

"Ah, no thanks. I'll have the ..." Edita desperately scanned the board above the counter. "Macaroni and cheese."

"Fine." The lunch lady used the soup ladle to plop a blob of mac and cheese on a plate. "Here."

"Thanks." Edita took the plate and went to the end of the row.

"I'll have the same," Dougy said.

Edita found a tray and put her plate on it. Then found a fork.

"If you like we can sit in the corner." Dougy pointed to a small table off to the side. "Less curious looks."

"That sounds good." Edita followed Dougy to the table and sat down.

"Why is everyone staring at me?" she whispered.

Dougy shrugged. "You're Dr. Mason's intern. A rare specimen. I'm not the only one who applied and was turned down. They're trying to figure out what made you different."

"Oh." Edita wasn't sure how to react.

"Just ignore them. They're probably jealous."

Edita tried not to think about it, but it was hard to shake the feeling of being watched.

"How is your internship going?" Dougy asked. "We haven't had a chance to really talk."

"It's very interesting. It's hard work. But ..." she hesitated.

"What?" he leaned in eagerly. "How is working with the legendary Dr. Mason?"

"It's not what I expected," Edita said. "I mean, I'm super stoked to have this internship but I thought the lab would be more, well..."

"More what?"

"Advanced! My computer is an antique. One hard drive and no cloud access. And Dr. Mason writes everything on paper! Sometimes I can't read her writing. Angus has better handwriting than all of us."

"Angus?"

"Angus is the mechanical arm. He writes poetry."

"Oh." Dougy raised his eyebrows. "An artistic arm. What else do you have in that lab?"

"There's Binder, an electric utility bot who is Dr. Mason's assistant."

Dougy shook his head. "Guess Dr. Mason does prefer bots over people. Except you." He added with an afterthought.

Edita's watch beeped. "Oh, my lunch is over. Eddy's calling me back to the elevator."

"Maybe I'll see you tomorrow?" Dougy asked.

Edita smiled. "Sure."

"*Soooooo* ... how was lunch?" Eddy asked as Edita stepped in the elevator.

"I had the mac and cheese."

"Good girl. Any other business I should know about?"

"Ah ... no."

"All righty, then," Eddy said cheerily. "Got to keep all systems in their place."

#

For the rest of the week Edita pondered the code in the embedded program. Binder selected an ensemble from Hayden while Angus wrote her a little poem of encouragement.

The code is complex, and I know you're vexed,
But you've got the tools, to unravel the rest,
Go, Edita!

Edita had the sensation that Binder and Angus were eagerly waiting for her to figure it out. They seemed to be holding their collective breaths. This created an even greater urgency to know more, so she dug out the programming textbooks Dr. Mason used when she was at university and began writing short programs to see what each function did in the layers of code.

She worked hard, her only breaks being to meet Dougy for lunch, much to Eddy's chagrin.

"Again? You ate there yesterday!" he complained. "And the day before that."

Edita laughed. "It's good to get up and walk around. I sit at the computer for hours."

"Hmmphf."

A man in a white lab coat was talking to Dougy as Edita entered the cafeteria. He turned to her as she walked over.

"Ah, this must be Dr. Mason's intern. The one I've heard so much about." He smiled at her. Edita had the creepy sensation he was analyzing her.

"Edita, this is my mentor, Dr. John Ramsay," Dougy said.

"Hello." Edita reached out to shake Dr. Ramsay's hand. There was an electric shock as their fingers touched.

"Oh! Goodness!" Dr. Ramsay apologized. "I guess there's a bit of a static charge on my clothes from this morning's test." He placed his hands in the pockets of his lab coat.

"We've been working on energy transfer," Dougy explained.

"Well, I'd better get back to work," Dr. Ramsay said. "Pleasure to meet you, Edita." With that, he turned and walked briskly away.

"I got us two mac and cheeses," Dougy said, pointing at the table. "Thought you might like skipping the line. And if you didn't show up, I can always eat it."

"Thanks." Edita sat down. She flexed her fingers. They felt numb. It had been quite the jolt.

"You okay?" Dougy asked.

Edita nodded. "I'm fine. So, what made you go into robotics?"

she asked, hoping to change the subject.

"I've always been fascinated," he answered. "But University is expensive. The only way I can do it is through a paid internship."

"The Uni has scholarships," Edita said. "I'm going to apply."

"With a recommendation from Dr. Mason, you'll get one for sure," Dougy said. "I have to work and go to school, so I need the job and the scholarship."

"Why?"

"I've got three siblings to take care of."

Oh, do your parents work away from home?"

Dougy's face clouded over. "My mother had a serious liver condition. She died while waiting for a transplant. My father didn't take it well."

"What happened?"

"He left."

"I'm sorry." Edita was embarrassed for asking.

He shrugged. "He didn't want the responsibility. But I won't let them be separated. I can take care of them. What about your family?"

"My parents died in a car crash when I was a baby. I live with my adoptive parents."

Dougy looked mortified. "I'm so sorry! Here I am grumbling about my siblings."

"It's okay. I don't remember them at all. My adoptive parents are very nice. They're paying for me to have private hovercar lessons."

"Cool! I hear it's like flying except close to the ground."

Edita smiled. "Yes. The hovercar can fly like a sailplane for short distances. It's really fun!"

"I wish I could do that," Dougy said wistfully. "Do your parents work in robotics?"

"They're dentists."

Dougy burst out laughing. "Well, at least now I know where to go if I get a cavity!"

Edita laughed. "I can get you a friends and family deal."

Dougy grinned. "I might just take you up on your offer."

They finished lunch in amicable silence.

#

That night Edita dreamt she was sitting in the back of a hovercar looking out the window wondering what the program did that Dr. Mason took so many pages to develop. *Energy transfer.* It was what Dougy said he was working on. That's what the program was doing! It was a large transfer of energy, but why? The transfer was not part of the 3D printer program. It was separate.

She fidgeted with the seat belt. It felt strange. She looked down to see she was in a harness strapped to a child's seat. She frowned.

A loud bang made her look up. The hovercar made a horrible crunching sound and folded all around her. She screamed as glass and metal collided.

She woke with a jolt.

She dragged herself into the elevator the next morning. Eddy sounded concerned. "You're late. Everything okay?"

"I had a bad dream last night. Didn't fall asleep until my alarm was supposed to go off. Slept through it."

"Oh, that's terrible!" Eddy said. "Ask Binder to play you some soothing music."

"It's okay, Eddy, I just need to focus on my work."

"Great idea."

He dropped her off at Level One. "Don't think too hard today," he said as he zoomed off.

Edita headed into the lab to find Angus busy writing on the board. *You're late. We were worried about you.*

"Had a nightmare and overslept, but it's fading now."

If you want to talk, just let me know.

Edita gave Angus a hug. "Thanks."

Edita applied her theory of energy transfer to the program. It took most of the morning, but she got it worked out just before lunch. The code that Dr. Mason was working on was designed to transfer a massive amount of data. But where did it go? Her antiquated computer could not handle that level of transaction.

At noon, Edita headed up to lunch. The other patrons had finally stopped staring. She found Dougy sitting at their usual table. His hair was sticking out at odd angles and his face was bruised and puffy.

"What happened to you?" she asked as she pulled up a chair.

"Eddy decided to show me the effects of G-forces on the human body."

Edita grimaced. "That doesn't sound fun."

"That elevator hates me."

"Oh, I'm sure he just . . . intensely dislikes you." Edita admitted.

"I don't understand why." Dougy stabbed his macaroni with his fork. "What did I do to offend him?"

Edita shook her head. "I don't know. But I'd guess it's because you work for Sloutech. You're technically working for the enemy. Dr. Mason refuses to have any of their equipment in the lab."

Dougy shook his head. "That's too bad. You could do your calculations faster if you had a Sloutech tablet."

"That's okay. I have Angus. He's as fast as any Sloutech computer."

"Say, do you want to grab some ramen, maybe after work?" Dougy asked shyly.

Edita felt a stir in her heart. "Sure."

Dougy smiled. "Great."

#

"So, how's *Dougy*?" Eddy asked as she stepped into the elevator.

"He thinks you hate him. Why did you squish his face?"

"I thought he would be interested in the principles of force vectors," Eddy said innocently.

"He looks terrible."

"Does he? Well I have a wonderful demonstration of the effects of zero G. Ever heard of the vomit comet?"

"Eddy!"

"I'm enhancing his studies!"

"You're picking on him. Why?"

"He works for the enemy. Need I say more?"

"He needs the job. He has three younger siblings to take care of."

"Does he now?" Eddy didn't sound convinced. "He's still your competition. Never trust anyone working for Sloutech."

"He applied to work with Dr. Mason, but she said no."

"That makes him even more suspicious."

"He just wants to learn."

"Then he'll appreciate my lessons!"

Edita shook her head.

That night Edita had the dream again. Only now she was in the hospital hearing voices. One of the voices sounded familiar. She opened her eyes to see Dr. Mason leaning over her. "It'll work," she said. "It has to. Tell Angus to get Binder ready."

She finally drifted off to sleep wondering what it was that Binder was supposed to do.

#

"I'm heading off to a meeting with the Public Health Counsel," Dr. Mason announced that morning as Edita arrived. "I'll be gone for two days. Think you can take care of the lab?"

"Of course!" Edita glanced at Angus who wrote, *Affirmative!* Binder beeped two C notes.

"Good." Dr. Mason grabbed a battered leather briefcase and disappeared out the hatch.

Edita turned to her teammates. "All righty, let's get to work!"

#

For the rest of the morning, Edita stared at the code, but didn't really see it. Instead she puzzled over her dream. She could understand that she might dream about her accident. It had happened before, when she was younger. But what did Binder have to do with it?

Her thoughts were interrupted by the lights flickering.

"What's with the lights?" Edita frowned.

Binder played a scared tone as the bot was lifted off the floor.

"It's okay, Binder, looks like the artificial gravity dampeners are glitching." Edita felt the sensation of suddenly being lighter. "The station's control center will fix it."

The lights went out.

"Or not."

Angus turned on a bright spotlight that was mounted on his arm.

There is a control panel for this floor at the end of the corridor, Angus wrote on the whiteboard. He was tilted slightly to the side as three of his wheels lifted.

"Let's see what we can find out." Edita went to get up and leapt one meter above her desk. "Whoops!" She grabbed the top of Binder and pulled herself down. Binder bleated three A notes.

"Don't worry, Binder. We'll get this sorted." Edita soothed the bot. "Probably a power surge on another floor. Dougy's lab is working with energy transfer, so who knows what the other labs are doing. We might be able to isolate our floor from the others."

You can wear the gravity boots that are in the desk drawer, Angus wrote. *They used to belong to the first intern.*

Edita pulled open the large bottom drawer. She put on the boots. "A little big, but they'll work." She reassured Angus and Binder.

Angus tried to roll towards her but as he was floating, his wheels spun.

"I'll help you." Edita grabbed hold of Angus' frame and steered him to the hatch. With the gravity going awry, he was easy to handle.

"Come on, Binder, let's go see what's going on." Edita grabbed Binder with her other hand and pulled the bot behind her. Binder responded with a B flat.

"It's okay," Edita said. She lifted Angus through the hatchway, then Binder. It was amazing how light they felt. She pushed them down the corridor as Angus shone his bright light. The boots felt like she was sticking to the floor with each step.

They passed Eddy's elevator door. There was no hum. If the power outage went throughout the whole station, Eddy would not operate. *Or, would he?* Edita hadn't asked him about that scenario. She still didn't know where the stairs were located.

She kicked herself. Right when Dr. Mason trusted her to take care of the lab while she was gone.

They reached the end of the hallway and Angus shone his light at a large panel. Edita pulled it open to see a dark control panel. "I was afraid of this. There's no power going to the systems at all. We need to get to the main station control and find out what's going on. Where are the emergency stairs?"

Angus pointed his light back toward the lab.

"Let's go." Edita steered the bots back down the corridor.

As they went along, Binder let out a C note and pointed at a tiny metal plate attached to the wall.

"That's the marker for the stairs?" Edita laughed. The sign was the size of the palm of her hand and level with the top of Binder. No wonder she didn't see it before. As she reached to press the button embedded in the plate, there was a commotion in the walls.

Edita's skin crawled. Something didn't feel right. She held her finger to her lips to tell Binder to be quiet and motioned Angus to shut off his light. Immediately they were plunged into darkness. Edita's heart thumped hard in her chest. She couldn't even see her hand in front of her face.

An oval-shaped panel slid open in the side of the corridor and a flashlight beam spilled out. Edita jumped back into the darkness and watched as two figures climbed out of the opening—a set of stairs disappeared behind them.

Edita's heart skipped a beat. One of the figures was Dougy!

"The lab's at the end," he mumbled with his head down.

"The intern should be upstairs by now trying to get the gravity controls fixed. We can grab the program while she's gone," the other one said. Edita recognized him. It was Dr. Ramsey.

Binder let out a low F sharp.

"Shhhhh," Edita whispered. She put her hand over Binder's speaker. She felt all her muscles tense. What was Dr. Ramsey doing?

She watched as the two men approached the hatch.

"I don't know about this," Dougy said. He sounded nervous. "What about Dr. Mason's bots?"

"This is not the time to get cold feet," Dr. Ramsey growled and pulled out a phaser. "We can stun the bots if they interfere."

Edita felt a surge of anger. How dare he threaten the bots!

"Psssst."

Edita froze. What was that?

"Pssssssst, Edita!" came Eddy's voice in a loud whisper.

"Eddy?" She hissed back. "You're online?"

"Yes. Quick, hide in here!" Eddy opened his doors and Edita pushed Binder and Angus through. Then he closed them to a small crack. "I run on an independent system."

Edita put her eye to the opening. "What's going on?"

"Dr. Ramsey wants to steal Dr. Mason's work! Once wasn't enough?" Eddy harrumphed.

Edita tried to formulate a plan. "We can't let them do that."

"Don't worry, her work is protected," Eddy whispered. "As long as I keep you all safe."

Binder let out a slight hum.

Just then there was a shout from the lab. "The data, it's gone!"

"What?" Dr. Ramsey said. "It's an antique! You can't run an old-school computer?"

"There was a virus hidden in the operating system. As soon as I tried to download, it wiped everything." Dougy sounded frustrated.

Dr. Ramsey growled. "I need that code, now that I know it works. We need to find Dr. Mason's intern."

"Oh, oh," Eddy muttered.

Binder let out a loud crescendo of an F scale.

"What was that?" Dr. Ramsey appeared at the hatch. "They're in the elevator!" He ran down the corridor.

Edita sucked in her breath as Dr. Ramsey's eye looked at her through the crack.

"Hello, Edita," he said calmly.

"You can't have Dr. Mason's work."

"I don't need her notes if I have you."

"Edita's just an intern like me," Dougy said as he ran up to Dr. Ramsey. "She doesn't know any more than we do."

"Oh, but she does," Dr. Ramsey said. "She just doesn't know it yet."

"What?" Edita said.

Dr. Ramsey took a step back. "Come out, Edita. Let's talk."

"No." Edita shook her head.

"Don't you wonder why you're the only intern Dr. Mason will work with?" Dr. Ramsey said. "Aren't you the least bit curious?"

Edita hesitated. "She was impressed with my computer and robotics skills."

"And…?" Dr. Ramsey sounded like he was trying to coach a cat out of a tree. "If you come out, I can tell you the rest."

Edita shook her head. "You're trying to steal Dr. Mason's work. I don't trust you."

Dr. Ramsey let out a heavy sigh. "Fine. Play it that way." He pointed his phaser at Dougy. "Come out, or I'll phase your friend."

"Hey!" Dougy held up his hands.

Angus wrote on the side of the elevator. *We need to get out of here now!*

"Yes," Eddy agreed. He slammed the doors shut.

There was banging on the doors.

"Oh, no, you don't," Eddy growled. The elevator shot downward very fast.

"Wait, Eddy, we need to get Dougy!" Edita shouted.

"Why? He betrayed us. We're going to the surface!"

The elevator shot downward, then suddenly jarred to a halt.

"What's happening?"

"There's a ship outside my cable." Eddy sounded nervous.

"A ship?"

"Probably the one they were going to escape on," Eddy growled. "I sure wasn't going to give them a lift!"

He shot upward. Edita found herself flattened on the floor.

"The ship's shooting the cable apart!" Eddy sounded furious.

Binder played a mournful tune.

"It's okay, Binder," Edita reassured the bot. "Eddy's elevator pod is equipped for space. We can lay low until help comes. Just engage your magnets, that'll keep you and Angus from floating around."

Binder made a clicking sound.

"We need to rescue Dougy," Edita turned her attention to Eddy after helping Angus get his magnets working.

"Why?" Eddy demanded.

"He needs our help."

"He's fine. Dr. Ramsey won't phase him—*much*."

"But the station just got severed from the elevator cable. It's not safe anymore. It will start to drift from orbit, and life support is failing."

"There are escape pods all over," Eddy said. "Dougy can take one of them."

I think Dr. Ramsey will leave Dougy behind, Angus wrote.

"It's a trap!" Eddy argued. "He's using Dougy to draw Edita out and then he'll grab her. We can't allow that!"

"Then we have to outsmart him. We'll make a plan," Edita insisted.

Binder let out a sad prolonged note.

We can't leave Dougy to die, Angus wrote. *Dr. Mason wouldn't want that. Her work's about saving people, remember?*

"Fine. We'll get Dougy," Eddy harrumphed. "But he's really going to love my next lesson."

How do we know what floor he's on? Angus wrote.

"I can scan for his energy signature—look he's in his lab—how convenient for an ambush," Eddy said sarcastically. "Now, let's talk about your plan."

#

Eddy parked the elevator next to a maintenance duct that Edita and Binder were able to crawl and roll through. Angus had to stay with Eddy, as he was too big to maneuver. Edita kicked out the grate at the end of the duct and lowered Binder to the floor.

Binder scanned the area, then let out a soft C note, then rolled down the corridor. Edita followed, her heart thumping hard in her chest. She strained her ears for any sounds but the station was silent. All of the escape pods had been launched. That meant they were the only ones left on the station.

There was no sign of Dr. Ramsey. *He's here somewhere.* Edita knew he was not going to give up so easily.

Binder rolled up to a hatch and beeped two C notes.

"Here?" Edita whispered. She turned the wheel. It rotated smoothly, not like the stiff one at Lab One.

The hatch swung open. Edita poised at the door. No one appeared, so she stepped through. Binder beeped again. Edita grabbed the bot and lifted it. The gravity in this area of the station was the same as on the moon.

Dougy was sitting tied to a chair. Edita approached cautiously. His head was down but snapped up as she got close.

"...raphhh!" he said through his gag.

"I know." She mouthed the words.

Binder rolled over and cut Dougy's bonds with a small laser torch, then zapped him with an electric prod.

"Hey!" he exclaimed as he pulled off his gag.

Binder gave him a B flat raspberry and jolted him again.

"I guess I deserve that." He wobbled as he stood up rubbing his backside. "Edita, I am so sorry. He said he just wanted to know what Dr. Mason was working on. I was supposed to get it from you during our lunch talks but I didn't want to pry. I ... was enjoying our lunches." His cheeks went pink. "Since I didn't provide the information, he decided to go and check her lab."

"You actually thought he would just take a look?" Edita said.

Dougy grimaced and sat down again. He put his head in his hands. "That's what I told myself. Dr. Ramsey offered me a paid internship and an endorsement for a full scholarship if I did what he said. Then he phased me anyway!"

Edita shook her head. "I don't get it. He could have broken in during our lunch breaks anytime Dr. Mason was away at meetings. Why now?"

Dougy shrugged. "I don't know, but the emergency stairs are sealed by Dr. Mason's coding, making Eddy the guardian of Level One. The only way to get the doors open is to cause a complete shutdown of the station—then a failsafe kicks in."

"And putting everyone on the station in jeopardy." Edita was disgusted. "Come on, we've got to get out of here."

"Not so fast," Dr. Ramsey said, stepping out from around a server.

Binder let out a sharp whistle.

"Is that an old utility bot?" Dr. Ramsay frowned at Binder. "I had no idea any of those things were still around."

Edita stepped in front of Binder, who immediately rolled around in front of her.

"What do you want?" Edita demanded.

"I want the information stored in your DNA," Dr. Ramsey said. "If I can't have the program, then I'll get it from you."

"What does that mean?"

Dr. Ramsey gave Edita a cold smile. "You haven't figured it out? You're the one that worked!"

"I know I have the first 3D printed heart," Edita said. "But so what? You can print as many organs as you want at Sloutech."

"You have a printed heart?" Dougy sounded incredulous.

"Get with the program, Dougy." Dr. Ramsey sounded annoyed. "Everyone knows a baby was brought into Emergency fifteen years ago and received the first 3D heart from Dr. Mason. But the hospital records were sealed and the child's name never revealed. I wanted Dr. Mason's research, so I bribed her intern into stealing what he could."

"You couldn't do it yourself, so you stole her work?" Dougy growled. "That's cheating."

Dr. Ramsey shrugged. "Why reinvent the wheel? I stole it and sold it to Sloutech. They made me head researcher of this station and gave me the best lab equipment money can buy."

"But you can't do anything without Dr. Mason's ideas." Edita clenched her fists.

Binder let out a disapproving tone.

Dr. Ramsey seemed amused by Binder. "Did you know that Dr. Mason and I went to university together? She was always pushing the boundaries. Why stop at printing organs? Why not everything?"

Edita's heart began to pound harder—something was tickling the back of her mind. The dream of Dr. Mason leaning over her, *get Binder ready.*

"I began to suspect that Helena had found a way to transfer a human consciousness," Dr. Ramsey continued.

Edita thought of the program that was stored in Binder. *Could it be?* She felt a strange sensation in her gut.

Dr. Ramsey took a step towards her. "There was something about you—the first intern since my spy. I figured you must be the child with the heart transplant. You were the right age. So I scanned you."

"The electric shock," Edita said, flexing her hand unconsciously.

Dr. Ramsey nodded. "Yes. It was a short burst transfer. Collected your DNA sequencing. Imagine my surprise when I deciphered it."

"What do you mean?"

"That you are the first 3D printed human!"

"I'm what?" Edita head reeled. The dream—the program she was transcribing. "How . . . how can that be?"

Binder let out a warning note.

"That's impossible! That tech doesn't exist," Dougy interrupted. "My project is about energy transfer and we have nothing that could hold that much data."

"Unless you repurposed an old power utility model." Dr. Ramsey tilted his head at Binder.

Binder let out an A sharp and hid behind Edita.

Suddenly it clicked. Binder had the capacity to store three lightning strikes. But was that enough to store a human consciousness?

Edita could feel it in her bones, like her whole body was resonating at a different frequency.

 "You're living proof it can be done. If we can reverse engineer what happened to you, we can replicate the process."

"Whoa!" Dougy said. "That sounds dangerous."

Dr. Ramsey ignored Dougy. "You can work on the program yourself, Edita. You'd get to work in a top notch research facility. From what I saw, Dr. Mason's lab should be in a museum!"

"And yet she out thinks you," Edita said. "I'm staying with Dr. Mason."

Dr. Ramsay pulled out his phaser. "No, you're coming with me."

"No, I'm not."

"I'm not giving you a choice."

"Did you know that Eddy is made of titanium-aluminum alloy reinforced with layers of Kevlar?" Edita said calmly.

"So?"

"It means he's more than just an elevator." Edita tapped her watch. There was a loud CRACK! and a shiny cylindrical object burst through the ceiling. Dr. Ramsey was knocked off his feet, the phaser skittered to the side.

A side panel opened.

Angus reached out and grabbed Binder and lifted the bot into Eddy. Edita helped Dougy, who had sprawled on the floor.

"You won't get far in an elevator," Dr. Ramsey shouted as Eddy closed the door shut. "I've got a clipper-class space craft. I'll catch you!"

"He's right," Dougy said. "You shouldn't have come back for me. Now you're trapped."

"Eddy is an escape pod," Edita said. "We can fly out of here."

"That's right," Eddy chimed in. "I'm space worthy. And, as you can see, as tough as nails!"

We need to get to the surface. Angus wrote on the wall.

"You bet!" Eddy said. "Just as soon as Edita straps herself into the pilot's chair."

"Chair?" Edita looked around.

A grating sound made Edita look up. The roof of the elevator slid to the side revealing a chair in front of a control panel.

"You've got a cockpit? That's so cool!" Dougy said in awe.

"Strap in," Eddy said.

Edita pulled herself up and strapped in. She had the eerie sensation of being back in the car seat with the harness. Only this time it was a space pod. "Okay, now what?"

"Now, you pilot us," Eddy said.

"Pilot?"

"You know, fly."

"Fly?" Edita looked at the controls in front of her. "Aren't you programmed to do that?"

"Me? I'm an elevator. I go up and down. I don't *fly*. Eddy sounded aghast. "You have to drive."

"I've never flown a space pod before!"

"How hard can it be?" Eddy said. "There's a manual somewhere."

Angus reached over with his mechanical arm and pulled out a booklet from a compartment in the pilot's seat. *Don't Panic: How to Fly the Emergency Space Elevator Pod.* Edita tried reading, then went straight to the diagrams.

"There, see, instructions." Eddy sounded pleased. "Now hang on, we're going into space!"

The escape pod shot down and out of the hole in the elevator cable and just missed hitting the ship flying straight at them.

Edita let out a yell and grabbed the controls. The book floated up past her nose. Angus grabbed it while Binder reached up with a small clamp and turned the pages.

"All right, this can't be that different than driving a hovercar, right?" Edita said. She glanced at the illustrations. "Thrusters—check. Altitude, very high—check. Push throttle forward for go—ah! Got it!" She pushed the stick forward and the thrusters kicked in—just as the ship behind them was reaching out with a grappling arm. It bounced off Eddy's smooth surface.

"Oh no, you don't!" Edita swung the pod around and shot past the side of the ship.

"That's it. You're getting the hang of it," Eddy sounded pleased.

Binder let out a flute trill.

We're being followed! Angus wrote on the wall.

"It's Dr. Ramsey," Eddy said. "I just scanned his ship."

Suddenly the escape pod accelerated very fast.

"Whoa! Eddy! I thought you couldn't fly." Edita held onto the stick with two hands.

"I can't. I'm just revving the engines. Weee!" Eddy said gleefully.

"Ahhhhhhhh!" screamed Dougy, who was clinging to the back of the pilot's chair.

In space they can hear you scream! Angus scribbled.

Binder started playing *Flight of the Bumblebee.*

The escape pod shot off towards the moon while Edita struggled with the controls. The ship behind them followed in pursuit.

"I don't know if I can shake him!" Edita was sweating now. The moon was getting bigger in her view screen. "Ideas anyone?"

Can you make him crash on the moon? Angus wrote.

"Crash?" Dougy gasped. "What about us?"

"That might work." Edita aimed at the moon's surface.

"Are you crazy?" Dougy shouted. "We're also going to crash!"

"Have you ever skipped rocks?"

"Ahhh, no. I mean, I can never get more than two," Dougy said. "But what's that got to do ... oh, no! You're not going to do that?"

Edita gritted her teeth. "This space pod is like a skipping stone. Its sleek surface is ultra smooth and virtually indestructible. That ship behind us is not."

"The beings inside are not indestructible!" Dougy countered.

Binder's C notes sounded in agreement.

"I got this," Edita said. "It's like flying the hovercar."

Edita concentrated—she would have to time this just right. She remembered her first hovercar lesson with her instructor. Just graze the surface of the road, he said. She would have to do that, but at high speed, on the moon.

The moon was growing larger in her view screen. The ship behind them was closing fast. The pod shot just above the surface—there was a loud scraping noise and the whole pod vibrated.

"The ship is right behind us!" Dougy yelled.

"They're trying to grab us with a tractor beam." Eddy sounded angry.

A crater loomed up ahead.

"Edita—" Dougy's face was turning green.

"Eddy, get ready to fire the engines full blast on my signal," Edita said. She jerked the stick and bounced the pod off the surface of the moon. The pod lifted up, then slammed back on the surface, then lifted again, only this time Edita pulled hard on the stick, forcing the nose of the pod to point up as the underside slid up the side of the crater. Rock and moon dust pummeled the view screen. The whole pod rattled violently. Edita gripped the stick. It shook so hard, she was afraid it would rip her arms out of her sockets.

The pod skimmed over the edge of the crater.

"Fire the engines!" Edita yelled.

The pod dipped for a heart lurching second, then shot up and away.

"The ship just fell into the crater!" Dougy gasped. "He's stuck!"

"We did it!" Edita cheered.

Yeah! Angus wrote.

Binder squealed.

"I want to be a space ship," Eddy said.

#

Dr. Mason returned as soon as she got the news. The elevator cable was going to take months to repair, so Dr. Mason moved the bots into the abandoned power station. The facility was big enough to fit Eddy as well.

Edita told her parents she was going to help Dr. Mason repair Eddy, though he suffered only minor damage to his outer plating. Her real job was to continue her internship working on the energy transfer of a human consciousness to a 3D printed body. Dr. Mason told the other researchers that Dr. Ramsey had destroyed her work by breaking into her computer, so she was going to start from scratch. But in reality all her work was stored in Binder.

Dr. Ramsey was arrested for destroying the elevator cable and trying to kidnap Edita, but nothing was said of his phasing Dougy. Instead, Sloutech offered him a paid internship and a full scholarship as compensation. He refused at first, but Dr. Mason took him aside and explained that he could still do some good from the inside. Edita suspected Dr. Mason recruited Dougy to be her spy.

Sloutech covered up the hole in the cable claiming it was the result of space debris from a defunct satellite. Dr. Mason and Sloutech negotiated an agreement that resulted in her getting new lab equipment in return for reinstalling Eddy as the space elevator.

They sat on the floor leaning against Eddy—eating macaroni and cheese that Dougy made as a peace offering. He was thrilled to get the opportunity to hang out with the team.

Edita finally had the chance to ask the question that had been weighing on her mind ever since Dr. Ramsey told her about the transfer.

"I don't understand. You told everybody I had a new heart, but it was more than that. Why did you keep it a secret?"

Dr. Mason chewed slowly. She took a full minute before answering. "When you were brought into Emergency, you were in rough shape. You needed a new heart, lungs, kidneys, spleen—basically everything. I had printed my first organs at that point, but the technology was still in its infancy and to transplant all those parts was not feasible."

She looked at Binder. "But I had been working on a much bigger project. It was an idea that I had been playing with since university."

"Dr. Ramsey said you were always pushing the boundaries," Edita said.

Dr. Mason nodded. "I was. I thought that if I could print single organs, why not print the whole body? The problem was how do you transfer something as complex as the human consciousness? That's when I found Binder. The power station was being shut down as fusion energy was taking over. I reengineered Binder for the transfer, but I had no means of testing it."

Dr. Mason looked thoughtfully at Edita. "When you arrived at the hospital, I knew your only chance was to do a transfer. It was incredibly risky. But you had such a determination to hang onto life that I was inspired. There was no family to talk to so I falsified the accident records to show only your heart was damaged. Then I went ahead with the procedure."

"That's incredible!" Dougy said. "Why didn't you share your breakthrough?"

"I didn't want to make a spectacle of Edita, as her odds of survival were unknown. It was an incredible feat just to use a 3D printed heart." Dr. Mason's face clouded over. "While I was writing the paper to publish the results as a heart transplant, Dr. Ramsey bribed my intern to steal my work."

"Dr. Ramsay didn't know what you really did?" Edita asked.

Dr. Mason shook her head. "Everything about the transfer process is only stored in Binder. The intern who betrayed me was working on the program for the 3D printer for the public health care sector. He stole that information, which Sloutech later used to build their own model."

"What happened to the intern?" Dougy said.

"No researcher or company will ever trust him again." Dr. Mason shook her head. "Dr. Ramsey set him up to take the fall."

"Oh!" Dougy looked pale.

Dr. Mason continued, "I was furious. There was no way I was going to share my research with Sloutech or anyone after that. So I kept working in secret and waited to see if Edita would be a success or not."

"You mean if I'd make it?" Edita said.

"Yes. As I said, it was incredibly risky. But look at you. You not only survived, you thrived!"

"And you followed in Dr. Mason's footsteps," Eddy chimed in. "You excelled at robotics and programming, and now you're learning bio-mechanics!"

"We watched you quietly," Dr. Mason admitted. "When you started applying for internships, I realized it was time for you to know."

"You wanted me to figure it out by working through the program," Edita said.

Dr. Mason nodded. "Yes. I collected all my old notes and then asked you to transcribe them. I felt it would be easier for you to digest the truth if you saw it could work."

Edita thought about it. "Yes, I think so."

"So, what does Edita do now?" Dougy asked. "Dr. Ramsey's in jail, but ..."

Keep working! Angus wrote.

"Yes," Dr. Mason said. "Dr. Ramsey is not going to give away Edita's secret because he wants to make the claim for himself."

"So if he says Edita exists, then he can't be the first one to do a transfer. The cheater!" Dougy growled. "My whole project for him was to find a device that could store an enormous volume of energy."

"It never occurred to him to use old technology." Dr. Mason gave Binder a friendly pat on the side.

Binder played a cheerful tone.

Dr. Mason addressed Edita, "I would like to keep you on as my research assistant after your internship. You can work and go to Uni like Dougy. It might not be with the fanciest computers, but I think if we work together, we can come up with a way to make future transfers accessible for the public and not a novelty sold to the rich."

What do you say, Edita? Angus wrote. *Will you continue to work with us?*

"It won't be easy and we'll have to keep our research close to the heart," Dr. Mason added.

"I can help with security." Eddy said. "I've got lots of great lessons to share with snoopers."

"There is the option of studying something else," Dr. Mason added. "It would be simpler, but I think you have a real aptitude for this."

Edita thought about what that meant for her. If she stayed on, she risked getting exposed. But what else would she do? Programming was her life—literally.

She looked at her hands, hands that were printed. Her whole DNA was something new, but without Dr. Mason's work she would have died as a baby.

"There must be a way we can help others," Edita said. "I'd like to do that. I accept."

Angus drew a smiley face and wrote:

Her heart's new, but genuine,

There are lives involved, but we've got the resolve,

Edita's here to stay, and the future she will pave the way!

The Murder of Crows
Paul Smith

Can a wrongly deposed leader overcome obstacles and rally his allies to victory? My story seeks to answer this question.

I found a clearing deep in the forest, made sure there was nobody around, and stepped out from behind the veil that had allowed me to move unseen through the greenery. I took a moment to rest and then began my work.

My name is Josiah Gray, son of the late, great squirrel, Edward Gray, and I am a wizard. To my knowledge, the only true active wizard squirrel left in existence and until recently, I was the senior educational member of the parliamentary council for Wizardry and the Mystic Arts. A lot I know, but in a nutshell, I teach magick. I say recently because now I'm a usurper, on the run.

It took me the better part of an hour to prepare the ritual I'd created. The final step, an effort of my will and the calling forward of the entity known as Cotton Tail. After three days on the run, it was time to get some answers, and Cotton Tail usually had answers with his unique access to various levels of the underworld. They would know something.

I stood accused of treason and labeled a usurper by the chief of Oak Tree Hill, Malin Neason, and like me, was a wizard also, or used to be. But luckily for me, he was not active. The house arrest

I was put under was a little suspect, especially when he sent four funny-looking assassins to take me out. It would have been better if he'd come himself. But the four he did send burned my house to the ground and I escaped under a veil. I've been hiding ever since. I began my ritual.

"I, Josiah Gray, wizard of the forest, call forward the spirit, Cotton Tail, and I bind him, I bind his will, and I bind his soul, to my circle." I repeated it a second time and I could feel the etheric energies begin to rise. I called a third time and a gust of wind blew through the clearing, and then calm.

Cotton Tail was a hideous low-level demon, spirit-eating cat. He had one good eye, the other glazed with cataract. His whiskers were bent out of shape and had a split in his left cheek that cut to the bone and was horribly infected. He had the worst case of mange on his back and legs I'd ever seen, ribs that must have been broken and healed badly, and the look of misery stamped all over his face. I don't know what kind of life he led when he was alive, but hell was home for this untrustworthy trickster now. We had worked together before, and by providing an offering, I usually knew what I was getting.

"Wizard squirrel!" shouted a voice from inside the circle. Then, like a Cheshire cat, the smile appeared and then the rest of the head; then the body, floating at first, but then settling down to the ground. It lay on its side in the most comfortable position it could find, "... and what can I do for you?" He took some delight in that question as he stretched. I nodded in the direction of a bowl. The contents I'd filled with one of the items I'd rescued from my house before it burnt down.

"Sour, rotten milk and old catnip. My, you do mean business," said the old cat.

"Do you accept my terms of offer, spirit?" I formally clarified.

"You had me at the catnip, young Mr. Gray. Now, what can I do for you?"

"You know what happened on Oak Tree Hill?"

"Goodness, yes! Old Malin Neason, with the whispers in his ear. They must have driven him mad, poor furry creature the spiders, whisper, whisper, whisper ..." The cat waved a mangy paw in front of its ear as it spoke.

"Neason has a governor?" During the Crow wars, their dark sorcerers found a way to weaponize spider embryos that delivered spider spawn floating in on the wind via a microscopic thread, unseen and deadly. Once in, the embryos would drive a squirrel mad. My father had a number of stories of men who would suddenly turn on their own in the middle of battle. Squirrels really didn't like that; as a result, crows no longer have dark sorcerers or magicians of any kind. We wiped them out. How long had Malin Neason had his? Had it been in waiting all this time? He hadn't been in the field for years.

"Hmm, Neason has a number of governors; he's quite beyond saving. So it seems is Oak Tree Hill as well." The cat groomed an infected area on its arm, just back of its paw.

"Not while I'm alive." Clichéd, I know, but it felt like the obvious thing to say.

"Courageous squirrel." The cat smiled and slithered over to the rotten milk and catnip. "Keep that attitude, you'll need it for what's coming."

"What do you mean?"

"Can't really say much, it's way above my pay grade. But something bad this way comes, Gray, really bad." He tucked into the rotten milk with great delight.

"Bad for who?"

"You won't understand this yet, but everybody." He took a deep sniff of the catnip. "All I can tell you is that it starts when there is a meeting of the original four, the four being those that signed the decree of Oak Tree a few years back."

"That can't happen." I shook my head.

"Why not?" the cat shrugged.

"Because at least one of the original four is dead." My father. One of the original four to sign the decree of the land that stated squirrels will always hold Oak Tree Hill, and ratified by the Goddess Demeter herself— and yeah, animal wizards—that's how we roll. "I'll have to worry about that another time. What's happening at the Hill?"

"Crows!" he said.

"Crows!" I echoed.

"... and Rats! Lots and lots of rats!" He cleaned the last of the sour milk off his rotting paw, nails broken and overgrown and twisted. I thought for a moment.

"You make it sound like the numbers are against us."

"An army of at least a hundred thousand rats, and crows never stay still long enough to count, but I promise you this, there are far more than before."

"We can't fight that many. I'm going to need help."

"You know you can count on me, dear boy. No one piles up a body count quite like you, squirrel. All those tasty souls in waiting." He laughed. I wasn't sure how to take that, although I'm sure he meant it as some sort of sick, twisted compliment, especially after our last encounter where I killed seven thousand rabbits; and no, I'm not proud, but they were trying to be conduits for some evil underworld menace.

"Until then, squirrel, you may want to head that way." He pointed in the westerly direction. "Your father had friends that way, that's all I can tell you." I looked at him like an empty wallet that produced a ten pound note, expectant of more but nothing more coming.

"One day, Cat, you're going to tell me how you knew my father and his friends." I gave him a look and clapped my hands together. With that, he was gone.

I brushed the circle away and cleared any obvious signs that magick had been performed, then I took a moment. I took a moment to eat and I took a moment to consider what was possibly ahead of me before I took off in the direction of the West.

#

I had walked quite some way before I'd got onto a straight path leading deeper into the forest. Being this far from Oak Tree Hill, I didn't have to worry about who saw me and it was a lovely day, so I was enjoying the walk, when a voice with a strong Scottish accent spoke out of nowhere asked, "Are you looking for me, pal?" I turned to see a large hooded figure seated between two trees. Not sure how I missed a guy that size, but I did. Now it seems, he was trying to start a fight. "I said, are you looking for me?" he repeated. When a guy's ten times your size and sounds like he's looking for a fight, it's always best to try the soft option first.

"Not me, buddy. Must have been someone else." I never stopped walking.

"Well, in that case..." With the blink of an eye, the stranger was next to me. I was startled and moved to a safe personal distance. "...we should accompany each other on the open road. It's not safe in these here parts. Would you like a drink?" He produced a large cup from under his coat, and although I had yet to see his face, I could smell the liquor on his breath.

"Not for me, and no, thank you. I prefer to travel alone." Just then, the strangest thing — I picked up the scent of another squirrel, multiple squirrels in fact. "Well, I suppose we could walk a mile or two together!" Squirrels this far out couldn't be a good thing, but the scent was off somehow.

"That's the spirit! I'll just get my staff." The stranger picked up a tall, straight staff that was bound in black cloth. Another wizard? We had moved only feet ahead when, appearing in front of us, were two rats dressed in squirrels clothing and covered in squirrel fur — well, that explained the off scent!

"What do we have here then! Looks like a treasonous member of the old Oak Tree Hill Parliamentary Council. What was it they said? Oh yes! On site!" Somehow, two became four and they began a slow approach towards us. I flashed a look back only to find four more, which meant there were probably twelve, maybe more. The stranger and I found ourselves back-to-back.

"We have no quarrel with you fine men. We are humble travellers in search of a place to stay and a warm bed for the night!" He took a last swig from his cup before putting it back in his pocket. "Is this your fight, little fella? Because I don't think they're going to fall for the crock I've just tried to sell them." The rats edged forward.

"It seems it is!" I replied, my hands started to glow with the energy I was about to use to defend myself. I began to slow my breathing and use my energy to connect with the energies around me, and then I found it, the unique energy signature that was being given off by the rats themselves. I tuned into the first four rats in front of me, and I held out my hand. Before they knew what was going on, they felt our energies connect and before I knew what was going on, the huge stranger swung his staff and smashed the first four rats into next week. If the others were dumb enough to stick around, and they were, their fate was going to be the same. He swung again and two more rats fell in the path of his heavy stick and on his final swing for the other two, his hood came off.

"Badger!" I exclaimed, much to my surprise. Then I felt it. I was still feeling for energy around me when I picked up the energy of a crow. We both hid low, searching for better places to hide in the undergrowth. Badgers are magickal from birth but are known to use it sparingly. He was aware of the crow too, probably even before I was. The crow squawked above our position but didn't see us. It would have stopped, but it must have seen the knocked out rats who met the badger moments earlier.

"The name's Archimedes. This way, little fella," said the badger, and he moved us to an underground hole not far from where we were. "This used to be a rabbit hole, but since the rats have been here, and they've been here a while, many of the creatures that walk this forest are gone. We'll be safe moving underground for a while." Archimedes the badger hadn't noticed that I'd stopped paying attention. I was just staring at him with one question.

"Why are you here, Archimedes?" I tried not to sound accusatory.

Archimedes shrugged. "What do you mean?"

"Seems strange to me that I should come across a badger now, of all days, when Oak Tree is under siege. Are the badgers planning something?" The badgers were major allies during the crow wars —we wouldn't have won it without them— and I was glad to see this one, despite him being a stranger to me.

"Well, if you must know, a mutual friend asked me to keep an eye on you. I've been shadowing you for the last day or so. Shoddy work on that veil, by the way. You might as well as had strips of meat strapped to your back in the hot sun, it stank so bad!" I turned to respond to his insult, but Archimedes had literally disappeared into thin air —no sign, no scent, no sound—where did he go? "I'm right next to you squirrel." His large, striped head poked out from his veil. Then, just to show off, he flashed in and out of reality with a veil so seamless he might as well have been standing behind trees.

"Who?" I enquired.

"What?" asked Archimedes.

"Who is our mutual friend?"

"Ah, that's easy. Robin!" In squirrel society, robins were the messenger service. We knew them on an individual basis and considered them friends, but Robin—the robin I knew—had clearly been very busy when not delivering messages. I wonder who else called him 'friend' in the forest? We had walked some way, and I could now hear the sound of rushing water. The river must have been close by.

We hadn't really spoken, Archimedes and I. He seemed to need to concentrate on getting us out of the tunnel, and I was preoccupied with the problem at hand —Malin Neason had a governor controlling his mind, and had been for years. It explains the changes in so many laws, and why he made such dramatic changes to the education system, especially with regards to the Academy of Magick. The head of the academy, Jamima Cleff, lost her job that day and seemed lost ever since. It was her disappearance that triggered all this. I hope she was safe. Vital moments could have prepared us, but Malin Neason had other plans. I could only hope he wouldn't go so far as to touch the magick students. My jaw clenched at the thought.

"Did Robin say anything about Tree Hill?"

"He said, 'Many squirrels in prison or exiled, some even executed. Dark times are upon you and your kin, make no mistake about that.' " And then I got really curious.

"What do you know about the signatures of the decree?" I wasn't looking for an answer, I was looking for a reaction, and bingo. I could hear him choosing his words very carefully, and he delivered them in an altered tone compared to the one he had been using thus far.

"I don't know much, just that there are only two signers left."

"Only two?" I wanted to know more, but then Archimedes told me this is where I get off. He pointed towards a narrow opening in a wall that let in daylight. I turned to see and when I turned back to carry on the conversation, Archimedes the badger had gone. I sniffed for the smell of alcohol, but nothing. He must have slipped away under one of those fancy veils of his. What happened to the other dead signature? And who was it?

I made my way through the very tight opening in the wall, only to find out that it didn't lead onto safe, dry land at all. Instead, it led to a nasty drop of thirty feet or so onto some rocks below, and then a raging river! Could the day get any better?

I hung out of the tight opening and squeezed the rest of my body through. If you didn't know, squirrels just happen to be great climbers. The sheer rock face that I had to climb once out of the hole would be an easy thing for a squirrel. However, no squirrel would or could be prepared for loose chipping. My hand came away from the wall and my body peeled off the wall along with it. I fell, and fell far. When I landed, I hit my head so hard I remember seeing blood before blacking out - and slipping, into the river!

#

I opened my eyes to two sleek-headed, whiskered animals staring down at me — otters. Twins named Sun and Flower, as I would find out later.

"Grandpa! The special needs otter is awake, just like you said he would. Can we take him swimming now?" Grandpa Otter was a formidable character and clearly a much distinguished elder of his community. I could tell that purely by how the children spoke to him.

"Run along, children, the special needs otter needs his rest and will come swimming with you when he can." He fixed his searching eyes on me as the children left.

"See you later special otter," they said as they left.

"My name is..."

"I know who you are, Gray." I wasn't sure if it was good or bad that he knew who I was, but there wasn't a lot I could do if things didn't go in my favour. Behind my back my hands had been tied. His stare didn't move. "At least your father could swim." And I was still uncertain. Otters can be very funny things when they want to be, and ruthless killers on ground and water. With a flick of his wrist, my binds were broken. I rubbed my wrists, while he stared.

"Is everything okay?" I asked. "The way you're staring at me, you'd think you'd seen a ghost." He snapped out of it.

"Based on your problems, sir, I'm surprised I'm not talking

to one.”

“You know what happened at Oak Tree Hill?”

“What happened, and what is happening — crows have taken the central forest and mean to spread their territory outward from there, rats hold the ground level. Malin Neason is still chief, but only just. A squirrel must hold that spot, it is decreed. But should that squirrel turn control over to another, all agreements would be broken, not just on the hill, across the land. Oak Tree is simply the linchpin of a much bigger problem.”

“Something wicked this way comes.”

“You’ve seen it too?”

“What? No, but a spirit I have contact with gave me a heads up, but I couldn’t say any more.”

“No. No I imagine not. Things are still forming on the other side. That is why it’s so hard to get a grip on it in this reality. Hate to tell you this, but what’s happening at Oak Tree is the distraction. There are forces at work here that are way beyond anything we could perceive. You do magick, don’t you, child?” I guess when you’re that old, everyone’s a child.

“Yes, I follow my father in that respect.”

“Many respects, it seems,” he smiled. “Tonight we get the final report. You’re more than welcome to join us for dinner. I’ve had the others acquire some berries for you. Fish doesn’t strike me as your thing.”

We stepped outside and Grandpa Otter was talking, when the strangest thing happened. A single drop of rain landed on Grandpa Otter’s cheek. He just stopped. Another fell, then another, and before we knew it, we were in rain! As I looked round, I could see they had all stopped. The rain fell on them all, those on the bank, those in the water. Those in neither place came out just to stand in the rain. Then it got really heavy, so I took shelter under a bush nearby.

The otters just stood there. I looked more closely at all the otters I could see. It was as if they were in a trance. They all seemed to be watching the same thing, their expressions wide-eyed in looking at whatever they could see. I seemed to join them just staring into space when flashing before my eyes was a beak and two beady eyes. But it was the flash of red on his chest that informed me who it was — my friend Robin.

"There you are, Josiah. I've been looking everywhere for you!"

"Wait a minute. Look! What are they looking at?" I pointed to the otters in total fascination.

"It's the Final Report. Each otter sees an aspect of his future, but sometimes it can appear to them as a collective."

"Can you tell which is which?"

"Nope!" The rain began to slow, and as quickly as it came, it stopped; and the otters began to move again, making their way to dinner and chattering about what they had just seen. Grandpa Otter came over and took my arm.

"Boy, you have no time. You must go back to Oak Tree, but first you must..." He bowed and whispered the rest in my ear. I looked at him hard.

"Why there? Why those two?"

"Because they have vital information regarding this war, and make no mistake, we are at war. The bad news, you can't reclaim the Hill by yourself. You simply don't have the resources. We shall help you, however, and you'll find help from a number of others. If we don't hold the Hill, the war spreads to many backyards and we simply can't have that. Now, hurry!"

There were discussions all over the camp. Whatever they saw, they needed to prepare too. Robin and I gathered some fresh supplies given to us for the journey, and off we went, all the way to Stone Henge.

#

We'd been walking a long time. The forest was a distant memory on our journey as we made our way across acres of open land. Robin spent most of his time looking ahead, making me aware of possible dangers. Stone Henge was still nowhere in sight. I collapsed, and I won't lie, I felt truly sorry for myself! My feet hurt, my legs ached, my back was going from days of walking. The food Otter gave us didn't last long and now I was really hungry.

Robin flew back and sat next to me.

"Josiah, you've stopped!" he declared, stating the obvious.

"I'm sick of walking, Robin. I've been walking for days now and I just seem to get further from my goal, plus a whole bunch of people all seem to know where I'm supposed to be, long before I even get there, and they all seem to know Dad." Robin could hear the sense of overwhelm developing in my voice. Too many questions, no answers. "...And you..." I started, "...more friends than a hedgehog's spikes and you haven't got one friend who can get us to the Henge any quicker?" I'm ashamed to admit it, but I was sulking and moaning like a brat.

"Of course, I do," said Robin. And as if by magick, a fox appeared out of nowhere. Robin flew over, did some sort of hypnotic dance, so good a hummingbird would have been jealous. It held the fox's attention perfectly. Moments later, the fox strode over with Robin on its back.

"My friend the Robin here says you are in vital need of transport. True?" The fox looked at me with huge eyes and a salivating mouth.

"Err, yeah, do you know the way?"

"No, that's on you." Fox had got me between his teeth and flipped me onto his back before I even registered what he had said. "I'm Mr. Fox. But you can call me Mr. Fox." I grabbed some fur on the back of its neck and held on tightly. Fox hit Mach 10, and Robin and I yeehawed our way for most of the journey. Before long Stone Henge was in our sights, but Fox had run himself out, and Robin and I would be on foot from here on.

We got a mile in and Robin said, "No further, for me, no further." I just looked at him. Knowing of the dangers presented by some of the protection spells over the last five thousand years, I shouldn't be going any further myself but I had to, for the sake of Oak Tree Hill and every squirrel who lived in its lush green forest. We made arrangements for after my meeting and we parted company.

I got a half mile in and began to prepare my spell. Once I had finished, I made my way quickly to Stone Henge.

Stone Henge is one of the spookiest places on earth. You can feel the presence of so many beings and entities that lived here, worshipped here, died here and all of them making their own inquiry as to why the living have come here today.

I started what I was about to do, first by clearing my actions with the spirit of Stone Henge. "Spirit of Stone Henge, I seek your permission to speak to the Crows." Nothing except the wind rustling past my ears. "Spirit of Stone Henge, I wish to commune with thee. I seek permission to communicate with the Crows."

Nothing. I stilled my mind and extended my awareness outward to see what I could feel around me.

"What are you doing now, squirrel?" I turned toward the voice around me, and I swear I almost wet myself in fear. The Owl. It stood there looking at me licking blood off its talons, waiting for an answer. When it comes to the animal kingdom and magick, there have been many great and wonderful beings that have become known for one reason or another —snakes for their knowledge, butterflies for their ability to control events— and they have all represented different forces in magick at different times. But there has only ever been one, owl, in the same place representing the same forces since the dawn of time. A silent and stealthy hunter, the owl represented wisdom and courage and it's not something you get past, or away from. "I said, what are you doing now, Squirrel?" He repeated.

"I wish to speak with the crows." My voice couldn't hide the fear.

"That's next, but when I first asked you, what were you doing?" The question was a curious one.

"I was extending my awareness, to see what I could feel." He would have known that, I wasn't sure why he was asking. I blinked and my eyes opened in time to see his wings, as we now stood face to face. I wet myself.

"Did your awareness tell you that was going to happen, Son of Gray?" I blinked again. He knew who I was too, and did Dad make it this far? We stood eye to eye. When you're eye to eye with an owl, you feel total exposure of your own soul whilst staring into the vastness of a black abyss hidden behind their socks. He didn't move, but I could feel his fascination. Then he just turned his head a full 180 degrees. "It seems you have visitors, Son of Gray."

Appearing on a stone behind him were two scout crows surveying the territory. They couldn't have seen Owl; if they did, they'd have stayed well clear. Owls use crows for sport and kill them as a matter of duty, which meant only I could see Owl. I looked at the crows and I looked at Owl. "Don't worry, Son of Gray. They dare not enter here. They can see you, but they feel me."

The crows stood on the wall and shuffled backwards and forward as if trying to get past an invisible net. Then they began to squawk, loud, incessant squawking. It wouldn't be long before others arrived, and they couldn't get in, but same goes for me getting out. I turned my attention back to the task at hand.

"Do I have your permission, great and wise owl?" The owl laughed.

"You squirrels, always in such a hurry." Other crows began to arrive. "Of course you can, Son of Gray" He smiled and moved to the side. More crows began to arrive, and Owl simply licked his talons unphased by what was going on. I took a seat on the ground in the centre of the stones, clapped my hands together, and focused my mind.

"I, Josiah Gray, protector of Oak Tree Hill and the squirrel wizard of the forest, seek audience with Hugin and Munin, Thought and Memory—Odin's Crows."

"Don't seek, demand!" proclaimed Owl, still licking its claws.

"I, Josiah Gray, protector of Oak Tree Hill and the squirrel wizard of the forest, demand audience with Hugin and Munin—Odin's Crows." My eyes still closed, I feel the hot bird breath of the crow known as Hugin breezing through my facial hair.

"You call the crows of Odin to meeting with you, a rodent and that owl!" The scowl in his voice was clear, as both Hugin and Munin stared in disgust at the very sight of Owl. Owl didn't look up.

"I have no quarrel with you gentlemen. Son of Gray wishes to speak with you." He looked up and said, "I needn't make such requests, I shall simply find you." His soulless eyes totally dismissive of any attitude the crows would present whilst also sending a predator's warning. More crows arrived and took their place on the stones. "You should listen to the Gray." He went back to licking his talons. Hugin and Munin simultaneously looked at me.

"Speak," they said.

"Oak Tree Hill, the greater forest, all territories assigned and agreed by decree. Why are the crows trying to break it for a second time?" Hugin looked up after my question and began to walk around the circle, looking at the crows arriving. There were nearly a hundred now and counting.

"Although it is nothing to do with us, the decree stands supported by our master and his equals in the realms where the land connects with the higher and lower realms. However, the crows stake a claim with a much older decree." My heart stopped. A much older claim that would give their action standing in any magickal court. They could probably even muster support for their claim, which would explain the rats. Simply put, this is a legal issue. One the squirrels, even the forest could lose. Otters go back to fighting with beavers, hedgehogs versus rabbits all over again, and squirrels go back to being the broken society of the forest. To hell with that!

"What decree?" Squirrel asked.

"A decree so old that your kind didn't even exist, a time long before the oaks."

"Supported by who?" Munin answered this time, as if to speak from the same mind.

"There are forces that exist that are so old, you could hardly identify them as forces any more. Some that are so old, their power creates new faraway galaxies. So old, that even the old ones amongst the gods don't know who they are. The decree of the crows allows their claim to stand, and the gods have decided that war will be the decider. You, squirrel, should be on the battlefield helping your fellow squirrels. Deserter!" Munin tutted.

"We were infiltrated. The elected chief had a governor in him growing and working away for the last five years. We weren't at war."

"When you war with crows, you are always at war with crows, squirrel." The two birds who had been walking around the circle came together as if ready to leave.

"Is there something going on that maybe you don't know about?" The crows laughed.

"No such thing, Squirrel. We are the eyes of the gods, we see all. Although this is a long way for you to come for such a short conversation that will most likely end in your death. At least you know now." Hugin bent over and put his wing out. "Your offering, squirrel." And then it occurred to me, all those spirits I could sense when I arrived, offerings, or very possibly, the lack of, and when all you have to offer is your life...! I reached round to my tail, pulled four hairs from the middle so no one would notice, and I handed them over. It got me an annoyed look.

"For your master." I said, and bowed, not daring to look up. They were, however, received with warm thanks. When I looked up, Hugin and Munin had gone and Owl had done licking his talons.

"Are you done, Squirrel?" he asked calmly, hundreds of crows now surrounding us.

"I am," I said resolvedly.

"Then just one last thing before you go — my offering." I don't know where it came from or how I thought of it, but I put my hands up and asked, "Who do you think the crows are for?" Those black soulless eyes seemed to smile at me, and the owl gave out an high-pitched screech, audible to only a few birds, and certainly not crows. All of a sudden, a plume of black feathers came floating down toward me, with no sign of the bird that had left them behind, and then it happened again on the other side of the circle; Owl took off, making his presence known to the crows. His talons deep in the chest and guts of one crow whilst swinging back for another to catch in his other talon, all this before the crows had even realised what was playing out before their very eyes. They gave flight only for another thirty owls to appear, each one arriving with a crow crushed between its talons and swiftly turning to get another. Black feathers littered the ground, along with the torn bodies of the crows that once owned them. Two hundred crows were quickly reduced to fifty escaping crows running for their lives. The owls shot for them like an air force squadron bombing them from above with superior force. Fifteen crows left, being chased by owls who had made very quick work of nearly two hundred of their brethren.

All over in a flash, the idea to leave the circle hadn't even entered my mind, it was that quick. Owl was nowhere to be seen. I made my way through the dead and the dying that lay all around, and made my way back to the Hill and eventually back to Robin.

"We've got problems Robin," I said, "but I think I know what to do. Time to head back to Oak Tree, and pick up some milk along the way."

#

A lot of people don't know this, but as aggressive as we are to others in the forest, squirrels do have friends. One of mine had a deep underground network that ran all around the entirety of Oak Tree Hill and far beyond in some directions. It just so happens that one of the holes that comes up for air was in my own backyard. If I was going to lead a war, I was going to need some tools for the job.

I got to the periphery of Oak Tree Hill and made sure the coast was clear before I began a series of small taps on a hollow tree trunk that led deep into ground. It was a special code that only my friends would know. And before long, ladies and gentlemen, I give you, General Clayton Sonic III, chief mole and master digger. I saluted and clicked my heels.

"General, it's me, Josiah Gray." He slowly poked his head forward from his little body.

"Josiah Gray, you've aged! But, being wanted for treason and being made enemy of the state will do that to you." I still held my salute. "At ease boy, and do come along. You know you're in the right place. You, and I do mean you, can always depend on us moles. Especially, the military underground."

"Thank you, General. Can we get off the surface? I'm literally in the belly of the lion right now."

"Of course, of course. Where are you headed?"

"My place. I need to get some things."

"Your place burned to the ground."

"That's why I keep spares hidden in the grounds. You never know when you need a spare." The General and I discussed plans and the role I needed the moles to play in the coming fight, but I needed him to be careful. Moles present no challenge for a rat and there were lots of rats, but the moles were smart, deeper, and masters of the underground game.

#

I got to my place through a hole that came up in the garden. I looked at the cindered remains of the place; nothing was retrievable. I made my way to the back of the garden to a pile of old cut grass and I began to dig. I soon hit wood and I pulled up a long box. Inside, wrapped in cloth, was a spare of the only weapon a wizard squirrel needed — my energy staff. It had the same marking as my original, but that got lost in the fire when the house burned down. I walked to the centre of my garden and dug my staff deep into the earth with crystal clear clarity and effortless will. I charged my staff with sacred energies of the earth; the rune-like markings etched deep into its surface began to spark and glow orange. I closed my eyes and poured more energy into the staff; the runes glowed brighter, embers floating away as the runes began to burn. I raised my hand and waited. I began to sway, which meant I was now in command with planetary energies needed to fulfill the charging of my weapon. It turned light blue and finally bright white — my energy staff was ready. Just one more thing to do. I took out a flask of milk I'd acquired on the walk back from Stone Henge, used it to soak a piece of cloth, and sat in the middle of my garden.

#

Later I met Robin at our rendezvous point as arranged, and much to my delight, he wasn't alone. There was Grandpa Otter and the otter twins, Sun and Flower, Archimedes, Mr. Fox, and a few other forest animals I didn't think I was going to see. He'd been really busy.

As I walked down the hill, I saw them all looking up at me as if I was the leader, and a voice in my head said, "If you're going to ask an animal to risk its life in battle, you'd damned well better be ready to lead it." My father's voice. We stood in a place where he and I used to play war games when I was a kid. I didn't realise it then, but he was preparing me for war; against any and all, our games carried a very real application.

We grouped round, took account of numbers, noted our positions, and agreed on our retreat/escape plan if things didn't go our way. But if things didn't go our way, we'd be lucky to get that far. With that, we separated. The others went to give word to their crews on the ground and I made my way toward the main road that led into Oak Tree Hill. On approach, I veiled and moved through to the main streets unseen.

I hadn't been back to Oak Tree since the parliament meeting where I got accused of treason and put under house arrest and my house got burned down fighting the assassins that came to kill me. Had I forsaken it? Had I left it to the hands of its abusers? Was I a deserter? I asked myself these questions because it broke my heart, but filled it with rage at the same time. What was a paradise was now a rat-infested hell hole. The rats had raided every shop, every store, and smashed anything squirrel without regard. The stench of blood from the body parts of dead and eaten squirrels, made blind by the crows and finished by the rats. Squirrels with their guts torn out and their limbs pinned to trees — a message to the rest. The bodies and the blood brought flies and other insects like cockroaches to feast on the remains of those who once walked these streets, who laughed, who cheered, who played. All gone, from here, anyway. I have no doubt many squirrels made it out, but those that didn't were now meals for rats and that enraged me like nothing else. Malin Neason, every crow and every stinking magpie was going to get blasted off the face of the earth starting today! And then the trigger.

I saw four rats trailing behind a CLASS 3 War Level Assassin Magpie. The single grey feather in the tail was the giveaway. And the size! They are much bigger than normal magpies, almost the size of crows and although not totally impervious to magick, they were damn hard to kill. In front of the magpie, a child, no older than seven, her voice choked from screaming as she ran from the monsters chasing her. Her parents must have been killed already. They would never have left her alone. And then the magpie picked out one of her eyes!

I stepped out from behind my veil, and without hesitation, filled my staff with energy and lashed the huge bird down the centre of its back with a laser-like energy lash that would cut most birds in half, but this was a CLASS 3. The bird spread its wings and squawked out loudly in tremendous pain. It hadn't even swung round before I'd hit it again, this time lashing across the wing. It stuck out awkwardly and the bird looked unable to use it. I lashed again, same place, just to make sure it couldn't be used, and then it turned to face me. "You die today Magpie," I told him, and he stared at me hard. He gave off a low rumble from his throat and the rats that were following him now seemed to be fixed on me also. "You too rats, you're getting it as well."

I placed my staff in combat position, ready for attack, maintaining a low vibrational energy through it at all times. You can do great things with an energy staff, but the energy required, if over-used, can burn out the energy meridians in the body, a very painful experience that could take me out of the game for far too long. I had to be careful. I didn't know what I was going to face when I got to the Great Oak.

The rats stepped forward, clear in their group effort, and in doing so missed the whole thing. I only saw a flash of the tail myself, but a fox ran through and snatched the bird and its life away from the fight. Then out of a bush came a badger that wasn't Archimedes, smashing the rats like it was workout day. He took all four at the same time and wanted other rats that were hanging about scavenging to know that he was coming for them next. He tore off down the street, fighting every rat in sight. I ran to the poor child in the street, but she had gone. Did the rats get her when I wasn't looking? I didn't have time to investigate. I could only pray she was safe, but this was a war zone. How safe had she already been? I looked up and noticed that crows were beginning to circle above the Great Oak, only a hundred or so, but it got my attention. I veiled again to avoid more rats; the crows would now be hiding in the trees on the run to the Great Oak.

#

By the time I got to the Great Oak more crows had gathered, circling, and it seemed, more rats! There was barely room to move, there were that many. I noticed, hiding in a tree close by, was the last fighting efforts of the soldier squirrels that stayed behind to defend their homes. Good luck, boys, I thought. Whatever their plan was, I hope they succeeded. I slipped past and made it to the Great Oak.

I made my way to the great hall at the top of the trunk of the tree. There was Malin Neason, the biggest crow I'd even seen, a magpie, and a rat. The four stood in deliberation. There was so much magickal energy in the air, I knew everything I did would be five times stronger. It must have come from what the crows were doing. No dark sorcerers didn't mean they couldn't still do magick.

"You're too late, Gray. In ten minutes, this entire area will belong to the crows and the rats," Neason said it with tears in his eyes. Neason must have been doing all he could to fight the governor, but there was no use. They had planned a genocide for the squirrels, with the rats on the ground cleaning up the bodies. Crows circled overhead. More and more came to join what was developing into a tornado of crows. Their squawks spread panic and anxiety through the forest. Their presence began to dim the skies as thousands circled above the Great Oak.

I became painfully aware of the situation and something inside me snapped. I clenched my fists, and as I did, they glowed red with the force of etheric power that was about to be unleashed on my foes. Neason had been a more powerful wizard in his time, but by law, inahadn't means you must be inactive. He hadn't practiced for years, but he may still have been a threat. I raised the energy in my hands and went for my first target—the CLASS 3, War Assassin.

"In the name of Edward Gray, I call upon the powers of the etheric realm to smite mine enemies!" I ran to the centre of the room and pointed my staff at the bird. The power left my body with the force of a bazooka missile. It blew a hole clean through the magpie and slammed what was left of his body onto a branch nearby, impaling the dead bird for all to see. "You're next, crow!" The bird fixed me with an evil stare before deciding this wasn't his fight and he flew up to join the now thousands of birds circling the tree. This was a weapon. I'd only ever seen it once before. They circle and then dive, killing everything in its path. I didn't have long, but first I had to deal with Neason and the rat.

The rat clearly hadn't been paying attention. He stood before me with a knife and his stained long front teeth dripping with saliva. I raised my left hand and connected my energy with his. I felt round his energy body until I felt the cavity in his chest. I used my energy to grip the cavity and the rat froze. "What are you doing? Unhand me!" he cried, and I squeezed. His panic becoming more desperate, and then he took a deep breath and coughed up blood. I squeezed more and he fell to his knees clutching his chest and desperately trying to scramble for breath. "You...," he literally dragged air into his lungs, "You!" He fell to the side, and breathed no more.

I went looking for Neason, who was hiding here somewhere. I looked over, only to see rats circling the tree the same way the birds were. I made my way to one side of the hall and said, "You can come out now Neason, it's over." The arrogant voice behind me said otherwise.

"Far from over, my dear Gray. This is a new time, and soon the crows will dive and Oak Tree Hill will be born anew." He stood at the other side of the hall with two rats in front of him, holding some sort of projectile device. Whatever it was, it was damn quick because I didn't even have time to flinch before the missile travelled across the room, and hit something before bursting into flames that held in the air for a moment and then fell flat on the ground ten feet in front of me. Stepping out from behind a veil, the badger, Archimedes. Archimedes, who dusted any burning embers off and held out a mug for me to take. "Hold my beer!"

More rats had come up into the Great Hall, poised for attack.

Archimedes cantered into the room and clapped three times. This did a great job at getting everyone's attention. Then he announced, "If any of you wish to leave the battle now, there will be no shame in it. You have families, and this is your last chance." Even I had a bewildered look on my face. "Very well!" He clapped again, three times. Every rat's eyes glazed over as their bodies seemed to twist in a sudden onslaught of pain before falling dead on the floor. Bottom line, Archimedes was badass.

We both set our attention to Neason, who looked at us and frowned, tears still in his eyes. Then, more rats. Twelve spilled into the hall, another one was ridden in by Sun and Flower, the twin otters. One with his teeth at the top of the rats' spin, the other with his teeth at the base of the spin. When they landed, they tore it apart and looked for the next before spying me. "Special Needs Otter, don't worry, we will protect you." Archimedes clapped his hands again and now the bodies were piling up. If rats were getting this far, it meant the forces on the ground were at their breaking point. Time to call in reinforcements.

"Archimedes, I need you to get a signal to all our forces out there. Can you do it? I need them to run as far as the ferns at the edge of Oak Tree. Those that can't make it that far need to get to the holes by the Sycamores. Tell them to leave no one behind." I hoped General Mole had done his job.

I looked out and saw a few brave warriors barely escaping the rush of rats that were now circling the tree, and there were so many crows, it was dark. I reached into my pocket and pulled out a small stench-filled rag. "Cover me?" I asked the Otters, and I made my way to the window and then the first squawk. Ten thousand crows all squawking together at the same time made the ground rumble and struck fear in everybody. There would be two more before they struck and we would all lose our lives. I looked at Archimedes.

"Hurry, squirrel, we don't have much time." I turned back to the window and held the rag outside, and passed energy through it.

"Cotton Tail, come and get paid!" My words rang out into a silence of their own. And I waited. In the distance, a small blue glowing light appeared, and then another, and then another, until all the edge of the Oak Tree began to glow. The glow moved inwards towards the tree, and then I saw it. A demon cat snatching the souls of as many rats as his happy excited little body would allow, and he wasn't alone. There must have been one cat for every ten rats, and there were thousands of rats. Some tried to dig their way out of the oncoming trip to hell, but they were never going to be fast enough. Then there was a sound that soberly reminded us that victory was yet to be ours, the second squawk.

Neason didn't move, he just stood there, frowning at our achievements, tears in his eyes. Archimedes waved his hand and that probably would have decapitated Neason, but all that happened were shimmering lights as his powerful magic bounced off Neason's protective shield. We both frowned at that.

"No time. Archimedes, can you isolate the air around the crows?" He stiffened for a moment.

"Done."

"Then let's hope this works." I could feel the area Archimedes had isolated for me, and it was huge, possibly even too big for my plan, but I had to try. I planted my staff on its point and closed my eyes and began to raise the energy around me, then it came up even more powerfully because Archimedes added his own energy to the process. Orange, red with flecks of turquoise light began to spin around me and spill from my staff. My hands began to ache as my energy meridians began to overflow. The lights spun faster and faster until they formed a cone, my elbows and shoulders began to ache now as the energy built up higher and higher and nerve pain ripped down my spine and nearly brought me to my knees.

I stood tall, my eyes still closed, and I called on the last energies my body could take. At this moment, I spoke the magick words. "With the power invested in me by the decree of the animals of the forest — Incinuratus." The third squawk rang out. I opened my eyes and looked up. Eighty thousand crows began their descent. Me, Archimedes, the otters, even Neason, we were all dead for sure. And then, as I looked into the eyes of the very first descending crow, ready to plant its futile strike, it burst into flames. Flames that spread so quickly to every other bird that got caught by the fire, that left a mushroom type cloud that could be seen for miles around. Every bird fell, flaming, smouldering or just plain dead in the sky. There were small fires everywhere, enough to burn the forest to the ground completely, and then ... then, the rains. It was as if the gods had been watching. I fell to my knees, barely able to stand, my meridians were burnt out for sure. Once again, our attention turned to Neason.

"Your call, boy!" declared Archimedes. I looked at Neason, and I could see nothing that suggested remorse or fear. He was always going to be a problem. The governor was tearing him apart inside and I couldn't stand to see it. I readied my hands for a spell that would have broken his shield and given us clear passage to him but I had nothing left, when a huge pair of wings spread through what was left of the smouldering branches of the tree and the owl's talons sunk deep into Neason's chest. Owl took Neason's eyes and then tore out his throat, and then opened his skull and feasted on the governors that had been hiding in Neason's head all these years. Myself, Archimedes, and the otters didn't even blink. Owl had flown away before we had time to react. "Never suffer traitors, Son of Gray, not for a second!" With that, he was gone.

Not sure how I felt about what had just happened, but it was over. That was my focus, that and the pain in my entire body. I made my way to the window to see what was happening on the ground. Carnage. Dead crow bodies piled up feet deep. Where there were no crows, rats. And then a blowing blue figure appeared from under the pile.

"Josiah! You're not going to be able to keep this quiet anywhere! Body count young wizard! Outstanding!" He licked his bloody paw and went back to taking the remaining souls left. He and his buddies would take care of the bodies that were left over and a clean-up would begin in the morning.

We had won back Oak Tree Hill, with the help of our friends of the forest. The decree was still intact and all was right with the planes of existence once again.

#

The next morning was the clean-up. Squirrels didn't waste any time in getting things back together. I stood in the street holding the sign to Mr. Billows grocery store, when I received a hard tap on my shoulder — Jamima Clef! If there was one person I wanted to see and know was still alive, it was Jamima Clef. Not seen since the start of all this, I gave her a massive hug and we rubbed noses. It's a squirrel thing. "Where have you been?" I exclaimed.

"I was there when Archimedes found you, and it was me that helped the little girl you saved from the rats."

"You've been following me?"

"Well, of course! How else would Archimedes know to help you?" Jamima knew Archimedes? I didn't want to know. "We are going to need a new chief now that Neason is gone." She said it rather loudly.

"You're the new chief. Well I couldn't think of anybody better. The position belongs to a Gray." There was something in that, I could feel it resonate within me.

"The new chief sounds right to me," said another voice, and another, echoes of agreement resounded through the helpers. I smiled.

"Well, then I accept." Jamima looked at me thoughtfully. As she did, we both noticed a sharpness in a southerly wind that blew through the camp; it gave us both chills. I looked around at the others who didn't seem to notice, and Cotton Tail's words rang in my head. Something wicked this way comes. Jamima looked at me uneasily, but mustered a smile to break our train of thought. We'd had enough for one lifetime, the next battle can wait.

"I think, dear Josiah, it's time you knew the secrets."

"Secrets?" I enquired.

"Secrets only the highest wizards are privy to, Josiah, no joke. Secrets." I eyed her suspiciously. "They begin, right now, and who knows. Maybe we can work on that rubbish veil of yours." She took me by the arm and led me to a place in the forest, and we began my training. And then it hit me—I was now the Chief and that was going to take some getting used to.

Mandarin: The 105th Story

Michelle A. Belgrave

What inspired this story was witnessing people in high positions removed for a few comments deemed offensive by others. For Mandarin: The 105th Story, *I asked myself, if a superbeing was in charge, how would they be deposed?*

"Who is Nicodemus?" Naman asked, head raised and cocked at an angle.

Amid the bustle and whirl of preparations, the soft voice barely pierced the commotion.

Behind Naman's long, lean form, two pairs of female hands fluttered nervously. They tossed synthetic microfilaments into the air. Initially undetectable to the human eye, the weaving pieces glittered and twinkled above Naman.

Within seconds, a rushing waterfall of platinum-colored liquid poured over Naman's head and tawny broad shoulders. Ivory sleeves puffed over bulging biceps, then clung like a second skin to forearms, as a white lacy ruff with a honeycomb pattern stretched from chin to collarbone, while white silvery jodhpurs flowed into shiny ebony boots at the knees.

The two older women tending to Naman made eye contact. Teeth bared, their heads tossed and twisted to and fro as though the answer was a rope in a tug of war. They settled down, tempered by the weight of Naman's stiff demeanor and rigid back.

"Answer me," Naman breathed impatiently, shoulders rising and falling, from behind a silken mask. "Now."

They glided around from the left and right sides of Naman. Together, eyes cast on the floor, hands clasped, thumbs facing outward, fingers curled and hidden, they bowed deeply at the waist. Slowly rising, in unison, they answered, "M'Sir, rumor say Nicodemus will harm you."

A startled murmur rose among the coterie in the massive room, echoing off the walls and magnifying their anxiety.

"Ridiculous," Naman scoffed. "It is impossible. Do not believe it." Addressing the disturbed group he waved a dismissal, then Naman glided forward, hovering above the floor. "Where is M. Darin?" The air rippled, distorting the protective barrier field, as a wave of motion caused by the parting procession trailed in Naman's wake.

#

Amanda watched the broadcast in her mind's eye, partially retrieved from her synthetic memory pool, and replayed events with exquisite detail. A dark spot appeared at the top left, which could be her embedded device misinterpreting floating vitreous. She held up a finger to focus. The shadow blew up, fanning outward, before sinking into Naman. It could be another fluke. Yet Amanda noticed a progressively awkward halting of Naman's flow. A careful speaker, the leader of Prasinopolis normally masticated and ruminated over every word.

"M'Sir is off script," she murmured.

Minute spasms made Naman grasp the lectern, eyes rolling back till silver irises gave way to sclerae. Pleasure tugged at the corners of Amanda's lips, pulling them into a wide smile, revealing large white teeth and long canines. The broadcast went blank. A sedate Naman spoke as though nothing untoward occurred. The curious episode happened within one hundred milliseconds, less time than the blink of an eye. Staring into space with her cat-like eyes, the pupils became tiny pinpoints. She clapped with enthusiasm and squealed.

"What is it now?" Amanda's unofficial guardian and honorary big sister Dollie Mercado grumbled. She reached out to put a hand on the diminutive girl's shoulder, but checked the affectionate gesture. Amanda didn't like to be disturbed during one of her reveries.

Placing her hands flat on the table, Amanda chuffed, imitating a satisfied tiger. With a happy expression, she turned towards a bemused Dollie leaning against the sink counter. "Guess what I saw?" she asked in a sing-song voice, and continued, not waiting for a response. "Remember the celebration on the third?" The date marked Naman's fourth year in office.

Dollie's brow furrowed. Unless it pertained to weather, traffic, weapons mastery, and martial arts, she blocked the broadcasts. "Are you talking about the latest?" Politics bored her silly, but this news penetrated. She walked towards the far wall to reach into the food generator. Retrieving a plate from the machine, Dollie placed it in front of a gleeful Amanda.

She beamed. "Naman is no longer," she chuckled. "I must tell Captain Harper."

Dollie shook her head. "Are you sure?" Out of habit, Dollie sought a dark corner in the bright yellow kitchen to check the broadcast.

When she turned back, Amanda was gone.

#

"We are not here to indulge in fruitless speculation, Amanda," Captain Scott Harper said gruffly. "QSPARC has a formidable track record."

Her wide-set eyes shone, reflecting light in the dark, dinky space. Shaking her head, Amanda held up her left hand and wagged an index finger. "It has a great record of solving crimes based on probability, and tracking individual criminal profiles since infancy. Monitoring people every moment of their lives, even the most ardent and law abiding are bound to have committed a few indiscretions. Yet the solve rate for serious crimes is only 33.87%." She smirked, scanning stats in her right field of vision.

Harper scowled.

Amanda's small pink tongue flicked at him, then disappeared behind a tiny smile.

Pushing back his chair, Harper began to rock.

Pointed chin thrust obstinately, Amanda wasn't going away until she aired her theory.

"But Naman is alive." Frustrated, Harper rubbed a hand through the black stubble over his scalp. It may as well have been a thicket of thorns.

Suspecting that her physical presence baffled Harper, Amanda savored needling him. The portal would have sufficed by saving time and presenting an appropriate guise or face filter. Amanda's hyper-cheerfulness was belied by an unwavering, steady gaze on Harper's uncomfortable, rumpled, and disheveled appearance.

"Where's Dollie?" He asked abruptly, sounding a tad wistful about Amanda's attractive, honey colored, long-haired companion.

Amused, Amanda jerked her head towards the door. "Outside."

No matter where she disappeared to, Dollie easily tracked down her location and vice versa.

Pulling his chair forward, Harper gestured. "I'm growing old here, Mandy."

She smiled brightly at having made headway. "Let me talk to Naman."

"Try again."

Amanda stood, not that it made any difference— the height of the desk reached her midsection. "Captain Harper, remember when I brought a spoofer to your attention?"

He blinked. "Yes, the Traveling Student Case."

A classmate of Amanda orchestrated a series of robberies by training security intelligence systems to avoid flagging him. The mastermind stuck to a fixed schedule while incrementally changing his routines, maintaining a staid and stable appearance, keeping indirect contact with operatives, and gaming the school's social merit system. Tantalizing aromatic hints of brine, cedar, pine, and orange citrus on his person triggered her curiosity. Clear evidence of extensive traveling, yet his attitude about it initially puzzled her. A normal teen wouldn't abstain from bragging, sharing and showing off his exploits. When he came in with a metallic smell, so much so she could taste it, followed by another day of smoke and acetone, it prompted her to act.

Clasping hands behind her back, a wheedling tone filled Amanda's voice. "Initially, you wouldn't take the word of a fourteen-year-old high school junior. After all of these years, you've come to appreciate my observational intuition." She tapped her temple. "Naman is possibly being spoofed, Captain Harper. I cannot do this without your permission. Let me begin by talking to Naman's staff."

Nodding, Harper jabbed at the keyboard. Pointing at her, he ordered, "Don't go ruffling any feathers," and turned back to his work.

An investigative consultant without a formal role, Amanda worked on an ad hoc basis. In this case, she would serve as a Brief, unable to petition for a warrant, make an arrest, or expand the investigation's scope. Relaying her findings to Harper was her sole task. The decision to proceed or end the matter remained in his hands.

#

"I like Naman's style," Amanda said, floating five stories above their heads in the book tower.

Cherie Oh and Patty Sazagawa, the household support of Naman, dipped their heads in acknowledgment and pleasure. "M'Sir has great taste."

The library was the last of the railroad cars, so to speak. Naman's house reminded Amanda of an old rail yard, with black shipping container cars, connected to an entrance hall resembling a grand central station. Rounded archways bore distinct names and numbers, leading to countless rooms of various lengths and directions on multiple levels.

Polished, marble gray slate tiles covered the ground floor. Large stretches of landscaped grounds, ornamental sculptures, flowered gardens or fancifully trimmed hedges, separated the black shipping container rooms. This allowed one to see many of the rooms running parallel from different angles and aspects. Amanda noted the lack of bird feeders, water fountains, flying or crawling animals. The subdued chatter of Naman's servants and

Dollie penetrated the silence.

Twirling leisurely, Amanda descended. Her eyes swept rows and rows of synthetic bound tomes, many untouched and unread. They filled the tower with the sweet smell of old books and dried ink. She could stay here for days, weeks even.

Like a thunderclap, the sudden hard clank and scrape of boots announced the arrival of Naman.

A startled Amanda turned her sharp, headlong drop into a graceful landing. Dollie smoothly glided to her side, standing sideways, acting as a shield. Amanda glanced up at her protector, lips pulling into a smile that transformed into a brief grimace. Dollie's presence comforted yet reminded Amanda of her vulnerability.

In a coming-of-age ceremony at twelve, most children of Prasinopolis elected to enhance their natural abilities or senses. Back then, Amanda's parents, concerned about her underdevelopment, wanted to boost her growth cycle. However, she had preferred eye augmentation, giving them cat-like qualities and appearance, along with a nearly limitless synthetic memory pool. Amanda's height and small build made her feel helpless at times. Despite her occasional discomfort, the same enhancements would have been chosen again.

Naman's long, lean frame halted, straightening at the sight of the assemblage. "Naman expects company?" The blurry voices of the self-referencing person sounded hoarse and a little bewildered.

Amanda stared. Entranced, she danced around Dollie's restraining arm. Moving closer, she maintained a discreet distance. Bowing, she executed a quick dip with her hands clasped at the waist. "I admire you, Naman, M'Sir." Turning on the charm with a broad smile, Amanda looked up, neck straining, seeking to make an impression.

Naman's suspicious eyes surveyed the room, eventually settling upon her. In a battle of wills, their gazes locked, each one refusing to yield by looking away first. Amanda knew she was being rude, but couldn't help herself.

Having lived in Prasinopolis her entire life, the city-state now bore the nickname Necropolis—"city of the dead." The country did not have a formal written constitution. Its system of government took form based upon customs, precedents, and laws by a willing, adherent bureaucracy. The governing structure used to consist of a few main branches: legislative offices seated by elections; public health, revenue and administrative positions chosen by lottery from professional pools; and the permanent security branch filled with appointees from the others for lifetime service. The last one served to maintain system continuity and preserve institutional memory.

The timeline of Prasinopolis evolved from BN—Before Naman —to AN—After Naman, as six branches shrank to two. The legislative and administrative branches became feeble appendages of the governing body called Naman. This transformation did not come by way of civil war, bloodshed or coup d'état. Naman's rule came by way of propaganda, persuasion, and being all pervasive. In a continuous communication cycle, like a conveyor belt with data flowing into and out of the broadcast, Naman's ideas were the public's ideas.

Three months into the new leader's term came the first upheaval. Naman announced the arrest of Mr. Cullver, charged with conspiring to sell preserved government land to a developer's consortium of which he was a member. Naman's dry and pitiless voice-over covered a live scene of officers marching into a stately brick house, followed by them leading out an austere patrician of above-average height with shoulder-length, fading, red hair. Mr. Cullver lost a seat in the legislature, a measure of his wealth, defending against numerous other charges, and public goodwill as the probe ensnared extended family members. Naman's broadcast devoted to Mr. Cullver's situation held the same weight as a trial and conviction.

Disquiet filled Amanda as Naman continued to study her like a biological curiosity under a microscope.

"Sit," Naman ordered, using telekinesis by waving a beckoning hand at the room across the hall. A bar stool skipped and skittered towards them, stopping with a noisy, grating half-spin in front of Amanda.

Desirous of being close to the most powerful being in Prasinopolis, she smilingly accepted the challenge. Amanda felt the weight of Dollie's stare, meeting it with a subtle nod. The gesture soothed both their nerves. She floated up, grateful for the assist from her boots. Amanda stood on the seat. The boots kept her balance and stability. Satisfied, she met Naman's eyes without the absurd height difference between them. Amanda wanted to touch Naman; somehow she would find a way.

"We came to speak with Madams Oh and Sazagawa," Amanda answered Naman's question from what seemed like hours ago. "It is a bonus that you, M'Sir, are here as well." She would turn on the charm offensive again.

Silver eyes flicked over Amanda's petite body, ultimately darting back to her small ears, pointed chin, and wide forehead. They crinkled with amusement at the corners. "You are no girl child.

You are woman, Amanda Elizabeth Harcourt," Naman stated in a matter-of-fact tone. The blurry voices were distinct now, perhaps two, but no more than four. One of them dropped the "H" in her name. She wanted to reach inside Naman, pull out one of those voices, and have a chat.

Naman's origin story began in a similar fashion to other super-beings: a projectile hurtling from the skies during a thunderstorm, erupting and coalescing from a pyroclastic flow, or being born of ill fated superbeings. Amanda suspected the derivation came the old-fashioned way: genetic manipulation and enhancement from a laboratory like everyone else. Yet, the boost was far more unique, a composition never encountered before.

It made her wonder: Who created Naman?

Amanda leaned forward, sniffed once, storing away the olfactory memory for later. "M'Sir, as I've asked your wonderful staff, have you been receiving any specific threats lately?"

Naman stared blankly at her, as though the lights went out. Nobody was home.

Madams Oh and Sazagawa finally gave Amanda the answer she sought. "Nicodemus."

Her eyes roamed over Naman's masked face, calculating features from the prominent brow, long nose, straight thick eyebrows, and fuzz of close-cropped black hair. Later, she would search for a smaller, younger face. Naman must be an exaggeration of someone more modest, albeit human, looking.

"Are you finished with Naman?" Amanda was asked, the blurry of composite voices gone, replaced with a strong deep one. She relaxed unconsciously, the voice a familiar narcotic from the broadcast.

"What did this Nicodemus say?" Tossing the question over her shoulder and starting to tremble from exertion, Amanda leaned back too far. In an instant, she found herself cradled in the arms of Naman, an experience akin to going from the frying pan into the fire. Naman's body radiated so much heat, she began to sweat. Amanda clasped onto a physique molded from smelting iron.

Madams Oh and Sazagawa exchanged stunned looks. During the time they served Naman, no one ever came close enough to touch. M'Sir avoided physical interaction.

"Put her down," Dollie demanded, lips tight. While no match for Naman, she took her self-imposed role as Amanda's protector seriously.

Naman's chest vibrated from a subdued chuckle. "Light as a feather." Amused, Naman transferred Amanda from one arm to the other effortlessly.

Playfully, the superbeing teased Dollie. "You catch her?"

"No!" They all shouted in unison.

Amanda wrapped her arms around Naman's neck. Guffaws filled the room as Naman pried Amanda off, gently lowering her to the floor.

"Never mind Nicodemus," Naman said, straightening. "Naman fears nothing."

#

THE PRASINOPOLIS PLEDGE

FOR THE BLOOD OF MY FOREFATHERS AND FOREMOTHERS

FOR THE LIFE OF MY PROGENY

FOR THE LIFE OF MY COUNTRY

FOR THE LIFE OF US ALL

For the protection of my ancestors

For the safety of my family

For the service of us all

I will sacrifice for our country

My word, my honor is the foundation

We must make Prasinopolis strong

We must make Prasinopolis thrive

"Did you enjoy your excursions among the locals?" Dollie asked, in the vehicle driver's seat, on their way home.

Amanda appreciated taking mass transit. Getting the feel of the city-state, riding like a regular morning commuter, observing the public and scenery, she wanted to take note of its changes. It gave Amanda an escape from Dollie's driving, which drove her to distraction. Living within walking distance of a stop, she took an autonomous vehicle for tourists to visit Captain Harper. It glided on a predetermined path, parallel to The Sturgis River, through the streets, bridges, tunnels, and main thoroughfares of Prasinopolis.

Over four hundred years ago, the city-state formed in a lush verdant valley, between two mountainous ridges, where most citizens lived. The little republic's name, Prasino, came from the Greek word for green. From snowcapped mountains, melting glaciers released bright blue waters to snake through Prasinopolis. The Sturgis River fed into a dammed Lake Matisse and flowed past two narrow strips of land called The Pincers into the Oyster Sea. The Pincers freed Prasinopolis from being landlocked with access to a free port and open waters.

The touring vehicle glided by bright, warm, classical-style government buildings, while skyscrapers made the temperature dip. Warming again as it moved past untended fields, farm lands and a park. The vehicle turned towards the newest development, buildings by the lake front with observation decks, restaurants, and other attractions. At the top of the hill, it provided a breathtaking vista of the lake and a glimpse of Naman's primary residence. Taking its last turn, the mostly empty vehicle entered the oldest section of Prasinopolis through narrow roads with its utilitarian office buildings, low-rise residential apartments, and manicured gardens of affluent and upscale housing on endless cul-de-sacs.

Engrossed in the scenery outside, Amanda thought over a response, turning away from the window to pontificate. "I use it as a quality of life survey. People spend at least three years in their lifetime waiting due to transport delays."

Dollie tossed her head, flipping amber- colored hair out of sight. "Do you think they're calculating that as they go about their business?"

"There are portals, the broadcast, and various entertainment options to keep them occupied."

"No one besides you would notice," Dollie noted wryly.

"Distraction time has increased by two minutes per week."

Leaning forward, Dollie looked up through the windshield, then at Amanda. She was going somewhere with this line of thought. "Meaning?"

"Quality of transport services have declined."

"No better than this." Dollie pointed at the traffic jam in front of them, as people gaped at a roadside distraction.

"It is an example of everything being off, out of whack, or off-kilter."

"And Naman is to blame?" Dollie began to yawn. If this was

about politics, she didn't want to hear it.

"Naman doesn't control anything. It's an illusion."

Dollie glanced at her, right before the traffic started to pick up speed. "Just what are you thinking?"

Amanda's little face was serious, her mouth downturned at the corners. "For this case, and piece of the puzzle...." She trailed off.

"Yes," Dollie prodded.

"Cannot be solved."

"Why?"

Amanda shrugged. "There is no evidence. In essence, it was the perfect crime."

"The host is present and still alive," Dollie answered.

Laughing, she glanced at Dollie's face. "What crime is personality snatching? It is impossible to prove." Amanda seethed. "Yet."

"There's more?"

"There will always be more."

Dollie nodded in agreement. "I agree. This this feels unfinished." She placed a comforting hand on Amanda's shoulder, patting her once. "Then we wait."

#

With a flexible intelligence design algorithm and mycelium-based cement-type cladding, their home could expand, contract, and contort into a variety of shapes, sizes, and colors. Amanda loved the current iteration of the house's exterior, resembling a small castle with large low bay windows on the first floor, and turrets with staircases in both wings of the building. A long driveway with tufts of grass between sand-hued, square, rectangle and odd-sized pavers led to a circle at the castle's wide, double-door front entrance. Their vehicle continued towards a portcullis-style gate that sensing proximity, pulled up into a courtyard with an attached three-car garage and modest living quarters atop.

Amanda decided to take a virtual memory walk. The usual method of examination consisted of skimming facts and logical breakdowns of a person, place, and things, but rarely about herself. She elected to do a virtual memory walk by dusting off old memories not viewed in years, if at all. The past held little interest for her, especially the formative years of high school. Yet her career as an amateur sleuth began there, the blossoming of a keen interest in problem solving.

If she wanted, the memory vault could be an in-depth tactile experience of all senses. The one-room apparatus hid behind a closet in the grand hallway. Amanda pushed at a door seamlessly blended into the wall, hinges tucked inside. Behind her, the door squeaked shut. On her left, she pressed a palm against the center of the wall. It separated with a soft hiss. A smiling Amanda walked into the memory vault, plunging into darkness as the virtual memory walk began.

The school's short, shrill bell rang out. This memory took place during her freshman year, the hardest one to remember. The hollow click-clack of her shoes echoed in the ensuing silence. Amanda walked past narrow, ceiling-to-floor windows, down a gleaming white hall, contrasting with a floor comprised of slender, dark wood slats arrayed in a herringbone pattern.

Swimming through murky depths would help her breach into the clearing of a restored past. Amanda started with the composition of spacious, faintly aqua blue classrooms filled with egg-shaped isolation spheres in a downward spiral towards the holoform at its center. Each capsule enabled students to experience immersive learning. Depending on the curriculum chosen, daily study time could take as long as twelve hours. The Scientific, Technology and Government High School, nicknamed "Stag" or "Stags" High, permitted students to schedule study hours and breaks based on exams, individual assignments, team projects, and a final thesis. Subjects came with a human advisor, working with a specialized artificial intelligence assistant, to constantly evaluate the coursework, mindset, and mood of students. Similar to a chef with a cooking team, the teacher and AI delivered a mental meal per student suited to appetite, nutritional need, and emotional well-being.

The air smelled like cut grass, heavy with pollen. With eyes and throat itching, Amanda adjusted the virtual memory stimuli to filter out allergens. Already a third of the way into her studies, far along on the curriculum path, Amanda remembers wanting to let her curiosity wander. Taking another step, the vista changed to a pale, cloudless blue sky, and school hall to yard encircled by an eight lane track field running parallel to Stag High's six-story, red brick building.

As Amanda walked across the field, it transformed into a cultivated garden. Winding, wide, crushed gravel paths led to wooden pedestrian bridges arched over kidney-shaped pools with spouting fish fountains. Alongside the walkways on large clear patches of trimmed grass, reflective sculptures loomed. Amanda paused before a bear sculpture, forward tilting, high as a street light, its small paws raised below a shrunken head. The reflective midsection distorted six shapes into long streaks. She glanced around, seeing nothing but an empty landscape.

Unhindered, Amanda stepped onto the grass to inspect the

streaky shapes. The imagery shifted, changing her location to South Trades Street, blocks away from Stag High campus, the demarcation of residential from downtown business area. Constructed in a classical style, the first building's two columns bracketed three flights of steps with a pediment surmounting a portico of four columns.

Amanda hesitated at the intersection of a manicured park on her left and a street of buildings casting deep shadows on her right. Blocking out the sun, they funneled drafts of cold air in her direction, leaving a chill.

Determined to keep going, Amanda stepped off the curb. A sharp pain pierced the back of her head. Amanda collapsed into a heap on the ground.

"Are you alright?" a voice, alternating in pitch between a squeak and basso asked. It belonged to a teenage male going through a hormonal growth spurt.

Amanda felt long, warm fingers skirt her forehead, travel to rest on her back, before pulling on her upper arm to move her into a sitting position. She couldn't see her savior, try as she might to make out the distorted image, head feeling light, giddiness made her blind.

Back in reality and present time, Amanda sank onto the shaggy-carpeted floor. Panting. Reliving this experience made her queasy. Legs pulled up and she cradled them in her arms. *Who helped me that day?*

She fell back into the memory walk. "I think I fainted?" Amanda sounded uncertain.

"I saw you collapse," he answered, moving closer, breath stirring the hairs of a bang brushing her eyelids. Yet he seemed so far, away as his face remained obscured.

Blinking hard, Amanda stared into luminous, large gray eyes, and lost consciousness again.

Amanda peaked through eyelashes as the sound of voices went from a husky whisper to a shout into her ears. Still within the depths of reliving her memory, they were in the school's infirmary. Her older brother, Robert James Dalton Harcourt, as a teenager, studied Amanda with an odd look on his tanned face: a mixture of consternation, dismay, and relief. Upon seeing her awake, his face transformed back to its usual jovial look; his voice laced with mockery.

"Thank goodness for your big hard head, Amanda, or you'd have suffered a serious injury."

She scoured the infirmary for those bright gray eyes. Her head began to pound as a shadow at the doorway caught her attention before receding. Had it been her imagination? No, the room was too bright, wide open, with free floating pads encircled by translucent monitors. What she saw had been real.

Amanda let her eyes roam over Robert's compatriots, a loose affiliation of people who called themselves The Hand. It would be more accurate to call them The Fingers. She didn't know the exact number of associates. Being the most popular student at Stag High damned near everyone wanted, or claimed, to be a member of Robert's secret society.

"Leslie." Someone tapped the redhead, seated and facing away from her, on the shoulder. Try as Amanda might, she couldn't make out a face. Back then, she hadn't considered the event important, making memory retrieval complicated. Amanda was surprised at how much she could recall. She circled, trying to get a better, more accurate picture of the individuals assembled.

The easiest person to identify was Francis, a close friend of Robert, standing at the window, absorbed with studying a device in his hand. The twins, Jacob and Paul, played a card game on a floating pad diagonally across from her.

Amanda froze all activity in the infirmary. Walking up to each figure, she tried accessing each face, especially of Leslie and whoever called his name. Yet obtaining more information from the memory vault eluded her. Sighing in frustration, Amanda went back to the floating pad, resuming the memory walk.

Robert followed the direction of her gaze, noticing the focus on his entourage. Deliberately, he blocked her line of sight. Hands in pockets, he leaned over to admonish. "You aren't going to wander off alone anymore."

"What did Poppa say?" she challenged.

Robert sniffed dismissively. "He would pull his hair out if he knew about your antics."

Amanda grinned in satisfaction. For all of his faults, Robert wasn't a tattletale. "I felt a little dizzy." Lacking a strong appetite for food, she ate one meal a day at dinner. For breakfast and lunch, she either consumed a beverage or ate nothing at all.

He pulled up to regard Amanda from a great height, which he knew annoyed her. "You forgot to eat again." Robert smiled, revealing perfectly even polished teeth, crinkles at the corners of long-lashed, deep-set light brown eyes under straight thick eyebrows – the symmetry of a handsome face. "Let's not repeat this, shall we? If I have to visit you in here again, people will know we're related." It was a joke, but it meant his collection of friends kept secrets and didn't gossip.

She reached for the bed sheet. "I'm fine," Amanda said and made a move to leave the floating pad.

Robert motioned for her to stop. "Eat first, then leave and go home early."

#

Mellow chimes filled the air as the portal blinked like a double-lidded animal, opening to reveal caller and callee.

"R.J." Dollie tapped a long, cream-colored fingernail on the desk in her room. On the other hand, she rested her chin.

Robert cast a casual glance over his shoulder, at the sleeping figure on the bed, revealing a receding V-shaped hairline and shiny bald-spot. Turning and hunching forward, he whispered conspiratorially, "Dorothy, it is rather late, even for you." The corner of his mouth pulled upward.

"You're a hard man to reach, R.J," Dollie drawled, writing invisible letters on the table with her nail.

They knew one another since Stag High. As a favor to Robert during his senior year, soon to graduate and unable to watch over Amanda, Dollie stepped up. Being sophomores, although Amanda skipped two grades, made it easy for Dollie to tag along—practically glued to her side. At first, the little girl would ignore Dollie, slyly dodging her and taking off, but gradually accepted her company. Amanda's burgeoning hobby started with finding lost or stolen objects, then into perilous situations thanks to her boundless curiosity. Due to her sharp wit, acerbic tongue and diminutive size, she became involved in a number of conflicts with classmates.

Dollie baldly stated the reason for calling. "She visited Naman."

Robert shot up out of his seat. The portal closed in a wink.

Waiting, Dollie studied her nails, tapping them on the table in a slow, precise tempo.

The portal chimed. Its lids pulled back to reveal Robert pacing before a wall of bare, mahogany shelves. Composure regained, Robert sat down, pulling at the cuffs of his long-sleeved, crisp, ivory shirt.

"Tell me everything, from the beginning."

Dollie gave him a brief overview of events.

Robert cursed under his breath. "I should never have allowed Captain Harper to give her such leeway."

She looked bored. "Amanda would have found some way to get involved. Besides, Harper doesn't know what happened."

"He will now."

Dollie pondered for a moment. "She's never wrong, R.J."

He smiled grimly. "There's always a first time."

"Listen, I share your concern, but I trust Amanda. I'm only telling you, because you have to be prepared."

Robert worked for the most indelible and enduring branch of the Prasinopolis government—the permanent security branch—which, by its very name, resisted change. Naman convinced the public of its elimination while overhauling and revamping the bureaucracy. Slamming both hands on the table in front of the portal, Robert no longer appeared concerned about waking his partner. "Why won't she let sleeping dogs lie, Dorothy?"

Dollie clasped her hands, answering solemnly. "The dogs aren't barking, R.J. Amanda's determined to find out what happened to Naman."

Robert fell silent, leaning back in his seat, frowning.

After the portal chimed, closing the connection, Dollie said over her shoulder, "Did you see that?"

"She was the reason you two broke up." Amanda responded.

Irritation made Dollie's throat tight. "Whenever R.J. is cheating, he's more attentive and buys more gifts. There's no way his wife doesn't have a new car and second home."

Without rancor, Amanda demurred. "Harriet prefers antique jewelry and classic art."

Chair squeaking, Dollie pivoted to peer at Amanda in the dark corner of her room. "I am surprised they never married. She seems to be his constant one and only."

"What is her name?"

"Monica Darin."

Emerging from the shadows, Amanda beckoned Dollie to send her an image. "Let me see her."

Dollie flicked her right hand in annoyance. "This is all I have." She held a palm up while running the other hand over it — a clean swipe gesture — in Amanda's direction.

"No face?" She peered at the image of a woman's back outfitted in a neat, tight, red pantsuit.

"I erased her." Dollie's upper lip curled in contempt. "Here," she added, making another swiping gesture. "Check out Stags High's collective cloud."

Amanda was not an alumna, and lacked access to the school's memory pool. Having deemed herself sufficiently educated and knowledgeable enough to finish the scholastic accreditation on her own terms Amanda left midway through junior year due to boredom. Only Mr. Harcourt made her feel trepidation over the decision. Bracing herself and expecting Poppa to raise a stink, he surprised her. Nodding, Mr. Harcourt arched his bushy salt and pepper eyebrows while coolly responding, "As you wish." His satisfaction laid with Robert pursuing a Master's Degree in Government and Legal Studies. Working for the Prasinopolis government, a Harcourt tradition, would be fulfilled by the oldest son.

"A student at our school. Indeed." Amanda said absentmindedly. She isolated the fan of straight ebony hair they saw on the bed behind Robert, patching it to the suited figure Dollie sent her. Rapidly, she flicked through thousands of shapes, sizes, and faces of people at various gatherings. Stopping at an assemblage of Robert with his coterie, Amanda shared the image with Dollie. The holoform of Leslie, Paul, Jacob, Francis, and Monica smiled at a fixed point above them, while a pale-skinned, lanky figure with luminous gray eyes stood apart watching.

"I cannot believe he's still with her." Dollie muttered in disgust, upon seeing her enemy's face in lifelike detail. "I thought R.J. preferred long-legged, light-haired women." Dollie's frame of reference came from dating men whose ex-wives or ex-girlfriends resembled her.

"He talks to you. Plus, Robert doesn't have a type." The difference between Monica and Harriet was night and day. A curvy, sepia-toned woman of medium height in contrast to an elegantly thin, long-nosed woman with chin-length, ash blonde hair neatly tucked behind small jug ears. Amanda liked her sister-in-law and honorary big sister Dollie. Both of them treated her well. She wondered, for a moment, if it would be the same with Monica. Although Robert may be hiding the relationship, she didn't suspect him of infidelity like Dollie.

"Does Mr. Six-foot-four-inches look familiar to you?" Amanda pointed at the teenage boy with the distant stare.

"The redhead?"

"No, I know Leslie." Seeing his face resurfaced forgotten memories, in particular of when he came to visit Robert. They stared coldly at one another. He greeted her politely. Yet the tilt of his head and aloof, haughty hazel eyes raised her hackles. Leslie Cullver, the redheaded scion of a founding family of Prasinopolis, and his air of royal superiority, rubbed Amanda the wrong way.

Dollie leaned closer, squinting. "Why am I not in this—oh, I see, I am in the background." She smirked at Amanda, wringing her hands in a worrying gesture. "The gang didn't like me too much, since I was a latecomer." Dollie indicated with her chin at the holoform. "That is Nestor Evans."

Pleased with the response Amanda smiled and revisited the cultivated gardens in her memory walk. Appearing before the reflective bear sculpture, she reached in, pulling out six long figures and fixing the distortion. Matching the image of Robert and his friends, the holoforms became complete.

Dollie watched the process avidly.

Amanda returned to the outside of Stag High's infirmary, at the side of the figure lingering outside its opaque wall. Gratified to see her savior's features, Amanda drifted close to the seated redhead Leslie, who faced away from her prone body on the floating pad. At last, she saw who tapped him on the shoulder—Monica.

The restored memories filled Amanda with satisfaction. "That's another piece of the puzzle solved."

Dollie yawned, stretching out her legs with toes pointed. "How does it relate back to Naman?"

"I don't know, but there is something here." She answered, looking at the holoform of Robert's group with a curious expression.

#

*Most societies will fight a war as bitterly, cruel and unyielding
internally as externally, perhaps with the former being more so as
fights among brothers have been the deadliest throughout history.*

—*Rudolph Harcourt*

Amanda went to visit Monica Darin alone. She lived in a five-story walk-up with a basement parking garage in the older, less developed section a few blocks from Captain Harper's precinct. Dollie insisted on accompanying her to the woman's apartment building, promising to stay in the parked vehicle.

A quarterly stipend from the trust fund left by Amanda's maternal grandmother barely covered the most basic expenses. With the steady rise in the cost of living, she required more funds, and needed consulting work, unlike Dollie. As the sole heir and Chief Executive at Large of the Echeveria Luna Foundation, an insurance and investment concern, Dollie simultaneously worked at her job and partnered with Amanda. Journalizing their investigations, masking the identities and various facts of cases, neatly dovetailed with Dollie's interests.

Yet questioning Monica would be a fruitless exercise with an angry Dollie dropping acidic remarks. Smiling fondly at Dollie's irascible nature, she reached for the doorbell.

The mahogany four-panel door whipped open. Monica's fleeting expression changed from hopeful to crestfallen then mildly annoyed.

"You were expecting someone?" Amanda asked, checking the ends of the hallway for lurking figures.

Fine black eyebrows arched over long, thick-lashed whiskey-colored eyes. Monica's small nose wrinkled up as though smelling a foul odor, before full lips curved upward into a smile revealing flawless white teeth and dimpled cheeks. Amanda could see why Robert remained fascinated by her. "I almost didn't recognize you, R.J.'s little sister." Leaning her head to one side, Monica perused Amanda from head to toe.

Aside from her uniform black outfits, favorite high-heeled boots, Amanda's height and heart-shaped face haven't changed since Stag High. Working to set Monica at ease, she said, "I apologize for showing up this morning unannounced. Yes, I am Robert's sister Amanda. You remember me, but I don't remember you or many of Robert's friends." Looking at Monica from beneath her eyelashes, Amanda tried looking shy and bashful. "He had so many beautiful girlfriends, it was hard to keep track."

Monica's lips tightened. Her fine brows drew together, bunching to create a long crease. "Why are you here?" She hovered between politeness, curiosity, or shutting the door in Amanda's face.

"May I come in, please?"

Stepping back to leave the door wide open, Monica sighed in resignation. Boot heels clacking on the basket weave, parquet flooring, Amanda stuck closely behind Monica, taking in the trail of her scent, discreetly inhaling and analyzing. The front door swung shut with a muted click.

Amanda took inventory of the dark, bluish-green apartment searching and storing every detail to her synthetic memory pool. A sparsely furnished living room bore no personal pictures, artwork, tchotchkes or trinkets. The windows were naked. A pine bar with a hidden sink and three matching stools, separated the living room from a mahogany kitchen wall. Cabinets and refrigerator door blended flawlessly into the wall, its continuity broken by the shiny surface of a food generator. Monica either liked the hermit lifestyle or getting ready to move. Amanda saw no suitcases; with the advent of synthetic micro-filaments, luggage would be overkill and unnecessary.

Monica leaned against an obsidian blue, high back sofa with bulky arms. "If you don't remember me, how did you end up coming to my place?" Displaying apprehension, Monica cradled her stomach. "What did R.J. tell you?"

In a flash, Amanda took the opportunity to turn right and dart down the hall. The layout of an apartment usually meant one could find a bathroom adjacent to the kitchen. She poked her head inside a white-tiled bathroom then scanned the spartan bedroom, sniffing the air and zipping back. Monica watched, mouth agape, unable to utter a word.

"Robert trusts you, Monica. He doesn't tell me anything."

"What did you do just now?"

"You seemed very worried. I wanted to make sure you weren't being threatened." Amanda began to pace, looking very much like her brother. "Robert doesn't even leave breadcrumbs for me to follow. However, if one takes enough time to work through the clues, an answer comes together. You used to work for Naman up until a few days ago. Indeed, you were one of the guiding hands that led him to head the government, but something changed in your relationship, so much so you contacted Robert out of concern."

Monica didn't deny it. "Yes, I worked for Naman. My job was

to assist him in governing."

Amanda tried a different tactic, "Who is Nicodemus?"

Her eyes widened a fraction, gradually resuming a blank, bland gaze of disinterest. "I don't know what that is."

"I hear that Nicodemus keeps threatening Naman." Amanda probed, studying Monica.

Shifting weight from one foot to another restlessly, Monica's body language indicated a waning patience wearing thin. "Naman enjoys immense popularity in Prasinopolis, unopposed by anyone. You are mistaken thinking Naman can be threatened or harmed."

"Darin is an unusual surname." Amanda noted, mentally diving through genealogical trees and historical records, while doing comparative genetic analysis with her olfactory senses. "Your family name used to be Mandarin, one of the founding families of The Republic." She didn't ask for reasons behind the change. Yet one particular scandal garnered scrutiny from her. "Your great-great-great grandfather was executed for treason trying to overthrow the head of state. The head of the permanent security branch, my great-great-great grandfather Rudolph Harcourt made the accusation and provided evidence." Her ancestor also founded The Invisible Hand, a secretive and covert agency within the branch. "Isn't it curious, as descendants of these two, we all find ourselves having a fate such as this?"

Monica sagged against the sofa, desperately needing to sit down, but putting up a strong front. "There are no special privileges being a founding family descendant. You have to make your own way, struggle like everyone else." The lie rolled smoothly off of Monica's tongue.

Amanda's outward appearance fooled people into thinking

her a simpleminded child. "Yes, yes, indeed." She agreed. If one's family fell out of the elite, shunned by polite society, avenues to top positions closed off, and unable to tap into networked circles, the best approach would be to start from scratch. To convince family no real damage or losses occurred, it made sense to pass reassuring fables down through the generations. "Why are you leaving?"

Monica laughed derisively. "I never said I was leaving."

"Is it because of the baby?"

She gasped. "How did you know?"

Amanda didn't explain. "It is best for you to go somewhere safe. Please do. Let Robert know where. He will take care of you."

"It is not him I will be hiding from," Monica relented. "It was getting dangerous to be around Naman." Resting a hand on her flat stomach. "I didn't want to endanger my baby's life."

Feeling sympathetic, Amanda left Monica with comforting words and a fond farewell. She compared the strengths and weaknesses of Harriet, Monica, and Dollie understanding why her brother chose Harriet. A simple woman, transparent as glass, and kind, she would not be involved in spying, skullduggery, or martial arts. When Robert got home, he likely didn't want to contemplate work, politics, or humor government related fulminations. He sought peace, and Harriet was a haven of tranquility.

#

The passenger door opened. Amanda reached for the grab handle, pulling up to climb into her seat.

Dollie waved at the vehicle's sensors to turn off the booming music. "How did it go?" Another gesture engaged the engine to drive.

Amanda listened as three steps underneath the vehicle

retracted with a faint whirl.

An agitated Dollie cracked her knuckles. Amanda felt the weight of her questioning stare. Dollie looked like she just rolled out of bed, her wild hair the result of twirling the ends and dragging restless fingers through it. Amanda sighed internally. Dollie needed more free time to pursue a stable relationship. She deserved as much. Unseeingly, Amanda glanced out of the window, mentally replaying the apartment visit. "Monica is pregnant."

"What!" The verbal explosion seemed to rock the vehicle.

Worried about an accident, though highly improbable, Amanda said in a soothing voice, "It is not Robert's baby. I repeat, it is not Robert. He is not the father." Telling Dollie about the pregnancy seemed like a bad idea, but it was better to rip off the bandage now.

"Did you know before you went there?" Dollie asked waspishly.

Why did Robert's women assume she helps to conspire against them? Amanda shook her head. "I wanted information about Naman. She worked closely with him for several years, and suddenly she's not around." She smiled. "Turns out Nicodemus is a what, not a who."

"Don't change the subject."

Amanda ticked off details, which provided clues to Monica's situation. A faint odor of vomit coming from the bathroom. Her elevated temperature bordered on, but did not surpass, a fever. In the apartment, Monica unconsciously cradled her belly behind folded arms. Instead of the ramrod posture from her pictures, she used the sofa as a stabilizing prop. With oily hair and a shiny face so early in the morning, Monica's appearance suggested a rough slog through a daylong work haul. Amanda's deductive reasoning exempted Robert of culpability. Fine red strands behind the toilet and under the pedestal sink, lay in stark contrast against a white-tiled bathroom floor. Monica's constant companion or frequent visitor possessed red hair. Robert was a brunette. As a serial monogamist, if he wanted Monica, a divorce from Harriet would have happened already.

"I'm not. Naman is in danger, and she no longer felt safe."

"So she decided to bail and not tell anyone," Dollie said scornfully, irked by Monica's disloyalty.

Amanda laced her fingers as the vehicle gained speed, pressing her against the seat. A moody Dollie driving at high speed, even with driver's assist, made her uneasy. "Rather a matter of luck on our part, or not." She chuckled at Dollie's glare. "She informed Robert. He was checking on her well-being, which means he has known about Naman's situation."

"The Invisible Hand at work." Dollie gestured at the vehicle to cruise slower.

Amanda sighed in relief. "Precisely." Leaning over, mischief gleaming in cat-like eyes, she whispered, "When was the last time you went on a date?"

Startled, Dollie snapped. "None of your business."

Browsing through the Stag High collective cloud, Amanda noticed Francis surreptitiously eyeing Dollie. "Francis is still single."

"Frank?" Dollie's voice and stare was incredulous. "What makes you think of him now?"

"You are an alumna. Isn't the reunion coming up?"

"For their class," Dollie shook her head, "and none of them will show up."

"Why not? Weren't you all thick as thieves?"

Dollie's extended pause hinted at a disturbing, old conflict within the well- knit group. "After graduation, everyone went their separate ways. A year later, they went out for a reunion celebration. I didn't go. I wasn't invited and wouldn't have gone if I was, since I had already broken up with R.J."

Holding her breath, Amanda waited for Dollie to continue.

"Imagine a group of young drunk guys with one woman as the center of attention."

"That would create a lot of friction."

Dollie sighed in frustration. "Monica always has to be the center of attention. Everybody has to look after her, listen to her and pay homage to her. Anyone who tried to join the group had to deal with her."

"Queen Bee syndrome," Amanda surmised.

"Either Leslie or Francis and Nestor fought. I blame Monica. She was the cause, according to the rumor."

"Get to the point, Dollie."

"Nestor had an accident, which almost killed him. After a long recuperation, I didn't hear anymore about him."

Amanda wondered, "Did you ever ask Robert about it?"

Laughing loudly, Dollie exclaimed. "He's the one who told me the story! R.J. said he left early, missing all the action. The twins—Jacob and Paul—gave him the rundown, but everyone was so plastered. Memories are fuzzy."

"Francis is a broadcast and portal specialist, Dollie. He enjoys martial arts like you."

She was intrigued. "Does he?"

"Pick his brain for me," Amanda proposed.

"How would I get him to agree to see me?"

With exasperated fondness, Amanda said. "Dollie, you are a beautiful woman. I'm certain if you called, any number of men would come running. Just get him to think about Naman. Find out if there's anything unusual about the broadcasts, and if Naman has been getting signals that are out of the ordinary."

Nodding slowly, she said, "Will do," as their vehicle pulled into the driveway towards home.

#

Deeply tanned with aqua-blue eyes, Francis "Frank" Antonin topped Dollie by a few inches. Her eyes drank in and savored areas where man-fur peaked from a plunging neckline, poked out from under cuff linked wrists, while whirls of chest hair created shadows under a white shirt. At four in the afternoon, stubble formed on his determined, dimpled chin, below a nose once broken and set incorrectly. His broad forehead with its straight hairline was topped by fluffy, sandy brown hair. Francis appeared a bit rough around the edges: spry, coiled like a spring, yet with an easygoing demeanor.

As Amanda suggested, Dollie contacted Francis. His enthusiastic response surprised her. They ate at an observation deck restaurant overlooking Lake Matisse. In the newest development at the lake district, a half-dozen skyscrapers by the scenic park lit up every five seconds mimicking a silent fireworks display. They sat in the less popular section of the restaurant with its view of a pristine shoreline at dusk, which suited them perfectly.

Francis and Dollie spent a little time reminiscing about the past, before they moved onto their favorite pastime of mixed martial arts with techniques from Krav Maga and Muay Thai. Francis confessed to being a secret admirer. Dollie wanted to ask why he hadn't stepped up, but remembered her near obsessive focus on R.J., his best friend.

Without hesitation, Dollie launched into her topic of inquiry. "You don't talk to R.J. anymore?"

Francis answered in a facile manner, having anticipated the direction of their conversation. "We talk on occasion. We met a few weeks ago, chit chat here and there." His brilliant aqua-blue eyes clung to her face while turning the subject around. "How about you? Still talking?"

"I work with his little sister Amanda. I rarely see him."

He sat back, assessing the restaurant's relaxed ambiance and tasteful decor. Brass chandeliers with amber crystals dangled over intimate and cozy booths on a plush, seaweed green carpet. Dollie sensed the wind in his sails ebbing. "I heard your specialty is the broadcast and portal." She continued, "Naman's a big part of the success of the broadcast, right?"

"Naman blew it up. Prior to him hardly anyone used the broadcast." In the two hours they spent together, Dollie could swear Francis's stubble thickened.

"How does Naman handle the bad feedback?" She preferred talking about the latest mixed martial bout, but needed to ask for Amanda's sake.

"That's a touchy subject of late." Francis cupped the back of his neck, rubbing it.

Dollie reached out to touch his hand. "I hope I am not intruding. It has me curious, that's all."

Francis stared at their touching fingers. Dollie was a member of their group. He wanted to win her over by confiding. "Lately, we've been seeing a surge of comments after every broadcast.

Complaints about public transportation, quality of service going down, people not feeling safe. In the beginning, it was all reply bots and easy to cull. But people are like ducklings, or sheep, and will follow the leader. Seeing the complaints is like an alarm. It wakes people up to make the same complains."

Dollie didn't consider the revelation earth shattering. "Maybe they are remembering what annoys them."

Francis held her gaze. "It should be a bell curve where it tapers off, since Naman has addressed those issues. But the wave doesn't crest, it keeps rising in a linear scale. The rate at which it keeps going will drown out any message Naman puts in the broadcast."

"What does that mean?" Confusion filled Dollie.

"We'll have to shut the broadcast down – like a time out."

#

"Did Francis strike you as the type to drink and start a brawl?" Amanda queried, studying the memory pool images Dollie shared from her date with Francis. Dollie said they made plans to meet again.

She plopped down on the dark gray sectional sofa next to Amanda, stretched out onto her back, and hugged a pillow. "He's very mild mannered, complete teetotaler, wouldn't touch alcohol."

"It could mean he used to drink and decided not to do it again," Amanda observed.

"That is true. No one gets religion like an ex-smoker or ex-drinker." Dollie rolled the thought around. "Frank is a fitness person, a martial artist. He's been like this since Stags. He is a walking deadly weapon. If he fought Nestor or any of those guys, it would be over with one punch." She shrugged. "Brawling wouldn't be his style. He's an efficient fighter."

Amanda looked at Dollie. "So he wouldn't loosen up and get wild."

"Just so you know," Dollie grinned, "he admitted he had a crush on me."

"Indeed, Francis only has eyes for you."

Dollie sat up. "That leaves Leslie 'The Red' Cullver and Nestor as the fighters."

#

A window was closing, and Amanda needed answers before it shut. She visited Captain Harper again, wondering if he would refuse to answer in the face of her brother's objections. Harper seemed unhindered by any restrictions, listening politely as she spoke about Nestor Evans.

"He went to Stags High like Dollie, Robert, and me. I heard he was horribly injured in an accident, but no one ever saw him again."

Harper frowned in concentration as he searched for information. "That night, about six years ago, he got into a one-vehicle accident on Stonemiller Road. Based on vehicle records, he was driving over the speed limit. It's a narrow road in a desolate location."

"Was he alone?"

"Strange. There's no data on that."

"A group of people show up to an event, either they came together in a few vehicles or alone."

"Emergency drones pried apart the vehicle. One transported him to the nearest trauma center, and the other gathered data from the scene." Harper swiped at the holoforms. "Can you believe it? The data collector drone got struck by lightning."

"That's as good as an EMP." Amanda smiled.

"Most of the pertinent details come from vehicle sensors." Harper typed on the keyboard, hammering the object. "No security cameras in the area, it's too remote. They must have gone to this place to say goodbye to the restaurant."

"Why?"

Harper swiped at the holoform. "See? Last night of business. It was closing."

"Where did Nestor end up after the trauma center?"

He didn't need to refer to the holoform anymore. "Nestor didn't have family to attend to him. The state assigned a guardian from the permanent security branch."

Amanda felt her ears burn. No one from The Hand stepped up? Robert had not joined the branch yet. Monica couldn't join. The twins left the country. Francis worked for a private commercial firm. The bad blood between Leslie and Nestor nixed that scenario. She drew a blank.

"Who could it be?" She asked aloud.

Harper cocked his head to the side, looking at her oddly. "Your father, Mr. Jonathan Harcourt."

For the first time in years, Amanda couldn't think of a snappy or witty retort. To wake herself from a daydream she slapped the table, wanting to shake off the sense of foreboding. Amanda needed to remain calm and logical.

"After the trauma center treatment, where does Nestor go for recovery and rehab?" Amanda felt desperate, her mouth dry as though stuffed with cotton.

Harper's expression, full of pity, created a sinking feeling in the pit of her stomach. She knew what was coming and tensed up, anticipating the blow.

"Sorry, Amanda. He didn't make it."

Her savior, all those years ago, a teenage boy whose face and kindness she forgot. She couldn't meet him today and say, "Thank you" or "Hello."

Numb for the rest of the day, Amanda rode mass transit, staring blankly into space. During that time, Naman's broadcast came on. She nearly shut it off, but her perverse curiosity kicked in. Since Nestor was deceased, and the accident happened over six years ago, all information from that night became freely available on the public record. Captain Harper transferred it all to her synthetic memory pool.

A frenzy seized her. Filling up with excitement and fear, Amanda clamped down to focus. Images of the wreckage did not interest her. She plunged that data deep into the memory vault, retrievable by a memory walk on a deserted road, shuttered restaurant, or bouquet of flowers at an intersection. What interested her came from Nestor's vehicle. The concerned teenage boy she saw in her freshman year at Stag High changed. Instead, a man stared back at her with intense, deep-set light gray eyes shadowed by thick straight eyebrows, a strong chin, full lips and a straight, long nose with a slight hump. His long neck, above impossibly broad shoulders, supported a well-formed head of short black hair.

Amanda studied Nestor's face then brought up Naman's face shrouded in a mask. She measured the size of their heads, finding Naman's head to be appreciably larger. Next, she measured the distance between pupils, discarding the result in disappointment.

Within a blink, she searched her memory pool. Naman kept his ears covered, but in one broadcast the mask slipped, exposing one ear, before it slid back into place. She captured the ear from tip to canal, minus the lobe. In the midst of working on genetic, physical and superficial cosmetic enhancements, the ears are almost always left alone. Amanda compared the ears angle by angle and swirl for swirl. They matched 100%.

Stunned, she stared in disbelief. Nestor Evans was alive.

#

Amanda lacked a predisposition to self-reflect, second guess or endlessly contemplate actions that would have arrived at a different outcome. Time was precious. Her philosophical bent focused on being devoted and dedicated to using every allotted moment of life.

She arrived home late in the afternoon tired, mentally and emotionally exhausted, but elated. Amanda wasn't surprised to see Robert waiting and Dollie cornered, appearing to be an unwitting hostage. She likely wanted to come pick her up.

They made eye contact. Amanda gave Dollie a reassuring nod. She visibly relaxed.

"Don't go see Naman again." The words burst out of an agitated-sounding Robert. Yet he appeared dapper as usual, wearing a navy suit, pale blue shirt with a red and royal blue candy-striped tie.

"You know that's the wrong thing to say to her, R.J." Dollie advised, chuckling. Seating herself across from Amanda, who curled up on the dark gray sectional sofa, hugging a large, worn, and woolly brown stuffed bear.

Robert pushed back his jacket, settling hands on hips, right leg thrust out. He shook his head, studying his laced, wing-tipped brown shoes, as he searched for words.

"Let my people handle this situation. This is an issue too deep for you to get involved with." He pointed at Dollie accusingly. "You are supposed to keep her safe. Keep her away from this."

She shrugged nonchalantly. "Top secret government stuff. The republic is in crisis. We can't handle the truth. Is that your story, R.J.?"

Quietly, her voice so low Dollie and Robert almost didn't hear her, Amanda said, "Why did you do that to him, Robert?"

He was taken aback. "Who?"

"Nestor Evans."

"Why are you so certain I have anything to do with him?" Robert evaded.

"The one-vehicle accident with no witnesses or surveillance cameras nearby. A drone, which mysteriously and quite fortunately, got hit by lightning."

"What are you getting at now?" he said, starting to pace like he did in Monica's apartment.

"I thought it odd that Poppa would be involved in Nestor Evans' care. He gave you the authority to use his name, since it was you overseeing this project."

That stopped Robert in his tracks. "Again, why are you so certain I have anything to do with him?" An edge of anger seeped into his voice. "Amanda, you're no longer a precocious twelve-year-old entering high school. You're twenty-two. This isn't the Tokada case where you find the solution in under thirty minutes. It's more complicated than that."

Dollie piped up. "Harper told you about that?" If Amanda faced dangers outside of Dollie's ability to manage, she conveyed information to Robert.

The Tokada case, a major first achievement and intriguing case to solve, almost made her famous—the intellectual equivalent of solving the puzzle of a room with no doors or windows. Amanda demurred from receiving accolades or the public spotlight. If not, she would be flooded with time-consuming false cases and publicity stunts. It hurt to hear Robert belittle her breakthrough feat. Perhaps he thought she was invading his turf. The future of Prasinopolis affected them all. She had every right to be involved.

Amanda ignored Robert's taunt. "Isn't he supposed to be dead? Yet here we are, talking about a man as though he is alive. Nestor had a tragic accident that night. He fought with Leslie over Monica. Let's look at it this way. Monica's family has been prevented from working in the government for centuries. Overnight, she's working with the most powerful being in Prasinopolis. Who would do that except for someone she knows personally from The Hand? As for Nestor, with his life ruined, his injuries so severe, you had this great idea – this project – to show Poppa that you could take over The Invisible Hand."

Shoving both hands in his pocket, Robert leaned back, cocked an eyebrow and smirked. "It was flawless, you must admit."

"Except your monster has a mind of its own," Dollie quipped.

Robert started pacing again. Amused, Amanda said, "Sit down, Robert. You are going to stroke out if you keep this up."

Scurrying to the kitchen, Dollie made a black coffee with a squirt of strong chocolate-flavored liqueur. Robert didn't have to ask. She knew his favorite drink.

As soon as she handed him the cup, Robert tipped back his head, polishing it off in five gulps. Dollie cast Amanda a quizzical look.

Amanda laughed silently, sticking out her tongue.

Robert handed the empty cup to Dollie absentmindedly. From behind, she pantomimed chopping him in the neck.

Amanda continued, "And someone or something is trying to wrestle control of Naman."

"Nicodemus," Dollie added.

"Threats from Nicodemus? Hardly," Robert said disdainfully. "It's a little as you suspected, but not entirely accurate. Nestor is Naman, and something more. We enhanced him. We rebuilt him. We nurtured it. We made it happen." Slapping his thigh, Robert admitted, "Then something happened. It's gotten away from us."

Amanda looked at Robert. "Nicodemus is the AI placed in his head. Nestor is a time bomb, set to explode any day now, isn't he, Robert?"

"He made us a promise government structure would stay the same, but he broke it. His word is what we relied on. A man must honor his word. It is our code and it ensures the stability of our system. Without that, things fall apart. Implementing changes to streamline our system from BN to AN cannot stand. It's not going to work."

"Your people wanted him to accept this, and he's not willing to go along with it. Instead, his psyche is breaking. Be honest with us, Robert. What is your contingency plan?" She knew it would be fatal if they ever deployed it.

"I can't divulge that." Robert's eyes shifted up to the right, scanning. He had been delaying them on purpose.

Amanda stood up, motioning to Dollie, time for them to leave.

#

In the vehicle, Dollie turned to Amanda. "And what is your contingency plan?"

Amanda said, "I need you to contact Francis. Tell him it is an emergency and bring him to Naman's place. The two of you don't need to come inside. I'll be in contact." Amanda spelled out for Dollie what she wanted Francis to do. Dollie nodded eagerly in agreement.

#

The setting sun left lavender and purple clouds to contrast against a vivid rust-hued sky. A street light beamed down on Amanda. She walked past open gates onto the red brick-paved driveway. Embedded florescent pebbles led a path split between a manicured lawn and a garage on her right. In contrast to the sleek, black modern style of the house, the garage came with a traditional, arched tiled roof and facade matching the driveway.

Baton-shaped, black sconces illuminated red brick walls surrounding the estate entrance and garden perimeter. Elevated three steps high, a black shipping container room sat on a stone deck with a modest outdoor glass-top table and two side chairs. Light from the interior shone through a large square doorway, casting a lone shadow onto the grass. The looming dark shape belonged to a waiting and watching Naman.

Amanda's cat-like eyes adjusted to the night, bringing the landscape into sharp relief.

Adorned in a black silky shirt, pants and boots, Naman's clothes appeared to twinkle and glitter. The silky black mask covering Naman's nose, ears, and neck seamlessly matched the outfit as one piece. The skintight shirt and sleeves extended over the back of Naman's hands, threading between the fingers.

"Naman sees you." Silver eyes peered down at her. A singular voice, though husky, betrayed no emotions.

"I missed your company, M'Sir. I had to see you again," Amanda answered flirtatiously, bowing, before swinging from side to side.

She stared at the unlit rooms of the house. Hearing no sounds of the night from crickets, nocturnal animals, or other movement, Amanda observed. "We are alone."

"Not for long," Naman answered coolly.

"Your staff went out and will be coming back?" She asked, moving closer to stare up at Naman.

"I sent them home. All that is left is me," Naman stepped down, reducing the height difference and strain on her neck, eyes crinkling with amusement, "and you."

Amanda swallowed. "I came here to warn you, M'Sir."

"You fear nothing like Naman."

"What I fear is not knowing. I do not fear what I cannot control, but I trust my reasoning skills."

"You trust your logic?"

Nodding, Amanda answered earnestly. "Yes."

In a casual dance of changing places, Naman stepped down, moving off the patio deck, while Amanda climbed up. Naman's outfit shone and glimmered with every move. "Logic did not bring you here to me. You are not always rational."

"I have a strong curiosity complex, which may override a normal sense of caution or hesitation."

Naman held his hands out as though to feel the air. "Naman is your object of attraction." It was not a question.

"You read my intentions well, M'Sir. Have we ever met, before you became—" She came down the steps to stand in front of Naman, waving a hand, trying to rekindle a forgotten memory.

Naman's head whirled, silver eyes shining as they searched the backyard beyond the garden wall, towards acres of untended grounds.

Amanda strained to listen, following the path of Naman's stare, but the distant thump faded.

"I was always me. I am always me." Naman turned back to Amanda, pinning her beneath an intense silver stare.

"Who may that be besides Naman? You were someone else with another name," she prodded, standing close enough to feel heat radiating from Naman's body.

Moving fast, startling Amanda into silence, Naman pulled her close. She heard the impact, a dull thud, and the clatter of objects hitting the patio stone tiles. Naman crouched over her, cradling, blocking the fusillade of bullets, while his protective barrier field deflected and decelerated the projectiles.

In the distance, Amanda heard a hoarse voice screaming, "Stop! Damn you. Stop, right now. Retreat. Wait until I tell you otherwise."

Naman unfurled from the defensive posture over Amanda, mask still in place, but the outfit from shoulder to shin in tatters.

Amanda trembled, squelching a horrified reaction. Blinking rapidly, she was determined not to cry, at least not now. Gingerly reaching out with a shaking hand, she asked, "Are you hurt?"

Naman's body showed no bruises or blood. Amanda forced herself to remain calm. She started to pant, anxious and fearful of fainting. Her legs shook. Dollie would be furious if she saw what happened, demanding that Amanda leave or take cover and hide. Francis and Dollie might already be at Naman's house and heard the onslaught.

"Naman will heal." Like a dinged metal surface, Naman's body filled out, smoothing imperfections, while the rented and torn synthetic microfilaments knitted back together. Within seconds, Naman's aura of unflappable, unruffled calm resumed as though nothing happened. Naman's even breathing and serenity enveloped Amanda, reducing her anxiety, making her feel stable again. She wondered if she was fooling herself. Perhaps traces of Nestor were suppressed, forgotten or entirely wiped away. Her eyes narrowed. If Robert was using standard, useless ammunition as his choice of weapon against the superbeing, that meant....

Excitedly, Amanda opened the portal. "Dollie!"

"Yes, we are here." Dollie's eyes gleamed, in the driver's seat, next to a bemused Francis. "We, I mean, Frank, did as you asked." Francis shut off the broadcast, removing tidal waves of reply bots sending confusing messages and bottling up the system. The chaos was caused by malware, because Nicodemus, Naman's AI implant, had been hacked into.

Ready to exit the vehicle, Dollie frowned and said, "I should be there with you."

Amanda and Francis shouted, "No!"

"No," Amanda repeated mildly. "Naman is protecting me. I am safe."

Dollie looked doubtful.

"I will give you a heads up when to begin," Amanda reassured.

The portal chimed, closing.

"You must leave now," Amanda urged, refraining from the desire to grab a forearm or hand and pull.

Naman didn't acknowledge her words, looking in the direction of the house grounds expectantly. A commotion in the distance.

This time, Amanda heard it too.

"I cannot leave. I have to stay." Naman gently pushed her away, nudging her up the patio steps. She complied, as self-preservation kicked in.

They listened to the thrashing of bushes being uprooted, and branches snapped off, to clear the way for the approaching visitor. The galumphing hulk stomped into the clearing. Darkness shrouded the body, an impenetrable black mist that gradually lifted and disappeared.

Amanda sighed, smiling and quaking in relief. At long last, Robert's contingency plan arrived in the flesh.

In a lustrous unitard, gangly, pale- skinned with shoulder-length red hair and silver eyes that shone, Leslie Cullver made the transformation to superbeing. He came to take Naman down. Only four times in the history of Prasinopolis has the country's leader been deposed. The events of tonight may determine if it would happen for the fifth time.

Naman glanced down at her, discomforted. Amanda realized she may be a hindrance. With a pleading look, she said, "Let me help you."

Brushing aside her concern, Naman asked, "Are your boots on?"

"What? Yes, they will turn on automatically," she answered absentmindedly. Yelping, as Naman casually tossed her onto the roof, one hand in a basketball-style layup, without so much as a backward glance.

Arms windmilling to keep her balance, Amanda floated. Her boots touched the roof with a fluid, binding click.

Naman kept a bead on Leslie the entire time, moving leisurely towards the ghostly figure as though taking a stroll in the park. Mid-step the superbeing stopped, clutching the sides of his head and falling to his knees.

Throwing back his head, Leslie laughed diabolically, revealing a mouth full of teeth capped with metal fangs. "This is going to be easier than I thought," he lisped, speech hindered by oversized incisors, striking the first blow.

It sounded like a wet towel wrapped around a bar of soap striking flesh. Amanda flinched, reliving a painful experience.

Pummeling Naman about the head and shoulders, Leslie's arms were a blur of motion. Naman struggled to his feet. The sickening thud of fists continued. With a raised arm over his head, Naman tried warding off the battery. He staggered back, punch drunk from a blow to the jaw.

"Nestor!" Amanda screamed.

Naman collapsed, arms splayed wide.

Leslie's force of impact was equal to, and quite possibly surpassed, Naman's strength. It would be over if Amanda, Dollie, and Francis didn't act now.

Throwing caution to the wind, Amanda launched herself off the roof. The boots worked with stone, metal, and wood surfaces, but she never tried grass. She landed next to a prone Naman, clumsily tumbling to a stop. "Nestor, can you hear me? It's Amanda. Let me help you!" Blood seeped from his temple, the clothing torn again. This time, no self-healing occurred.

"Get out of my way, little girl," Leslie warned, fists clenched, trembling with explosive rage. Amanda sensed his restraint, a grace period granted due to Robert, wouldn't last long. He panted with impatience.

Touching Naman's exposed cheek, the remaining piece of mask crumbled away. Amanda slapped a hand across her mouth, stifling an empathetic moan. "How could they have done this to you?" Those naked features horrified and haunted her. Deep groves caused by embedded spikes cut jagged trails over Naman's cheeks. A wire mesh device made of piercing metal prongs and a web of glimmering, flesh-colored, synthetic material hid the curve of his full lips.

Amanda cupped the back of his head, careful not to touch a wound or the metallic muzzle. Whispering in those familiar ears, she uttered the words, "Let me help you." His eyes opened. Twin silver beams of light touched her features with a soft glow. She could feel tension building in his neck.

"What can you do, Amanda?" He asked, frowning, voice laced with pain.

She opened the portal, per audio channel, to Dollie and Francis. Leaning down, her lips brushed Naman's earlobe so Leslie couldn't hear. "Release yourself, Nestor. Come back. Take control from Nicodemus."

With the acute auditory enhancement afforded a superbeing, Leslie heard her.

"Why don't you tell me where Monica is, Nestor?" He growled, triggered by the names. Leslie charged. No longer concerned with holding back, his feet hit the ground in an ungainly stride. Lacking sufficient training, Leslie was unaccustomed to his new powers. Thus, he wanted a fast fight and quick defeat of his enemy.

Quivering, Amanda put herself in front of Naman, hoping to dissuade Leslie from attacking.

Moving her aside, Naman sat up, simultaneously catching

Leslie in the shin with his right foot, temporarily disabling him.

Amanda beat a hasty retreat, climbing onto the patio chair then table to boost her leap. She caught the edge of the roof gutter, lifting one leg over, using the momentum to reach safety.

Naman had a lot going for him: speed, strength, stamina, and a touch of telekinesis, yet it meant little against another superbeing like Leslie who boxed at an early age. Naman wasn't a tactical or skilled fighter.

Taking his time while healing, Naman rose.

On the rooftop, Amanda rubbed her hands together, smiling at the frisson of excitement.

Putting his hands up, partially shielding his face, Naman moved into a fighter's stance. Naman gave Francis access to the mesh device and used him as an avatar. With permission, Francis controlled Naman's movement, which he could break free from at any time.

The aura around Naman pleased Amanda, because it meant Nestor had returned.

Robert spoke into her ear, using an encrypted audio channel of the portal. "I can't hold them off forever."

"Give him a few more minutes. Please."

"His time is running out, Amanda."

She decided to feel out his intentions. "Leslie was your contingency plan."

Feigning ignorance, Robert sounded evasive, issuing the standard plausible deniability. "I have no idea where or how Leslie got this way. We are not accountable and will have to deal with him after Naman. He's unregistered, and it's illegal."

"Only one other person could have enabled him, Robert,"

Amanda pointed out. "Leslie asked Nestor for Monica. I believe, in the process of helping Leslie transform, he became unstable. She had to run away."

"I will deal with Monica. You worry about Naman. Even if he wins this battle with Leslie, he still has to leave."

Amanda said, "I understand," somber at being on opposite sides of the situation with her sibling. They didn't speak again for the rest of that night.

Naman completely healed. Back in place were the silky black mask and glittering outfit. In a face-off between the two, Leslie bounced with nervous energy. Locked into position, the superbeings gauged each other's weaknesses. Francis tempered Naman's impulses, steeling his calm. Naman would let Francis make the next moves, deciding not to second guess his expertise.

Leslie grimaced, flashing his jagged teeth, the signal Francis was waiting for. Naman sidestepped Leslie's deadly combination of feint right jab and rapid left hook.

Struggling not to override Francis's control, Naman heard reassuring words in his head. *Trust me.* Relaxing his shoulders, twisting his neck, flexing and stepping back, Naman smoothly danced out of reach of Leslie's advances.

A volley of hammering fists came fast and furious at Naman. Raising arms, taking shelter, Naman buried his head into the crook of his elbows.

At a distance, a person with normal vision would see the outline of two glowing, silver-eyed, giants tightly stalking one another in a circle. The disturbing sounds of pummeling and punching loud enough to wake Necropolis "city of the dead."

Leslie closed in to hug Naman in a tight clutch.

Naman's knee found its target, driving hard to crack Leslie in the ribs followed by a sucker punch to the solar plexus. He wanted to deliver a kick to the back of Leslie's head. Francis stopped him. Executing a full rotation with that amount of force requires proper balance and deft execution. Naman might overextend his leg, miss, and fall. Instead, when Leslie leaned over, winded, Naman's elbow slammed into his neck.

Leslie choked, wheezing for air, evading the next blow by scrambling away.

'*Don't,*' Francis warned. They struggled over which direction to take. '*Relax, be like water.*'

Limping, Leslie backpedaled and jogged backwards. His cockiness waned while growing alert and watchful. Leslie noticed Naman froze after fighting. Looking indecisive about his next move or listening to someone. Either way, it worked to his benefit. Leslie grinned. Boldly coming up to Naman, who appeared distracted, he aimed for the jaw, an area below the ear, which would knock anyone out—even a superbeing. While bringing up the right hand again for a punch, Leslie let his left his hand hang unconcerned about protecting that side.

Naman grabbed Leslie's right hand, using the momentum to flip him over his shoulder. Francis had no control over Naman using telekinesis to throw Leslie far, and forcefully, into the ground. The bone jarring pain made him buckle and writhe trying to escape the agony. As the aching subsided, a determined Leslie crawled on hands and knees to get back on his feet.

A rapid back and forth, a fury of fists slamming into each other's faces, wild swings, open-hand slaps, a couple of tight clutches ending with violent push offs, and constant pounding of flesh happened in a blur. With the superbeings barely out of breath, and mutual assault unflagging, the slugfest continued.

Repeatedly, Leslie went for the right jab feint and left hook. Francis noticed his dependency on the boxing go-to move. Using a repetitive, familiar, or trademark move made sense. In a short skirmish, a one-two punch was enough. Yet in a long, wild, drawn out contest with no rules, mixed martial arts required different tactics, techniques, and skills.

Francis aimed for the unpredictable. Naman shot off in a sprint towards the backyard, and wilderness of the house grounds.

"What?" Shocked, Amanda watched Leslie hesitate before running off in hot pursuit.

Naman knew every tree, bush, dip, and swell behind his property. Surprises awaited Leslie.

Without hesitation, Amanda stepped off the ledge, floating down to the stone patio. Raising her head, retrieving the memory of Naman's scent, Amanda took flight after the fleeing superbeings. Their scent left a clear trail like a light beam across the dark landscape. To her cat-like eyes, it was as bright as a night of the full moon.

Amanda found Naman crouching behind a tree, alert for signs of an approaching Leslie. She tapped him on the shoulder. "Found you."

He pulled Amanda down beside him, enveloping her in the invisible shield. Sensing Amanda wanted to talk, Naman covered her mouth. Their eyes locked for a quarter of a second in silent combat. Her teeth nipped Naman's palm. He snatched back his hand. She grinned, sticking her tongue out.

Leslie might have heard her. Naman couldn't locate him. The advantage over Leslie was lost, unless.... "How did you find me?" Pulling Amanda closer, he whispered in her ear, making them burn. The tips felt hot enough to singe.

She indicated her nose, wrinkling it. "I stored your scent when I first came to visit."

His silver eyes gleamed. "Can you tell where Leslie is?"

Silently, Amanda pointed up at a tree. Perched on a branch and partially hidden behind another, Leslie hungrily scouted the area.

Naman clasped Amanda's little hands. "Are you willing to be bait? Will you leave as soon as it is safe to do so?" His silver eyes also telegraphed, *Don't wait for me. Don't look for me.*

They stared, gazes unwavering.

Amanda swallowed, "Yes."

After squeezing her hands in gratitude, Naman wrapped an arm about her waist. He jumped high into the tree, planting her on a branch.

Grabbing his forearm, Amanda pleaded, "Don't kill him."

Her unwavering faith humbled Naman. Nodding curtly, he released her and floated down.

Leslie heard Amanda. His head bobbled, swiveling around like an owl spotting prey. He snarled, "What are you doing here?" Swinging from branch to branch, Leslie exuded menace. Landing with a hard thud, he didn't see or hear Naman.

Now, Francis said.

#

Standing triumphant over an unconscious hogtied Leslie, a bruised and bloodied Naman began to self-heal again. *Thank you, Frank.*

Great fighting with you, Nestor. To protect his friend, Francis terminated the Nicodemus implant. It dissolved, along with the broadcast, wire mesh, and tracking device. You are not alone, he reminded. Their connection cut off. Exhausted, Francis slumped down in his seat.

Dollie sensed the adrenaline, strain, and energy seep out of his body. "Frank!" Dollie quieted upon seeing his smiling, sleeping face. With two sweeping gestures, Dollie set his seat to fall back.

#

Blades chopped the air. Overhead drones illuminated treetops, punctuating undergrowth with glaring spotlights. Thrashing sounds grew near. Robert couldn't hold back his team or cohorts any longer.

Amanda climbed down, running from the scene, making certain not to look back. It would fill her with regret; she might not leave.

Hard footsteps pounded the ground, gaining speed and coming closer. Each thudding footfall fell into sync with her heartbeat. Amanda heard a rustle behind her. A tall, lean, figure burst out of the bushes in a leap, arms winding and swinging up to straighten. The body sailed over her head, flying, going far past the point where she could run and catch up. Amanda suppressed the urge to follow. Naman knew how to disappear without her, having done it before. He didn't need her weighing him down, being a hindrance, encumbering his freedom.

"Nestor," Amanda sighed at his fading scent, certain she would never see him again.

#

A few days later, at 6:00 a.m., a brand new broadcast announced Naman's resignation from office. Within seconds, a round of candidates declared their intentions to run for Head of State. None of them presented as superbeings, simply average politicians.

"Naman is no longer," Amanda said aloud to herself. Dollie was spending time with Francis. She chuckled, recalling the cheekiness of coercing Nicodemus' creator to help Naman. It made sense. Francis never stopped being a member of The Hand, no matter where he was or what he did. He owed it to Nestor.

#

Weeks later, Amanda rode in the tourist vehicle. Sitting in a window seat, she stared unseeingly. At the moment, she couldn't tell where the mostly empty vehicle drove past. A dull ache replaced the pleasure she used to feel on these trips.

A tall man, dressed in silky black shirt and pants, with shiny black boots, walked down the center aisle. He stopped next to her row seat.

The familiar scent made her cat-like eyes widen. Amanda's pupils expanded, her nostrils flared. Joy and elation shot through her when she looked up at his bare face.

Smiling, he asked politely, "Is this seat taken?"

Omri

Steven L. Rosenhaus

The idea of a golem — an artificial being brought to life using basic elements and kabbalah rituals — has always intrigued me. Combine that with my penchant for playing a game of "what would happen if" in my writing music or prose, and you get the story of a rabbi overwhelmed by his charge to lead the Jews of a colony on Mars. He creates a golem as an assistant; creating a golem on Earth is dodgy enough, but on a different planet?

Rabbi Yosef ben Mordechai, aka Joseph Loew, was in his twenties when he received his *smicha* (ordination) and first gained some experience with congregants assisting Reb Moishe ben Meir in Borough Park, Brooklyn. His first rabbinical position was in Florence, Italy. It was an eye-opening experience, starting with learning Italian. He stayed in Florence for four years, moderately successful in ministering to those in the Jewish community who did not feel comfortable praying in the *Sinagoga Ebraico di Firenze*. Then the call came from the Chief Rabbi back in New York.

"We've decided you've proven yourself and are ready to lead in an area best suited to a rabbi of your learning, your talents, your ability to adapt," the Chief Rabbi said. "We are sending you to look after Jews on Mars."

"I'm sorry, Rabbi," Joseph said, taken aback, "but did you say

Mars?"

"Yes, the New Brooklyn colony there; they have a large Jewish population. And, God willing, you'll bring us closer to *Moshiach* with your work." Joseph sat in silence, nervous and trying to make sense of what he was hearing. "Of course, you'll have to go through training for space travel, and the trip itself will take about six months." *Six months? Training?*

"I'm not saying 'no', Rabbi," Joseph finally said, "but shouldn't someone with more experience be going?"

"Absolutely not. Your youth is in your favor, Yosef. You will get there in good health, God willing, and perform acts of loving-kindness for years to come."

A year later, well, here he was. It wasn't Brooklyn, and it certainly wasn't Florence. It was as different in every way Joseph could imagine and some he couldn't have before setting foot on, literally, alien soil. Maybe not so alien. By the time Rabbi Loew arrived, most of the colonies, including New Detroit and the first one, Perseverance, had done to Mars what Israel had done for the Negev. Martian land was being rehabilitated to grow crops and increase the oxygen levels in the atmosphere. Exosuits and portable breathing apparatuses, at first necessary at all times, were rarely needed now. Joseph didn't understand it, or why there was reddish dust *everywhere*, but *Torah* he knew. And he was here to bring the light of *Torah* to anyone who wanted it.

He slowly got used to living in New Brooklyn, getting to know the colonists and working on building a congregation. He was the first rabbi on Mars; it didn't take long for word of his presence to get out. The first few days were tough and hardly anyone showed up for morning prayers. Gradually more came, and some thirty people came to the first-ever *Shabbat* at the *shul* — it wasn't large enough to be called a "synagogue" — on Mars. There were children in New Brooklyn, all born on the red planet. Joseph, becoming known as "Rabbi Joe" to the Jewish locals, set up a Sunday Hebrew class for the children. Several adults also wanted lessons, so he set those up for right after the children's classes.

The excitement of it all — being on a different planet, being the rabbi for a new community — started taking its toll though. *Who has time to appreciate it when everyone demands your time, when you are wholly responsible for every aspect of running things?* And the questions! Moses himself would be beside himself at such questions, but at least Moses appointed judges from each of the tribes to take some of the burden of responsibility off him. Not that Joseph didn't try to get assistance.

"Please, Rabbi," he pleaded during one of several calls to Earth, "can't you send someone to help? Must I do this on my own?" He waited minutes for his signal to reach its destination and to receive a response. The waiting was close to agony. Then, finally:

"I understand, dear Yosef, I really do," the Chief Rabbi said, "but we don't have anyone young enough with the right qualifications we can send. Even if we did it would take more than a year to get him to you. Something about the orbit of our two planets making it difficult at times. I don't understand it..." The Chief Rabbi went on, encouraging Joseph to maintain his resolve, his belief in *Hashem*, and to do whatever he needed to do. Joseph half-listened at this point, his mind wandering. Then the Chief Rabbi ended the call, but not before adding he would be sending the books Joseph had requested on the next transport. "I must tell you I am not happy there are books on *kabbalah* among them. No one's ready to explore the connections between *Hashem* and the universe until they are at least forty years old." The Chief Rabbi sighed. "But then you are a special case, always have been. *Shalom,* Rabbi Yosef." That was that. Joseph was on his own.

Earth's year is measured as twelve months comprised of 365 days, 366 every four years to account for slight variations in the planet's rotation. Jewish calendars are lunar based, with the occasional leap month (Adar 1 and Adar 2) instead of a leap day. A year on Mars, on the other hand, averages 687 days, not quite twice as long as on Earth. Adjusting to the slightly longer days of Mars — by about a half-hour — was difficult enough for Rabbi Joseph, but a Martian year? *Oy, gevalt. What do we do about holidays? Do we follow the Jewish calendar twice to follow Earth months? Do we stop part way the second time through or eliminate months in the middle? Do we add leap months? We observe Rosh Hashanah and Yom Kippur only once a year, but how do we determine when? So many questions!*

New Brooklyn's rabbi sent those questions, and others, back to Earth for guidance, but he knew it would be a long time before his elders came to any decisions. They would study all of the texts, compare their findings, and discuss. And debate. Coming to a consensus would take a long time indeed. Rabbi Joseph had to make decisions *now* though, on top of dealing with the day-to-day issues of his congregants.

"Rabbi, my wife…"

"Rabbi, my job…"

"Rabbi, my husband…"

"Rabbi, I have a question…"

If Job could be patient, so could Joseph. Still, the challenges increased. He eventually convinced one of his better adult Hebrew students to help with *Shabbat* services. It helped, but not enough. It all began to overwhelm Joseph. The worst of it came on a Wednesday. It began with the funeral of a congregant that morning.

The man had been ill for some time and died the night before. Rabbi Joseph supervised the ritual washing of the body by a couple of congregation volunteers, and helped wrap the deceased in a white shroud. The next morning Joseph led the funeral service, then supervised removal of the body to cold storage until the next transport could bring it back to Earth for a proper burial. Meanwhile, he helped the widow sort through the numerous forms and permits required to return the body to Earth. While dealing with the funeral and its aftermath, Joseph missed a planning meeting with one of the New Brooklyn Catholic priests for an interfaith service. He barely made it to the afternoon prayers on time, and when those ended he was inundated with questions and requests from congregants. Joseph hadn't even had time for lunch, and his stomach growled in annoyance. No matter. He had to work out how the widow would observe the seven-day *shiva* mourning period. "Normally, you begin *shiva* right after the burial," he explained. "But as your late husband, of blessed memory, won't be buried until he lands on Earth, it would be appropriate to start *shiva* as soon as the transport leaves."

From there, Joseph rushed back to *shul* for the evening prayers. He was beyond tired, and his stomach was still growling from hunger. *If there were two of me, maybe I could see my way clear.* He had no idea what to do, but he knew how to start figuring it out. *When in doubt, there is always Torah.* Once home, Rabbi Joseph quickly put together a meal and ate it as he pored over the *Talmud* and other texts, comparing what he found with *Torah* portions to look for clues. He found nothing useful. A few months later, a supply transport arrived and with it, a container with books the Chief Rabbi had promised. There was a cookbook of vegetarian Italian meals — Joseph had developed a taste for Italian food while in Florence —as well as a hefty tome on the creation of calendars, and several books on *kabbalah* that the Chief Rabbi wasn't happy about, including the infamous *Zohar* (Radiance). All the books were available digitally, but for Joseph the concept of a book was important. *A real rabbi, a real Jew, studies anything important from real books. What, you're going to read Torah from a pad?*

Rabbi Joseph didn't bother finding space on bookshelves for his new acquisitions. He put the cookbook on the counter in the kitchen; the others he stacked on his desk. He sat for a while, just staring, unfocused. *I need a walk.* He left his residence and walked around the colony without a particular destination. Only half aware of where he was going, he soon found himself at the eastern edge of New Brooklyn. This area was mostly agricultural; there were greenhouses, fruit trees, fields growing various vegetables, and even a field blanketed with sunflowers like those Joseph saw during his time in Italy. *Now this is a miracle, that such things can grow in such a...different place.*

"Blessed art Thou, O Lord, our God, King of the Universe," he intoned in Hebrew, *"who has granted us life and sustained us, and allowed us to reach this moment."* Taking it all in, Joseph thought: *Indeed. Who ever thought I'd be praying on another planet?* He made his way home to find Rachel Leib waiting for him at the entrance. Rachel was the daughter of Michael Leib, who had

helped him with the funeral. Michael was a structural engineer and one of his better adult students learning to read *Torah* at Saturday services. Joseph didn't know much about Rachel except she was in her twenties and worked in biochemistry.

"Good afternoon, Rabbi," she greeted him. "I received one of your books by mistake in the last transport." She handed him a copy of *The New Zohar*. By tradition, he wouldn't normally accept anything from a woman in public, lest anyone get the wrong idea, but on Mars everything was new, including traditions.

"Thank you," he said. "This will help in my studies." She looked at him in a way that both pleased him a lot and bothered him a little. He looked down at the book to avoid staring at her. "Yes, this will help."

"Yes, okay then," Rachel said, "I have to get back. Good to see you, Rabbi." With that, she turned and walked away. Joseph watched her depart for a moment, shrugged, and went inside with his book.

That evening, he spent reading various texts, making notes on his pad, and thinking. Everything he read, everything he knew, came down to one solution to his problems: he needed help, rabbinical help. Again he thought: *If there were two of me, I could see my way clear.* He flipped through one of the books on *kabbalah* and stopped at one page. *No, I couldn't do that. That would be beyond nerve; it would be chutzpah. But I'm drowning here without help and there's no one who can come to my rescue. Maybe Hashem has shown me the tools I can use to rescue myself then. I can create a golem.*

The thought was both revolting and exciting. *I have no right to create something like that, but I have no choice at this point, do I? A creature made from the dust of the...earth? The earth? I'm on Mars. Could it work?*

Over the next few weeks, Rabbi Joseph studied when he wasn't giving Hebrew lessons, planning talks on the week's *Torah* portion, and advising people who came to him or called with questions. He taught himself as much as he could about the process of creating a golem; the ritual cleansing he had to do first, the materials he would need and, most importantly, how to form the golem's body and animate it. The first step was to determine the golem's size. Too big and it would scare people; it could even become dangerous. Too small, and it wouldn't be useful or be taken seriously. Joseph settled on making the golem about his own height and general build. *People feel more comfortable seeing something a bit like them,* he reasoned.

This would take a lot of Martian soil, which was plentiful but difficult to collect. He thought about getting it from one of the farming areas but decided against it. The first reason was practical: *We need that soil for crops to grow. Anything else would be a waste or worse.* The second reason was what he had learned about farming on Mars, and from the writings of Eleazar of Worms. Soil used for agriculture on Mars was processed to match that of Earth, and it even contained a small percentage of Earth soil in the mix. Making a golem, according to Eleazar, required virgin soil, so the blend used by the colony's farmers wasn't acceptable. The next day he made arrangements to borrow a shovel and a couple of pails from one congregant, and a small electric cart from another. Neither asked for the reason the rabbi wanted these things. *We're a colony on a new planet, he thought; just about everyone has a project to make life here better. Besides, who questions a rabbi?*

The rest of that week and through the next, he went out once a day after morning prayers, except on Shabbat. He rolled the cart to an uninhabited area to the south of the colony. There he was like a child at the beach, loading Martian soil into pails with his shovel. When the pails were full, he covered them with a tarp and rolled the cart back home. Once there, he emptied each pail onto the floor of an unused room in the back of the residence, forming a pile that grew with each day's trip. He covered the soil with a tarp to keep the pile intact.

The other major ingredient for creating a golem was water. The water, according to Joseph's kabbalistic sources, had to be pure. Mars has water — that much was proven as far back as the twenty-first century — but it was scarce. With no rivers or lakes on the surface, let alone seas or oceans, any native Martian water had to be obtained through very deep wells. Wells were few and not very productive. All water used for food, drink, and agriculture, for now at least, was recycled, filtered, and purified. Those processes made potable water available but not in large quantities. Joseph had to conserve water as much as possible and save what he could in containers. In less than two weeks the back room had a large pile of Martian soil under a tarp and many containers of different sizes filled with water.

One day during all of this, sometime after evening prayers, Michael Leib knocked on Rabbi Joseph's door. "Rabbi, Shara and I would like to invite you to our place this Friday evening for Shabbat dinner," he said. Joseph was about to say something, but Michael stopped him. "We won't take 'no' for an answer." Joseph thanked him and accepted the invitation.

Dinner at the Leib's that Shabbat was unpretentious and lovely.

In addition to Michael and his wife Shara, there were David and Lynne Smith, recent arrivals from Earth, and Rachel Leib. The wine, Michael joked, was guaranteed to be imported — from Earth. Rachel made a mock sour face at her father.

"You know we're working on growing grapes here, Dad, —" she started to say.

"It's just a matter of time," Michael finished for her. Clearly, they had had the conversation before. At Michael's suggestion, Joseph taught the Smiths the ritual for handwashing before the meal, and his hosts gave him the honor of saying the blessing for the wine. The food was simple, but tasted better than anything Joseph had eaten since his arrival on Mars. The wine was good, maybe not as sweet as what he was used to, and the company was delightful. This was the first time Joseph felt truly comfortable, *relaxed*, on Mars. Some of this was due to Rachel's presence. Everyone talked throughout dinner about a variety of things and Joseph, not just being a rabbi but *the* rabbi of New Brooklyn, found himself dominating the conversation.

"I used to question, why would *Hashem* want any of us to go to another planet? And do you know what? I found the answer in the *Torah*."

"What do you mean, Rabbi?" asked Rachel. "The *Torah* doesn't mention space travel or colonizing another planet at all."

"This is true," Joseph said, "but it says in a number of places, and in a number of ways, that we are put on Earth with responsibilities, not just to ourselves and each other, but to Creation itself. To me, it means not only protecting our environment, but also colonizing Mars; it's taking responsibility for the value of human life. Only *Hashem* can give life, and only *Hashem* can take it away."

Everyone nodded in agreement, and Joseph allowed himself a moment of self-satisfaction before the hypocrisy of what he just said, compared with what he was planning on doing, hit him. He must have looked distressed; Rachel leaned over to him and quietly asked if he was all right. "Thank God," he replied, "I'm fine." Dinner over, the guests thanked the Leibs for a lovely time, and everyone bid each other "*Shabbat Shalom.*" The Smiths left, but Joseph stayed behind to ask Rachel a question.

"I didn't get to ask you at dinner," he began, "but what is it you actually do? I know it has to do with biochemistry but nothing beyond that."

"My specialty is biodiversity," she said. Joseph looked puzzled. "Biodiversity is the study of life in particular habitats or ecosystems. My work is exploring not only what we're bringing to Mars from Earth, but also the variety of life that was already here before we arrived."

"Mars had life before we came here?"

"For a long time, we couldn't find any evidence of anything living, either in the past or present. Then we began terraforming to allow colonization —"

"Terraforming?"

"That's creating an earth-like environment where it's not normally supported. My job is to see that the environment we create or adapt is biodiverse enough to become self-sustaining. Here's an example..." She described how Mars' first settlers had to live in special quarters and could only go outside wearing full protective suits. Within fifteen years, just before the New Brooklyn colony began, enough earth plants and trees had been planted and were growing to release more oxygen into the atmosphere, to capture and disseminate sunlight and its heat, and to raise the base level temperatures enough to sustain human life with less severe restrictions.

"Now," she continued, "the oxygen levels are high enough that we can mostly go without exosuits or even breathers. We're also introducing less-hardy crops and raising a small number of farm animals, like chickens and ducks, to help maintain balance in the ecosystem. It's too slow a process for some people, having to wait for, let's say, grapes." The reference to Rachel's father made them both laugh.

"But you said we couldn't find Martian life from before we came. Has that changed?"

"We're not sure," she said. "We're still investigating." The rabbi thanked her and his hosts again for a pleasant evening and took his leave. He had much to think about, but the mental image of Rachel kept interrupting his thoughts.

Saturday was, of course, Shabbat with its full schedule of morning services. Afterwards, there was a small *kiddush* with pastries from a regular attendee who loved to bake, and then a discussion of the day's *Torah* portion with whoever was interested. When everyone else had left, Joseph closed up the *shul* for lunch and a well-earned nap at home. Later, he went back for afternoon and evening services. After Shabbat and the ritual of *Havdalah*, he and the congregants exchanged wishes for a good week. Once again, Joseph locked up and headed home. *I love what I do. I love being a rabbi. There is still too much, though. No one person can do it all.*

Sunday followed the routine of morning prayers, children's Hebrew class, and the adult class after that, followed by a light lunch for the overworked rabbi. He spent the rest of the afternoon in his study, reading and rereading the information he had collected for creating and controlling a golem. The next day, after morning prayers, Joseph went straight back home to get started. First was the necessary ritual cleansing. For Joseph, this meant bathing in a mikvah, a pool of natural water, to achieve a ritual purity. But on Mars there were no pools of water, natural or processed.

These were unusual and extenuating circumstances, which Joseph felt allowed him some freedom in interpreting the texts. Using water he had saved, he gave himself an old-fashioned sponge bath. He was also required to immerse himself but, there being no way to do that, he immersed each limb one at a time in the biggest vessel he had. Then he held his breath and dunked his head so that even the hair on the back of his neck got wet. He didn't notice that, as he pulled his head out of the water, he had nicked a finger on the edge of the vessel. It didn't hurt and was tiny, just enough to draw a drop of blood. He couldn't immerse his torso, so he did a second sponge bath instead. The blood was washed off, but the tiny wound was still there.

Dried off and dressed, Joseph referred to notes on his pad for the next step. He pulled the tarp off the Martian soil he had collected and started fashioning it into a humanoid shape about his own size. The reddish soil had dried out, so he added water to make it more like clay. Another drop of blood from the earlier nick on his finger got mixed in as he worked. Joseph still hadn't noticed the nick, but stopped working when he saw the soil bubbling slightly. The bubbles subsided quickly and, after a moment, Joseph returned to fashioning the golem. It took less time than he anticipated to get the basic shape right, and the more his hands went into the Martian clay the faster things seemed to go. It was almost as if the clay was helping form itself.

Joseph wasn't particularly artistic, although his Hebrew calligraphy had allowed him to earn some money creating lovely *ketubot*, marriage contracts, for newlyweds in Florence. He was surprised now with how well and quickly the golem was taking shape. This wasn't one of the grotesque *things* he saw depicted in his research; it was more...man-like. When he was satisfied that the golem was formed properly, Joseph stopped working and brushed the clay off his hands. He stood over the figure. The clay fell off his hands and onto the figure, where it was quickly absorbed. Joseph noticed, but didn't think about it. He covered the figure with the tarp, turned off the pad, went to the bathroom to clean up more thoroughly, and from there, to bed.

Tuesday was busy. Michael Leib came late to *shul*, just in time to make the morning *minyan*. Afterwards, he asked to speak with Rabbi Joseph privately.

"Is everything all right, Rabbi?" Michael asked.

"Oh, yes, Michael. I'm just a little tired, that's all."

Leib checked the time. "I can't stay long," he said. "I have a meeting in twenty minutes, but I wanted to ask you something." He hesitated. "I've been thinking about getting our community more involved here. What do you think of us organizing a group, a committee, to help you run things?"

"Well, I have asked for a second rabbi," Joseph said, "but he might not arrive for at least a year."

"That would help, but it's not what I meant," Michael said. "You need to delegate some responsibilities instead of trying to shoulder them all yourself. Yes, some of us assist in services, but you haven't let anyone *do* anything with any other aspects of our lives as a Jewish community. You know I'm a structural engineer, right?" Joseph nodded. "My job is configuring structural elements to resist accountable forces."

"I have no idea what that means."

"It means, Rabbi, that I design things to be built so nothing they interact with tears them apart. The way I look at things, your responsibilities are exerting forces on you that can tear you apart, and you have no way to counteract them. You need shoring up, as it were. You need help." Joseph didn't respond for a long time, but when he did, it wasn't what Michael expected. Rabbi Joseph laughed.

"Thank you," Joseph said when he stopped laughing. "There is a lot to do, and even with the longer Martian days, there's not enough time to do it all. Yes, I can use the help." They agreed to meet, along with some other congregants Michael had in mind, in a few days. With that, Michael left. Joseph sighed in relief. *That will help, but it still leaves religious duties. With more families getting involved every week things are becoming overwhelming. In Florence, I at least had Rabbi Dinowitz to assist me; here, no one yet, not for at least a year.* Joseph determined to go on making the golem. He went home and straight to the back room. He picked up the pad and read the next step in the process, performing a verbal ritual.

According to most sources, he first needed to meditate, something he learned to do in his training for the flight from Earth to Mars. He would then need to recite a special array of Hebrew letters, or a combination of several names of God, or both. It was a complicated procedure. There had to be a name or separate letter combination for the head, the torso, and for each of the golem's four limbs. If he used letters, each was to be paired with a different vowel sound. There are twenty-two letters and five vowels in Hebrew, so there would be one hundred ten possible combinations from which to choose. Joseph would have to memorize everything and recite it while walking seven times around the golem in one direction and, if necessary to undo the golem's creation, he would need to recite the incantation in reverse, walking around the golem seven times in the opposite direction.

Rabbi Joseph considered other ways of creating a golem; there were many, of varying complexities. Instead of choosing one method over another, he used what they all had in common. The only thing he couldn't do was create the golem with anyone else. Most texts suggested that a group of learned men perform the ritual. Presumably this was to ensure that nothing went wrong. *But if I had other rabbis here, I wouldn't need to make a golem in the first place.* Joseph wasn't ready yet. He had to make sure the incantation was correct, and then he had to memorize it forward and backward. *The sages knew what they were doing, he thought, when they made things this difficult. I trust them.*

The Chief Rabbi's message came the next morning. "Good news, Yosef," it read. "We found someone to assist you. He can be on Mars just after *Pesach* next year." *After Passover, next year. No, I have no choice now.* He went back to the sanctuary and carefully removed the *Torah* from the ark. He carried it home, holding it close to him both to protect it and because of his love for all it represented. On the way he met Rachel.

"Is it a holiday I don't know about, Rabbi?" she asked

"No, I'm just taking the *Torah* home to study." There was a moment of silence before she spoke again.

"I enjoyed talking with you at Shabbat dinner last week, Rabbi."

"Please, call me Joseph."

"Joseph then. Maybe we could have a cup of tea or something another time?" He unconsciously pulled the *Torah* a little tighter to himself for comfort; he wasn't used to a woman being so...direct.

"Normally I would insist on having a chaperone," he began, "but we're adults and can be expected to behave. Besides, we're on Mars! I've begun to think a lot of things here can't work the same way as on Earth. I don't think *Hashem* would have a problem with it. Yes, let's have tea. When are you free?" They settled on the following Monday to meet. Joseph left. Once home, he placed the *Torah* on the desk in his study. He was distracted, unfocused, and lost track of time. Later, he almost missed evening prayers, and while he didn't rush them, he didn't linger over them either. He didn't give a mini-lesson on *Torah* as he would sometimes do. Once prayers were done, he wished everyone a quick "good night" and headed straight home once more. His thoughts were all over the place. He thought about Rachel, about the golem, about the assistant rabbi he would get in a year, Michael Leib's offer of assistance, about — *everything*. Thoughts arrived and flew away; they tumbled in various permutations with others. He paced the room for some time.

"*Genug*!" he said aloud in Yiddish. "Enough! I must focus." With every bit of information he had available in piles over half his desk, along with the sacred *Torah* taking up the rest of the space, Joseph created the incantation he was to recite. Kissing the *Torah* scroll, he rolled it up and covered it. He would bring it back to *shul* in the morning, when he would lead the *minyan*. For now, he needed a meal, and then rest.

Thursday morning *minyan* went smoothly. There were twelve congregants that morning including a new member who was saying *kaddish* for his father who had recently died on Earth. Joseph spoke with him after services, gave his condolences, and told him he would stop by later to check on him. Then everyone left, and Joseph closed the *shul* and went home. It was time.

Setting his communicator to "silent," Joseph retreated to what he now thought of as "the golem's room." He pulled the tarp off the figure. Using one of the containers of water, he washed his hands. He focused on the ritual he was to perform. He picked up a *Chumash*, a book version of the *Torah*, from the table. He began walking around the figure, carrying the book close to his body and reciting from memory the incantation he had devised. As he completed his seventh incantation and seventh circuit around the figure, he opened the book to Genesis, Chapter 2, verse 7.

"And God made man from the dust of the earth," he read aloud in Hebrew, "and He blew into his nostrils the breath of life, and the man lived." Nothing happened, not for seconds or maybe minutes. Then the figure gave tiny twitches in the extremities. Joseph leaned over to observe and noticed a warmth, mild at first but intensifying, emanating from the torso. It became hotter and started glowing red. Joseph, concerned, backed away. The twitches became more pronounced, and the torso shook noticeably. As it shook, the heat dissipated, the reddishness of the clay paled, and it took on a very different texture. From where Rabbi Joseph stood, it looked more like skin. *I'm not done yet,* Joseph thought. *Neither is my friend here.*

Joseph walked over to the table and took a small piece of

paper he had prepared. On it, in Hebrew, was the word "*emét*," or "truth." He approached the golem, which had stopped spasming and cooled; he leaned over to get a better look.

"It looks like a man," he said. The golem, otherwise completely still, slowly opened its eyes and looked directly at Joseph. *What is it thinking? Can it think?* The rabbi of New Brooklyn Colony inhaled and exhaled slowly to calm himself. He held the slip of paper in front of him. He didn't know what to expect, but he talked to the golem.

"Please open your mouth," he requested, pointing to his own mouth for emphasis. "I need to put this under your tongue. It will allow you to speak." *Does it have a tongue? I only fashioned the outside.* The golem in fact did have a tongue and, aside from some slight oddities of proportion, looked quite *human*. The paper was under the golem's tongue for less than a minute when the golem spoke.

"Master?" It was a simple question with much meaning behind it. Joseph nodded. The golem's voice was a little rough, but not unpleasant. The golem's movements were awkward at first, as one might expect. It took a while for Joseph to get the golem to even stand up, but by the end of the evening, and with Joseph's direction, it was able to walk around the room unaided, albeit stiffly.

The golem responded to directions immediately, without hesitation, and literally; it made for confusion at first. When Joseph told the golem to sit down, it did, on the floor. The rabbi then pointed to a chair and suggested the golem sit there. It tried sitting on the back of the chair, causing both chair and golem to fall to the floor. The golem wasn't hurt or embarrassed, of course, and said nothing. Joseph patiently showed the golem how to sit on the seat, which the golem then did perfectly. As the golem sat, Joseph watched. *I did this. With Hashem's help, I did this.* Next, Joseph handed the golem some of his own clothes and showed it how to put them on. The clothes fit because the golem's proportions were similar to the rabbi's own. By the time the golem was dressed, it was time for evening prayers. Joseph would have to leave the golem alone until he got back from *shul.*

"Sit in the chair," Joseph quietly ordered. "Do not go anywhere. I will return in a while." Later, when the rabbi returned, he found the golem sitting completely still in the chair.

"Do you sleep?" Joseph asked.

"I do not know, Master," the golem replied. "What is sleep?"

"It is...a way to rest. You close your eyes and allow yourself to rest like that."

"Should I do that, Master? Should I sleep?"

"Yes. Go to sleep. I will wake you in the morning." But he didn't wake the golem in the morning, nor during the day. It was Friday, with morning prayers to be said and preparations for Shabbat to be made. And Shabbat was, well, Shabbat. *You just don't do anything on Shabbat.* But Joseph had questions, a lot of them. *I thought I had thought this through, but I have so many questions. What, exactly, should I have it do? How can it help me? More importantly, I've given it existence; I have a responsibility to it. Do I treat it like a thing? A person? And — why didn't I think about this! — how do I explain the golem to others?* He would know more once he prepared the golem for work, but first, there was Shabbat.

Friday evening and Saturday passed as they should, quietly and with focus on *Torah.* In *shul* at the end of Shabbat, he celebrated *Havdalah,* the break between Shabbat and the new week, reciting the blessings over wine, the special three-wicked Havdalah candle, and the box of spices. Afterward he met Rachel as they were both about to leave.

"*Shavuah tov*, Rachel," he said.

"*Shavuah tov* to you as well, Rabbi," she replied.

"Please, it's Joseph."

"Joseph. Are we still having tea on Monday?"

"Yes. Where should we meet?"

"How about on your street? There is a new place not far, that we can try." They agreed and set the time. Then he excused himself to go home; he had a project waiting for him, he said.

"Are you writing a book?" she asked.

"No, but I want to get back to it. I will see you on Monday." They bid each other another "*Shavuah tov*" and left the *shul*, walking in opposite directions. Joseph felt excited, but whether it was from his conversation with Rachel or from what awaited him at home wasn't clear. Maybe it was both.

The golem was exactly where Joseph had left it a little more than a day ago, sitting completely still in a chair with its eyes closed. Joseph took a moment to look closely at his creation. *Is it growing hair? That's odd.*

"It's time to wake up," Joseph said gently. "Open your eyes." The golem opened its eyes but did not move. Since Friday afternoon, the creature's exterior had definitely taken on the look of skin. Daring to touch it for the first time since he molded the clay, Joseph discovered it felt like skin as well. Other things were also new or different. The golem's eyes, at first like baked enamel and Martian-mud colored, now looked more human. The "whites" still had a reddish tinge, like someone was overtired, but the irises had taken on a deep brown much like Joseph's own eye color. And hair –yes, hair– was growing on the creature's head and eyebrows. *It has a head but thinks not*, Joseph mentally quoted from the Passover *Haggadah. But it can talk, so it must be able to think.*

This week's Hebrew lessons for the kids, normally at *shul*, were held in Joseph's home. The adult class was cancelled for that day. Nobody minded the sudden changes or questioned them. As the children sat in the rabbi's main room, the golem sat in "his" room with the door just slightly ajar. Joseph had told the creature "I want you to listen to the class and try to learn to say the aleph-bet." The golem listened and learned, taking in everything that transpired. After the class was over and the children had left, Joseph spent time talking with the golem. He was quite pleased when it recited the *aleph-bet* perfectly from *aleph* to *tav.*

"What did you think of today's lessons?" Joseph asked the golem. "I give you permission to speak as you wish."

"I understand that learning the aleph-bet is important because letters make words." Joseph nodded. "Master, I would like to ask a question." Joseph was surprised at the golem's initiative.

"Go ahead."

"I heard you call the children by different names," the golem said. "Why?"

"Because this is how each of us distinguishes ourselves from each other. Many of us go by several names depending on the situation. My Hebrew name is Yosef ben Mordechai; my everyday name is Joseph Loew. Some people, including the children who were just here, call me "Rabbi Joe." In the Hebrew class, we have children with names like Robert, Keith, Sarah, and Ruth."

"Do I have a name?" the golem asked. *That's another thing I didn't think about before*, lamented Joseph.

"Not yet, but you should have a name. It is a tradition among Jews to name our offspring when they are born. You are not my offspring, but I did create you, so I should give you a name." The rest of the day was spent with Joseph tutoring the golem in basic human behavior, learning the English alphabet, and reading and writing in both English and Hebrew. The golem's ability to learn, to absorb knowledge, was to Joseph's mind, extraordinary.

"You did very well today," Joseph said.

"Yes, Master." Joseph thought about the golem's response. *He calls me "Master." That would make him—*

"I have a name for you," Joseph told the golem. The golem looked at him blankly, as it looked at everything. "I name you *Omri ben Adama*." The newly named Omri turned his head as if in thought, his mannerism surprisingly human.

"Thank you, Master," the golem replied. "I know the name is Hebrew, but what does it mean?"

"Your name has many meanings," Rabbi Joseph explained. "To some it means 'servant' such as you are to me. To others it means 'my sheaf' or 'my bundle of sticks,' and for others it is the name of an ancient Jewish king. To exist in this world, we are different things at different times."

"Like you are 'Master' to me," Omri postulated, "but to others you are 'Rabbi Loew' or 'Rabbi Joe.' To yourself, and in your prayers, you are Yosef ben Mordechai." Joseph was surprised by Omri's ability to reason, but chose not to show any reaction.

"Exactly, Omri. And 'ben Mordechai' means 'son of Mordechai.' Mordechai was my late father's name, of blessed memory."

"And my name, 'ben Adama' means...?"

"In your case it means 'son of the earth' because you were made from the soil of this planet."

"But you told me we are not on Earth," Omri countered. "We are on Mars."

"That is true, but we don't have a word in Hebrew for 'Mars', so I adapted the language to suit you." Joseph yawned. "It's getting late, Omri, and tomorrow will be busy. I need to sleep, and I can only guess you might, too."

"Yes, Master. I do not know if I am tired, but I would like to close my eyes for a while."

"Then sleep, Omri." Omri closed his eyes and went perfectly still. Joseph covered him — no longer "it" — with the tarp draped up to the golem's neck. *What an extraordinary conversation. What an extraordinary creature.* Joseph yawned again and prepared for bed.

On Monday there were seventeen people for morning *minyan*, the most Rabbi Joseph had seen. Later there were forms to fill out and questions from congregants to answer. A young couple stopped by to announce they were expecting and, if it was going to be a boy, they wanted to know if the rabbi could perform the *brit milah*. He explained that he couldn't, but he had been consulting with one of the colony doctors. "He is Jewish and comes to services when he can," Joseph said, "I'm guiding him in doing circumcisions using the traditional methods."

Although his workload wasn't any lighter, today *felt* lighter to Joseph. Once home, he cleaned up, and was just drying his hands when there was a knock on the door.

"Let me guess," Rachel said when he opened the door. "You forgot we're having tea." Joseph's face went a deep red.

"Well, I didn't, I mean—" he stammered. She smiled.

"It's okay, Joseph, I was teasing you. Shall we?" There weren't many places to go in the colony just for relaxation or food you didn't make yourself, but there was an actual coffee shop down the street from the rabbi's residence. There they enjoyed a couple of hours lingering over cups of tea and talking about all sorts of things.

"You say Mars once held life?" Joseph asked at one point.

"Yes, we've known that since the mid-twenty-first century, but we didn't know — and we *still* don't know — if there is still life here, and if there is, what form it takes. We can only guess that whatever is here exists on a microscopic scale." He didn't understand some of the concepts but Joseph was fascinated by the conversation, and more so by Rachel. She continued. "So let me ask you: what is this project you've been working on?"

"Excuse me?"

"You hole up in your quarters if you're not at services; I never see you outside anymore. I assume you're working on something. Are you writing a book?"

"Oh, nothing like that." *What can I tell her? The truth is always best, but the whole truth?* After some hesitation, he said, "I'm training someone to be my assistant. It's taking a long time, and he's not ready."

"Someone from the colony?" she asked. "Someone I know?"

"It's not anyone from the colony."

Rachel nodded. "Oh, I see," she said. "He's coming in on the next transport, and you're communicating with him as he travels." Joseph didn't answer, which Rachel took as a confirmation of her assumption. "Great. I look forward to meeting him." The next transport was due in six months. It would be the last one for a long while, as Mars' and Earth's orbits were moving out of phase. *Will Omri be ready by the time the transport arrives?*

Saying Omri was an exceptional student was an exaggeration. In less than a month he mastered reading and writing in two languages, although his Hebrew was stronger than his English. His use of spoken English, by contrast, was better than his Hebrew. He spoke Hebrew a little slower than most humans would, and with a slight unidentifiable accent. Omri was learning more about human behavior too, not only from Joseph's teachings but from observations of his Master. He didn't feel or demonstrate fear, sympathy, love, or friendship, but he learned what they meant and what they mean to humans. To expand Omri's abilities, Joseph encouraged him to ask questions.

"Master, why are we here?" Omri asked one day after his lessons.

"How do you mean? In New Brooklyn? On Mars?"

"Why are we alive? I think of such questions when I close my eyes for the night."

Joseph sighed. "I don't know, Omri. No one really knows. We believe it's *Hashem's* plan and desire that we exist. As to why, we can only guess. Many of the sages say, and I agree, that we are here to honor Creation itself. We have responsibilities to ourselves, to each other, and to life all around us. We learn what we can about what is expected of us through *Torah*, and through the writings of the sages. Then we do our best to live the way *Hashem* would want us to live." Omri turned his head, the mannerism that Joseph had learned meant the golem was considering what he heard.

"I would like to learn *Torah*, and *Talmud*, Master," Omri said.

Joseph smiled. *Now I can really train him to help me, and if I can get him to a certain point by the time the transport arrives, all the better.* The next few weeks were intense for both rabbi and golem. Every spare moment was utilized in learning to not only read *Torah*, but to interpret various portions and compare those with the commentaries of the sages in the *Mishnah*.

By the time the next transport arrived with new colonists and supplies, Omri was ready. The golem wasn't anywhere near as knowledgeable as a full-fledged rabbi, but he certainly knew enough to pass as an assistant, someone in training with a lot more to learn. At the same time, Joseph's relationship with Rachel was growing. The coffee shop down Joseph's street saw a lot of Rachel and Joseph during that time. The day after the transport arrived, Joseph asked — not ordered — Omri to wear new clothes he had given him.

"We're going outside, Omri," Joseph said.

"I have never been outside, Master."

"I know, but now you are ready, if you want to go."

"I would like to go outside, Master. You have told me a lot about what is outside, and I would like to see it."

"Very good. If we meet anyone I know, please call me "Rabbi" instead of "Master." I will introduce you. I may say something you know is not true. Do not say anything about it until we are back home."

"Yes, Master."

The two walked around New Brooklyn, Omri seeing everything for the first time and Joseph remembering what it was like when he first set foot on Mars. As Joseph anticipated, they hadn't been walking before they ran into Michael Leib.

"Hello, Rabbi!" Michael greeted. "The committee is meeting tonight. You're welcome to come, but it's not necessary." Since Michael and the others formed the committee, dealing with most documents and the logistics of running the *shul* were taken off the rabbi's duties. It made Joseph's life easier and less complicated. He only had to attend a meeting once a month, and most of that time he only had to listen to reports. Michael, having finished talking business, finally realized there was someone else there.

"Hello, I'm Michael Leib," he said to Omri. "And you are...?"

"I am Omri—" the golem began, but Joseph interrupted him.

"He is here to be my assistant rabbi." Michael smiled.

"So they finally sent you someone?" Michael asked. "*Mazel tov!*" With that Joseph and Michael said their goodbyes, and the rabbi and the golem resumed their walk. They walked east so Joseph could show Omri the farming going on, and then south. When they got to the edge of the colony, they stopped.

"This is where I got the soil to form you, Omri," said Rabbi Joseph.

"Yes, I know, Master."

"How? How could you know?"

"I do not know. I *feel* it somehow. This is where I come from." They walked back home in silence.

Joseph slowly introduced Omri to life outside of their home, but more intensely tutored him in *Torah*. Like Joseph, Omri took to wearing a *yarmulke* for much of the time. His hair had grown long enough for a haircut. Omri studied the various services; he practiced them as best as one could alone while Joseph led the same ones in *shul,* until Joseph felt it was okay for Omri to attend in person. Omri was introduced to the congregation at morning services one Shabbat by his full name, Omri ben Adama, as Rabbi Loew's new rabbinical assistant. "He did not grow up with our particular traditions, so he is learning everything from the beginning," the rabbi said. "For now he will mostly observe."

Everyone wanted to meet the new assistant, and almost all of them had questions.

"Where are you from originally?"

"What do you think of New Brooklyn?"

"Are you married?"

Omri, preternaturally calm as always, didn't answer right away.

"I am not married," he said, eventually, "but I am still too young, too unformed, for marriage. I think New Brooklyn is a—" he searched for a word — "wondrous place, and I am glad to be here."

"And where are you from?" he was asked again.

"I am...from the south."

"Oh, I thought so. That explains your accent." And so it went. Omri was accepted without hesitation by the congregants. Most of them, anyway. Rachel, for one, was unsettled by Omri.

"There is something 'off' about him," she confided to Joseph the next day when they met yet again for tea.

"Oh? Oh, I see what you mean," Joseph replied. "Omri is not used to being around a lot of people. He has been spending most of his time studying. He needs to interact with other people more." This seemed to mollify Rachel, although Joseph could see she was still uneasy.

As weeks passed, Omri's knowledge of *Torah* grew exponentially. He became more human-like in his mannerisms, his gait when he walked, and even in his speech. The more Omri learned, the more Joseph shared his duties with his handmade protégé.

Soon Omri was leading the children's Hebrew class, as well as the first part of the morning prayers. Joseph observed as one of the children asked Omri a question about the story of Jonah and the whale.

"Why did God let Jonah get swallowed by the whale?" the child asked.

"Because *Hashem* wanted Jonah to do something, but Jonah didn't want to," Omri replied. "I think *Hashem* had the whale swallow him to give Jonah time to think, in private, about what he needed to do." Then Omri led the next day's morning prayers flawlessly, calling out the page numbers for each section to keep everyone on track. Joseph had never thought of that, relying on congregants to help each other find their place. That evening Joseph and Omri sat at home and talked.

"You have exceeded my expectations, Omri," Joseph said. "I have always questioned that story about Jonah myself."

"Thank you, Master," the golem replied. "It is pleasing to know that. I would like to ask a question, if I may." Joseph nodded. "You refer to me in public as your assistant. I interpret that as 'assistant rabbi.' Am I correct?" The rabbi nodded again. "If that is the case, can I become a rabbi?" Joseph's reaction was sharp.

"No! You can *not* become a rabbi," his voice rising in pitch and volume as he spoke. "You look like a human being, you speak like a human being, but you are not a human being. You can not become a rabbi!" Omri was quiet for a moment.

"I have studied *Torah*, *Mishnah*, and the other texts you have had me read, and I cannot find anything that says a rabbi must be human."

"You've thought about this, haven't you? You've researched it."

"Yes, Master, I have. I may not feel as humans do — I think a human being would have been angry or upset with your reaction before — but I do feel things. Each day I feel more things and feel them more intensely. One thing I have come to feel is a love of *Hashem*, and for that I thank you. You have given me the second greatest gift someone could receive."

"The second greatest?"

"Yes. The first was you creating me." Joseph calmed himself before speaking.

"You still can't become a rabbi, Omri, I'm sorry."

"Why?"

"Because despite all of your training and your love of *Hashem* and *Torah*, you're simply not—"

"—a human being," Omri finished for Joseph.

"No, Omri. It's because you're not a Jew. But we can do something about that." They talked through the night, exploring ways to get around what seemed to be an insurmountable problem. *Can a being become a Jew without a* brit milah? *After all, one does not include a male organ when fashioning a golem. Of course, women have converted to Judaism for centuries. We can't have beit din, a rabbinical court, because we don't have enough rabbis!* They discussed and debated other issues and possible solutions until Joseph realized it was almost morning.

"We will figure this out, Omri," Joseph said. "For now, please, go to *shul* and lead the morning *minyan*. I will be there in time to say *kaddish*." Omri left; Joseph set an alarm to go off in a half-hour and lay down on his bed, still dressed. When he awoke, he felt disoriented; he looked at the chronometer and realized he slept through his alarm and had missed Shacharit altogether. He got up, took off his clothes from the day before, washed up and dressed in fresh clothes. *There's no point in rushing right now, is there? I've failed. Omri will be discovered.* Joseph ate breakfast and left for the *shul*. He arrived in time to see congregants leaving and chatting with each other.

"He's good," Joseph heard one congregant say.

"I never really understood that *parsha* before, but Reb Omri made it very clear," said another. *'Reb Omri'? And he's giving d'var Torah?*

"Oh, hi, Rabbi Loew," called Michael Leib as he left the *shul*. "Are you feeling better? Your assistant said you were tired from studying last night and needed extra sleep."

"Yes, yes, I'm feeling much better, thank you."

"Omri is really turning into a good speaker, Rabbi. You should let him give the sermon next Shabbat."

"I just may do that." Michael left and Joseph entered the *shul*. He found Omri stacking prayer books onto their designated shelves.

"Thank you, Omri," Joseph said. "This could have been very embarrassing for me, but by all accounts you did a splendid job."

"I have determined something, Master."

"What is it?"

"I do not have to convert; I am already a Jew."

"How so?"

"I have lived as a Jew from the moment you started teaching me all that I needed to know. I have feelings — I have *love* for *Hashem* and for the *Torah*. I know more *Torah* than anyone on Mars except for you. All I need is to make it official that I am a Jew." Joseph couldn't think of any reason to deny what Omri was saying. The rabbi thought for a moment.

"You are correct, Omri. But to make it official..."

"We need three rabbis, a *beit din*, to convene and declare my conversion."

"Yes. But we can't because—"

"We can, Master. You can convene a *beit din* by yourself." Joseph remembered he used the phrase "unusual and extenuating circumstances" to justify creating Omri in the first place.

"You're right, Omri, we can do this. And more." Two weeks passed. That Shabbat, Rabbi Joseph paused services just before the *Torah* portion to make an announcement.

"I want to let you all know that as of yesterday we welcome Mars' second rabbi ever, Rabbi Omri ben Adama, who received his *smicha*." The congregation spontaneously burst into cheers of "*Mazel tov!*" and "*Yasher koach!*" When the din died down Joseph continued. "Now I would like to allow our newly minted rabbi to lead the *Torah* portion of our service."

The congregation, even Rachel, soon got used to the rabbi's assistant in his new capacity as "second rabbi." Joseph got used to it too, very used to it. Meanwhile, Joseph also built up enough nerve to ask Rachel to marry him, making sure it was all right with Michael and Shara Leib first before he asked.

"Really, Rabbi? Of course!" Michael teased. "What took you so long?" Joseph proposed to Rachel in their favorite coffee shop, and she said 'yes'. Joseph suggested that Omri perform the marriage ceremony, at which Rachel laughed.

"Well, you can't officiate at your own wedding," she said. "Besides, you trained him well. You've made him into your own image." Joseph was startled by her last comment, until Rachel added, "You've given him the education he needed to be a good rabbi." Joseph relaxed, and Rachel smiled. Joseph and Rachel didn't want to wait, so they made the arrangements to wed in two weeks' time. At home, Joseph told Omri the news.

"Mazel tov, Master," Omri said.

"Rachel and I plan on going to one of the other colonies a few days after the wedding, Omri. I would like you to take over as rabbi for the time we are away. It is a lot of responsibility."

"I understand, Master. I will do my best."

The wedding was joyful, traditional but with adaptations for the new world of Mars. Rachel and Joseph left a week after the ceremony and reception. They would be in Perseverance for two weeks on their honeymoon.

#

Three months later, a transport arrived. One new arrival was a young man with payess and traditional Jewish garb. He was greeted by Michael Leib.

"Welcome, welcome," Michael said. "I'm Michael Leib. I'm chair of the *shul* committee. You're going to love living here in New Brooklyn."

"Thank you. I thought the rabbi would be here."

"The rabbi extends his apologies; he had a wedding to perform. He will see you back at his residence."

"I've heard so many wonderful things about the rabbi. I hope to learn a lot from him."

"Oh, that you will."

"So, what is Rabbi Loew like?"

"Ah, my son-in-law! He married my Rachel. They're in Perseverance."

"I don't understand. You said I will be meeting the rabbi. It's not Rabbi Loew?"

"It's a long story. Rabbi Loew had an assistant before you; Joseph trained him himself. His assistant officially became a rabbi while he was here, and we love everything about him. He's so down to earth. Or Mars." Michael chuckled at his joke. "Anyway, while Rachel and Rabbi Loew were on their honeymoon Rabbi Omri took over and, well, I shouldn't say this about my son-in-law, but everyone agreed that Omri is a better rabbi than Joseph." Michael blushed. "When Joseph and Rachel returned, I was the one who had to tell Joseph that he was fired, from his own *shul* that he had basically built from scratch. He didn't talk to me for a week."

"So...?"

"So it seems there are enough Jews in Perseverance to start another *shul*, and they asked Joseph to be their rabbi. All things considered, it turned out all right. The only thing Joseph said about it though was odd, 'I won't be digging in the dirt any time soon.' I have no idea what he meant by that." Michael Leib and the new assistant rabbi walked down the street toward the *shul*. "Come, I'll introduce you to your new home, your new *shul*, and your new boss."

Proxy
Michael Ben-Zvi

What happens when the revolution is over, the hopes and dreams come crumbling down, and the bastards end up winning? Do we give up? Or maybe we just find something else to believe in. Perhaps even the smallest of victories, that last sliver of hope, is the one thing we can hold on to.

In the Eternal City of Tannapol, a man had many ways to start the morning. Before breakfast, the pious would begin with the Dawn Prayer, facing old, faraway Earth. Those more practical than observant would greet the morning with a shot of *kafa* and cream. The even less pious would add some *kohol* or honeywine to their *kafa*, an extra spark to start the day off.

Tam Ergun didn't bother with the *kafa* these days. Honeywine on its own was enough for him.

It was a hot and dry morning in the Eternal City, as it usually was eleven months out of thirteen. But early *Avra* was the right time of year. Tam was not so far gone that he would drink alone in his apartment. Like bread and meat, alcohol was best for social gatherings. He mused with regret that the ones he most wanted to share with did not keep regular morning hours.

It was a typical morning for Tam, sitting outside at Breha's Cafe with bread, cheese, and honeywine, watching the rising sun banish the light of the three moons. He would look out upon the merchants setting up their stalls in the Royal Bazaar and listen to the call from the Gold Tower, beckoning the faithful to the Dawn Prayer, and give thanks to the Twelve Angels for another blessed day.

And Tam would wonder what it was that any of them had to be thankful for these days, as he took in the sights of the city that he both loved and hated, that warmed his heart each morning and broke it every night.

"Some things I can always depend upon," he heard a familiar voice call out. "Tam Ergun at Breha's. That, the sunrise, and the call to prayer."

He laughed as he saw an older man in a tattered old red *djellaba* held together by a rope, barefoot, and a patched-up cap to keep the sun off his head. It was Filo, or Filo the Unshaven, as they called him around the Bazaar. He was the friendliest of fellows, near and dear to all, right before he would beg for money.

Tam was lucky he was a mere working man and not someone blessed enough to live in the Estates or to have dinner with the Kalif in the palace, or Filo the Unshaven would resort to his other profession of pickpocket extraordinaire.

"*Salam*, Filo, old friend," Tam greeted him. "Join me for a morning toast?"

"*Wa-salam*," Filo replied in kind. "And to what are we drinking this morning? As if I should be surprised?"

"Why, what else should all good residents of Jiballah and the Eternal City drink to?" replied Tam. "To the People's Regime, of course. *Samat!*"

"Oh, my friend," said Filo the Unshaven, "you drink too much. More than I can recall you have before."

"It *is* my profession," said Tam. "Just as begging is yours. Do you see me judging you on how you earn your money?"

"I would never judge a bartender, my friend. After all, I'm not too proud to beg for drinks as I am for coins."

"Yes," said Tam. "As Big Sallah is well aware."

"But *you*, my friend," said Filo, "I can't help but be concerned. A bartender who drinks is like a hash merchant who enjoys his smoke too much—his own best customer and the one guaranteed to put him out of business."

Filo came over to join Tam at his table, no doubt to mooch a few morsels of bread and cheese as much for the pleasure of his friend's company, Tam thought.

"Don't you have to be at Prayers this morning?" asked Tam. "Isn't that what you promised when the Peace Troopers missed you after the last roundup?"

"I prayed yesterday," said Filo. "Surely the Angels will be happy enough with that from a poor wretch like me."

"You're supposed to pray at dawn *and* dusk," said Tam.

"Eh," Filo shrugged. "The Angels are supposed to be eternal, aren't they? They can afford to be patient."

They conversed effortlessly in Marketspeech, which Tam preferred among his friends, rather than the more formal use of Tuka or the flowery phrasing of Farras. Marketspeech always felt more natural to Tam. You knew when people were lying to you.

It was funny that he was thinking of lies just as he heard a rumble coming from the far end of the city, seeing a white column of smoke reaching out past the Gold Tower.

More of Jiballah's wealth, going off to enrich those who now ruled the city.

"Do you think our Kalif times the launches with the Dawn Prayer?" Filo laughed. "Give the faithful something heavenly to look at when they're supposed to be facing Earth?"

"I wouldn't be surprised," said Tam. "He has that kind of ego. Soon enough, he'll be declaring himself the Thirteenth Angel, and his Squattie friends will back him up on it."

"Tam!" Filo looked around. "Be careful. There are snitches everywhere. Even I have the good sense not to be so careless in public."

"And you're too anxious," laughed Tam. "That's why I cut out *kafa*. Who needs more anxiety in these times?"

Filo laughed at his friend. "Oh, Tam. I worry about you only because you are a far more respectable man than I. You have far more to lose should you offend the wrong people."

"I don't offend anyone," said Tam. "The city has long forgotten about me and the other partisans. That's how comfortable the people in the Estates are."

"I don't just mean politics," said Filo. "I'm talking about money. If someone were to levy fines against you—"

"I'm not worried about that," said Tam. "You're the one who needs to be more careful, especially after last week's sweep."

"And what do I have to worry about?" said Filo. "I have nothing to tax, nothing to take. I am free and clear of all debts. And that's how they get you! But you, old friend, you have an apartment, a job with such loveliness all around—"

"It's not like that," said Tam, "not at all." If anything, Big Sallah's House was a sad and desperate place to work, filled with the most miserable and hopeless people he knew. Even the beggars who slept on the streets lived happier lives than the girls at Sallah's or their customers. Of course, none of them seemed to think so. They drank and hashed enough to hide the sorrow.

"Oh, I've touched a sore spot, haven't I?" said Filo. "As soon as I talk about loveliness, your thoughts always lead towards—"

"I told you it isn't like that," Tam repeated himself, this time with more annoyance.

"Of course not," said Filo. "And I don't mean to imply anything disrespectful regarding the delightful Miss Jaya—"

Tam said nothing. He could deny as much as he wanted, but he doubted that Filo would ever believe him. He couldn't even convince himself that there was nothing there between him and Jaya.

"—I would never insult anyone so lovely, one for whom you have such obvious affection," Filo prattled on. "And after all, she is a mother. The Blessed Lady of Tears would curse my soul were I ever to speak ill of—"

"You know, Filo," Tam finally said, "you're not as clever and observant as you like to think. Jaya is my friend, and that's all. Even if I wanted more from her, it would be the last thing she could think of right now. She has to earn a living and take care of Little Soo. And I'm hardly the man who could fix her problems."

"She could do far worse," said Filo. "I mean it. You have steady work, and you keep your drinking to a minimum. You're already a father figure to Little Soo. You're honest, reliable. And I'm certain I've told you how respectable you are."

"You have. Whenever you need money."

"*And* generous to your friends," he added. "What woman wouldn't find such a charitable nature to be desirable?"

"Security," said Tam.

"I beg your pardon?"

"She wants security," Tam elaborated. "I can't give any woman that. Not Jaya. Or Little Soo."

Filo sighed. "Security, in these times? That's too much to expect from anyone who doesn't live in the Citadel. Even those useless slugs in the Estates tremble in fear every night that they might lose all their privileges tomorrow. No, my friend, the only man in the Eternal City with any security is our dear Kalif himself. The Squatties and their filthy offworld money see to that."

Tam could hear the Bazaar coming more to life, the stalls fully assembled, the wares and dishes placed for display. Spices wafted through the air, and handwoven rugs hung on their racks. There were aisles of glassware, leather goods, sandstone carvings, and polished stones from the mines. Those accursed mines, once Jiballah's blessing, now a burden that summoned the worst of scattered humanity from across the Diaspora.

#

In Tam's grandmother's youth, they lit the streets of Tannapol at night with candles and oil lamps. Families kept warm with fireplaces using straw and flamestones. Food was simple, cooked by wives and mothers, raising the fortunate few children that survived past infancy. The kings and princes of the Eternal Satrapy in the Citadel all lived and ate well and extravagantly, of course, but they were still Jiballan, as trapped in this world as the people they ruled. But so much changed after the Reconnection, when the first emissaries from the Society Worlds landed, bringing news of the Diaspora and the scattered worlds of humans now rising and reconnecting.

Now everything was different, Tam mused, yet not as different as he'd once hoped. Offworld technologies, things Jiballans could never hope to make for themselves, were finding their way into the markets. But they were toys for the wealthy, doing little to raise the quality of life of the poor.

It wasn't that Tam cursed the changes that had come to his world, but rather that the changes had not come fast enough. The Society Worlds told of places where there was no poverty, no ignorance, no hunger or sickness, and especially, no Satraps. It had been a time of great promise, a promise that remained unfulfilled.

Such abundance and opportunity might have been the truth among the Society Worlds, but not so on Jiballah. The Satraps and the Church of the Angels kept offworld visitors at bay, wanting their tools and toys, but not the changes that came with them. But the changes were impossible to keep out once the jumpknot that tied Jiballah to the worlds of the Diaspora was open. Soon it wasn't just the Society Worlds that came. Other cultures, some allies of the Society Worlds, some neutral, some not. Many had ideas and agendas of their own for Jiballah, particulary its mineral wealth. And soon enough, Jiballah and its mines attracted the bottomless greed and avarice of the Cartels of Lyr.

#

"*Yallah*," Filo beckoned to Tam, standing up from his seat and tugging at his sleeve. "You'll want to see this."

"See what?" said Tam, waving him off. "I haven't finished my breakfast."

"You'll have enough honeywine when you go to work," said Filo. "How often will you get to see this?"

"What are you talking about?"

"The Port," said Filo. "I have it on excellent authority that Akka'haman himself is making an inspection."

That jolted Tam out of his listlessness. "Are you sure? How do you know this?"

"I hear things," said Filo. "The marketplace is all abuzz. Lord Squat himself. Aren't you curious? Don't you want to look?"

Tam shook his head but did not feel the commitment in either direction. "Why? What good would it do? It's just asking for trouble. Besides, it's not like we'd ever get a close enough look. Pendrago will have the entire Port covered with Peace Troopers. And Akka'haman will likely have his own security. You know, the kind with actual competence and experience at killing people. It's not worth it, just because you're feeling bored and curious."

"Well, I've never seen a Squat up close before. I want to see—"

"Fine," Tam sighed. "I'll go with you. I don't have to be at Sallah's until 10. I'll go just to make sure you don't do or say anything to get yourself killed."

"I knew I could count on you, old friend," said Filo. He tugged on Tam's sleeve again as he left a few coins on the table for Breha to cover his bill. How much time and effort did he exhaust just to keep Filo safe from his own worst impulses, he thought.

More merchants were up and about with their stalls as they crossed the Bazaar and into the city's commercial district. He considered hailing a pedicab to take him to the Port, but he knew they'd never stop to pick up anyone who looked or smelled like Filo. And he wasn't in the mood to pay their increasingly exorbitant prices. No, thought Tam, he'd walked the length of this city back and forth his entire life. His own two feet were good enough.

As they crossed into the mercantile wards, Tam could see the change in the character of the neighborhoods. The dust and graffiti were left behind. Pedicabs rode down wide boulevards lined with palm trees, and glass and steel towers stood gleaming in the sunlight. He saw patches of exotic plants imported from far-off worlds in tended gardens, using far more precious water than the long-adapted Jiballan species. Tam could see the construction of a new tower, a mix of native physical laborers and strange offworld exomechs carrying metal pipes and timber. The Kalif's plans for a resort for offworld business interests. Why any offworlder would come to Jiballah for a vacation was beyond Tam. There was only one business on Jiballah that was of any value to visitors. The mines. Those accursed mines.

Just past the commercial wards, the buildings grew denser and uglier. They were industrial wards, which everyone called Greytown. It was a relatively new part of the city, just a few decades old, no older than the Port itself. But it had been all thrown together very quickly as the mining industry in Tannapol changed from gold, silver, and precious stones to a much larger industrial export market for offworld. It was also here that the Peace Troopers' presence became more pronounced. A few of them had eyed Tam and Filo suspiciously in the commercial wards, seeing them right off as not belonging, but as long as they didn't approach any of the towers, no one would do anything further. But in Greytown, it was a different matter. Here, the output from the mines was refined and processed for shipment to the Port. Beggars and suspicious persons could have some sort of nefarious purpose. And if that happened, the Peace Troopers might not get paid. And that certainly couldn't be allowed to happen.

"We should stay clear," Tam cautioned his friend, pulling on the sleeve of his *djellaba* to steer him in another direction. "It will be safer this way."

"Right," said Filo. "I'm sure that with Lord Squat coming down, everyone's feeling a bit anxious. Anxious troopers like to stomp on things to take the edge off. Better than drinking, not that that stops them."

"Look," said Tam, "if Akka'haman is here, he probably already landed by the time you heard about it. He might have even come down overnight. So there's nothing to see—"

"Let's try over there!" Filo darted to a nearby railing, one that offered an expansive view of several Greytown structures, including a wide-open circular pit with pipes and belts. A steady stream of lifter trucks was pulling up alongside and dumping quantities of dirt down into the hole, with streams of greenish foam jetting out from the pipes and filling the pit after each load. The acidic stench hit Tam right away, along with the harsh metallic taste in the air. He realized it was a remediation tank, where they separated super-heavy elements from the low-grade ore. Here, the refinement and purification process would begin before being shaped into high-density bars for easy transport to orbit.

"It's been a long time since I've been this close to one of the refineries," said Tam. "You couldn't pay me enough to breathe this air every day."

"You think this is bad?" said Filo. "Imagine what it's like for those poor *gandu* who have to dig this stuff out of the mines."

"It's too unpleasant to think about," Tam said solemnly, folding his arms. "They should be importing machines to do this work. Or at least give us the means to build them ourselves. Surely the Kalif's Lyr friends can afford to do that easily enough."

Filo shrugged. "Machines brought through the jumpknot cost money. Jiballan labor is cheap. Jiballan lives are even cheaper.

Surely you know what a bargain the Squats are getting by being here."

It was then that Tam saw something near the remediation pit, an assembly of some sort. He reached for his belt and pulled out his battered old opticals, a piece of offworld tech he'd had, well, since he'd fought for the Regime. Was it more than twenty years already, he thought? The opticals were probably long-obsolete to the mercenaries who'd once used them. However, the microstatic field that acted as a focusing element was still active, as was the battery inside. He held the goggle-shaped mask to his eyes and focused on the crowd. Right away, he recognized the polished blue and white armor and full-face helmets of Azrali soldiers. They were mercenaries whose homeworld sold the services of their well-trained warriors to offworld clients like the Lyr, instead of having to field and maintain an independent army.

"Is he there? Is it him?" said Filo. "Let me have a look."

Reluctantly, Tam handed the opticals over to Filo. His friend jumped with excitement as he focused his attention on the crowd. "He's there! Both of them! Oh, forgive me, but if only the Angels could make for a terrible accident, right here and now. Our lives would be so much happier!"

Tam took the opticals back and saw for himself. He focused the microlens and saw two figures more clearly. The one to the left was unmistakable. Pasty white, balding, and heavier than the last time Tam had seen him in public. His Excellency, the Grand Kalif of the Eternal City of Tannapol, and all of Jiballah, Mott Pendrago himself.

Seeing him again, it stung Tam even more that this pitiful declining portrait of decadence had led the forces that had toppled the People's Regime and now enriched himself at the expense of all the gullible fools who'd once seen him as a liberator.

But next to Pendrago was a creature Tam found even more appalling yet unbelievably still human. Akka'haman, the Lord of Cartel Bountiful of Lyr, the Kalif's sponsor and ally. Tam felt the bitter taste in his mouth, not from the processing pit. The Lyric tycoon had been one of many that had financed and invested in the Regime's overthrow, replacing it with a government more favorable to their commercial interests and profits.

When the *jinn* had remade the worlds that comprised the Diaspora, none started as fit for Earth-based life. Only ancient Earth itself, according to legend, could naturally sustain humankind and the flora and fauna they needed. But some worlds supposedly were more of a challenge to the *jinn* than others, so they found it necessary to change the humans settled there to meet the transformed planets part way. Such changes had been minimal for the first settlers of Jiballah, and they were reasonably close to their ancestors from ancient Earth. But humans needed more modification to survive on worlds like Lyr, the result being a breed of human with thick, leathery skin, small eyes, heavy jowls, and dense rolls of fat that grew heavier as they aged. And the Lyr supposedly lived much longer than any Jiballan. Akka'haman must have been quite old for one of his kind. He looked so heavy he was dependent on some kind of lifter platform to move without assistance, with an entourage of younger Lyr and machines to spray his skin to keep it moist in Jiballah's arid climate.

It must have been serious business, Tam thought, to bring someone so powerful all this way from home into such an uncomfortable and alien environment just to check in on his investments.

If only he'd kept more of his old gear from the war, thought Tam, weapons like his trusted flame pistol. And if only he'd thought to bring it here for this moment.

"Hey!" Tam heard a voice from behind him. "*Ki mada?*" He recognized the slurred attempt at a more formal Tuka speech. He turned to see a trio of Peace Troopers in green battered and mostly ill-fitting armor plates. The leader wore a helmet and visor, and the other two had makeshift cloth caps with the Peace Trooper emblems stitched on. The sloppiness of the three contrasted the crisp professionalism of the Azrali mercenaries below. The Peace Troopers weren't actual soldiers or law enforcement. They were thugs handed whatever uniform was available. Their job was to stamp down on whatever they were told to, as long as they didn't steal from what they collected and could remember to show up for their shift without being drunk or stoned. That looked too stringent a requirement for these three.

"You causing trouble, *gandu*?" the leader went on, pointing at Filo and Tam. "Think you can beg for coins in front of the Kalif and his guests? Embarrass our city like that?"

"You're the only embarrassment here, *kahlet*!" Filo swore at them, and Tam gasped in alarm. Calling Peace Troopers a bunch of dirty bastards was a singularly bad idea. But then Filo didn't end up in his station in life by making the smartest of life choices.

And it was clear just how wrong a choice that was when the other two troopers pulled out their batons, with their leader soon joining in. Peace Troopers didn't carry guns as part of their regular duties, mainly because no one trusted them to shoot straight, and it would cost more than it was worth to train them properly. But the batons didn't need much skill to use, especially with their pain settings switched on. And from the crackle of ionized air at the tips of their batons, the troopers looked eager to test the high-end features of their weapons.

"Uh, we're not looking for any trouble, *sahi*," Tam spoke in his most respectful tone, despite wanting to scream *kahlet* at these degenerates just as loudly as Filo.

"Oh, you found it, *nikwad*," said the lead trooper with menace, his activated baton raised above his head.

"Sirs," said Filo very quickly. "For your time and efforts in our city." He reached for the pouch tied at his waist and unfurled it quickly. At least thirty coins shimmered in the air before scattering across the pavement. The troopers' were distracted as they dove to gather up the fallen coins, stumbling over each other in the process, quickly forgetting Filo and Tam.

Tam and Filo ran as fast as their legs could take them out of Greytown, not daring to look back at any pursuit.

"Relax," said Filo between breaths. "We're nothing. They forgot about us ten minutes after they met us. I doubt they were sober enough to remember how we look. We were just sport to them."

"Filo," said Tam, "that must have been your entire take for the morning."

"Oh, it's nothing," said Filo. "It was my fault for bringing you here. And besides, there was less than twenty *bira* in the entire pouch. Those fools can share a cup of *kafa* with that." He then patted proudly at his chest. "I keep the valuable stuff here."

Tam shook his head and laughed. "I should have known. Always a contingency with you, isn't there?"

"You've always underestimated me, my friend, just because I'm a beggar," said Filo, as the blocky gray buildings gave way to the more polished streets of the commercial wards. "Oh, I take no offense. You think I don't know how many thieves and pickpockets there are in the Bazaar? I *should* know. I'm one of them!"

\#

After crossing from Greytown, Tam flagged down a pedicab and parted ways with Filo. He wasn't happy about paying for a ride, but it was a reality of life in Tannapol. The cabmen were an influential cadre in the city, and they dealt harshly with any driver that dared to undercut their prices.

Sallah's House was an unassuming place from the outside by design. It looked like any other rundown three-story apartment building in the Shallows. Only at night would the red lights and the sleazy posters of half-naked women and ladyboys be unfurled. A few of the other Red Ward brothels and fleshpits had invested in offworld holographic projectors to advertise their talent. Big Sallah's contribution to the art of management was to make sex work look as mundane and cheap as possible.

Tam stumbled through the vestibule and down the stairs to the bar and storeroom. He'd hope to enter unnoticed, but luck wasn't on his side. Sallah was seated at one of the barstools, going over one of her ledgers. The Twins were standing at her side as if waiting for his arrival.

"You're late," Big Sallah snapped. "Ten minutes. You were supposed to unload the stock from the back room. You expect it to sit there waiting for you?"

"I'm sorry—"

"Shut up, *nikwad*! I'm sick and tired of it. Everyone has excuses, but no one gives a shit about doing their fucking jobs and making me some damn money!"

Tam thought it best to keep silent and ride out her tirade. Big Sallah was, for lack of any better words, he thought, delightfully profane. He had known a few women taller than Sallah, but none occupied a room as fully as she did. Her bulk and thick tattooed arms were all muscle, bone, and pure spite. And most likely a good portion of synthetic biotech from offworld. Sallah had spent a small fortune at some point in her life and, painfully, so he heard, transformed herself into what she was now. It certainly made her memorable. And strong. He'd seen more than one occasion where Big Sallah had broken a customer or employee's wrist or a jaw with one hand just because she felt like it.

"I swear—" she went on, no longer talking to Tam or anyone in general. "I'm losing money every night because of pitiful, lazy drunks behind the bar, thieves working the front room, and a stable of the dumbest whores that ever popped out an angel's shithole onto this forsaken city."

"Hey—" Tam spoke up while walking towards her, his tone sounding weak even to himself.

He never got any closer. The Twins quickly stepped into his path, and both shook their heads, warning Tam to step no closer. Whatever Big Sallah had taken to remake herself, the Twins must have tripled the dosage. Rami and Zuro, the two bodyguards, known around the Red Ward simply as The Twins, weren't actually twins or biologically related. But their enormous, neckless, over-muscled shapes and similar facial tattoos had given them interchangeability, to the point where no one bothered to call them by name, and they had stopped answering to them.

Tam then heard light footsteps from the stairs leading to one of the connecting apartment blocks. A significant part of Big Sallah's income came from being the landlady of apartments rented out to the staff. He turned to see who was approaching and saw her, long flowing black hair, her face light with blush. She wore a silky red *kameez* that ended just above her knees, with a matching sash, a diaphanous caftan, and dark red slippers. His breath stopped for just a moment, as she was the one ray of light and beauty in this dark and unfeeling pit within a wicked city.

"*Sala*, Tam," she greeted him with a warm smile.

"*Wa-sala*, Jaya," he returned her greeting with the respectful reply a civilized man gave to a lady.

"Well, aren't you two adorable," Big Sallah said with cruel laughter. She then turned to Jaya. "Didn't expect you to be up this early. You had quite the busy night." She arched an eyebrow at Tam, her words a subtle jab to remind him who Jaya was and for who she earned her money.

"You got your piece," said Jaya, her earlier gentleness now taken on a veneer of ice. "And I had to send my daughter off to classes."

Sallah spat on the ground and dismissed her words. "At least you didn't bring the damned brat here. I warned you about that."

Jaya's eyes narrowed coldly at Sallah. "The last thing I want is for Soolein to see more of this place than she has to."

Big Sallah perked up and strode over to her. Tam's eyes widened in alarm, seeing just how tiny and frail Jaya looked against Sallah's towering mass of muscle and rage. He feared that Sallah would strike Jaya or break her jaw. Instead, she stood over her menacingly, running her fingers threateningly along her jawline. "Quite a mouth on you, pretty little thing. Think you're a queen in the tower, don't you, just because you're the top earner. Just you wait, pretty mouth. Wait until someone younger comes along, someone hungrier, someone—" Sallah then smiled even more cruelly and glanced over Jaya's body, with particular attention to her hips. "Someone less . . . *used.* Then maybe something will happen to that pretty mouth. Something nasty. Then how's the little sprout supposed to eat because Mama can't work? Then she'll have to be the one who brings in the money." She then stepped back and paced around Jaya, who had gone silent but concealed a tightly controlled rage within.

"Maybe I'll be hiring," Sallah continued, "or maybe Chikki down the street. Your girl's about the right age for some of his customers. You think about that next time you want to open your pretty little mouth." Sallah then dismissed Jaya and turned her attention towards Tam. "*You.* Get the crates unloaded and the bar stocked. I'm expecting a caravan of PTs in tonight."

"Something going on?" Tam asked, trying to put the earlier conversation out of his mind.

"The rumor on the street is that one of the Squats is in town. They're all acting crazy around the Port."

Tam considered chiming in that the rumor was fact, but thought it best not to admit anything. "I . . . I heard something similar," he said.

"Anyway," Sallah shrugged, "if it's true, it means the Kalif will make the PTs do some real work for a change. So by tonight, they'll all want to get drunk." She then glared at Jaya. "And they'll want to be happy."

Jaya nodded at her cooly. "They'll be happy. And you'll get your piece of it, don't you worry."

Big Sallah snorted and waved them both off dismissively. The

Twins moved in tandem, reinforcing Sallah's mandate that both Jaya and Tam were dismissed.

Tam sighed, slumped his shoulders, and made his way to the back room, where the morning deliveries from the distilleries would be waiting for him. He noticed that Jaya was following him. What a pair the two must have looked like together, he wondered. She, so flowing and elegant, far too graceful and ethereal for a place like Big Sallah's. And then there was him, at least ten years older, with an unshaved rounded face and too much weight around his middle, his clothes ill-fitting and rumpled, looking just like as Jaya often jokingly described him, an unmade bed.

"You didn't have to get in the middle of that," said Tam as he bent over to pick up the nearest crate. "She's in a mood. She could have hurt you."

"She wouldn't dare," said Jaya. "I'm no good to her with a wrecked face, and she knows it."

"One day, she won't care or think that far ahead," he said. "She'll just act."

"I know," said Jaya, sighing at first, then gesturing her arms in anger. "It's just that I get so . . . so frustrated. With her. With everything. This business."

"I know," said Tam. "You shouldn't be living like this, you and Soolein—"

"I mean the way she runs everything! She's so cheap, so tawdry. It makes her small and the rest of us even smaller. There's just so much we could be doing with this place, the location, the opportunities. There's money coming into Tannapol, real money. And she can't grasp any of it. She can't see past being the tiny little queen of her sleazy little kingdom, and you and I and the others all have to be her subjects! It's infuriating! How do I make a better life for Soolein, give her a real future, with that pumped-up freak holding us all back?"

"You could leave this place," said Tam. "You could make another life—"

"Where?" she laughed. "She'd send the Twins after me if I ever walked out. And every other place in the Red Ward is just as bad. Chikki's is worse. Far worse."

"You could—" Tam put the crate down and tried to give her some kind of reassurance. But what could he ever offer her?

"I could *what*, Tam?" she said, as frustrated as she was resigned. "Seriously? On Jiballah? In this reality? What opportunities are there *really* for a woman who doesn't have family in the Estates? With a child with no father? With *my* life?" She sighed again, but her expression then softened as she came closer to him, and like always, instinctively straightened the collar of his *kurta*. "Oh, Tam. You're still the dreamer, aren't you?"

He cast his eyes downward, not sure of how much of a dreamer he was anymore. "Things can still change," he said softly. It was the only answer he could give her.

Jaya looked at him thoughtfully as she stepped back. "What was Sallah was saying before, about the Squats?"

Tam looked about nervously, making sure no one else was within earshot. "I saw him. Akka'haman is here on Jiballah. He was making the rounds with Pendrago in the refineries in Greytown."

She looked at him with alarm. "What were you doing there? If they spotted you—" She then eyed him warily. "Were you there with that beggar friend of yours? I hope you didn't bring him around. You know what Sallah said she'd do if she ever saw him mooching—"

"Relax," Tam chuckled. "Filo has better survival instincts than that." He then looked at her more seriously. "But I meant what I said. Something's going on if Akka'haman himself has to come here. It could mean something's about to change."

"Yeah," said Jaya. "Maybe something worse." Her eyes then widened. "That reminds me of what I wanted to ask you. When I heard you come in, I mean, I didn't expect to get into it with Sallah—"

"What is it?"

"It's Soolein," she said, fluttering her eyes as she spoke. "If the PTs are coming out tonight, then the other girls and I are going to need a lot of prep time, and I won't be able to get away for lunch. Would you mind, terribly mind, if you picked her up at Primary and got her lunch before bringing her back to the apartment? I don't—" She then glanced away from him. "You understand I don't want her around. Especially today, and after what Sallah said about Chikki—"

"Of course, I don't mind," said Tam. "I'd be happy to. It's just, since when have you ever needed, well, you know, prep time? The doors don't open until after the Dusk Prayer."

"I know," she said. "It's just that, well, Merrek will probably be coming tonight—"

"Oh," said Tam. "I see."

"Don't be like that," said Jaya. "Merrek, he...he's not so bad. He's—"

"Please," said Tam, looking back to the crate and picking it up, "please don't say he's *nice*. He's a Peace Trooper. They don't get to wear the green helmets by being nice."

"I was going to say he's not . . . terrible," she said. "He's a squad leader. He might go a lot higher. That's someone good to have as a friend. I might need one in the right place one day. You never know."

He had already started unpacking the bottles when he finally turned to her. "You could do so much better than 'not terrible.'"

"Oh, Tam," she answered with a girlish giggle and gave him an affectionate peck on the cheek. "Always looking out for Little Soo and me. So I can count on you to pick her up?"

He looked at her sadly, his eyes telling her everything she wanted to know. Of course, he would, he thought. She could always count on him.

#

It was with all the boundless energy and optimism of a five-year-old that young Soolein pulled on Tam's sleeve and dragged him through the Royal Bazaar. He might have been the adult, but she was the one in charge.

"*Rafi* Tam!" she called out, bestowing upon him the title of an honorary uncle.

"Easy, easy, Little Soo," Tam said with laughter. "I'm an old man. I can't move as fast as you."

He promised Jaya that he would provide Little Soo a healthy lunch before bringing her home. But it seemed like the only thing the child was interested in were the stalls of candied yams, dates, and sweets.

"Why don't I take you and get you some falafel or roasted vegetables?"

Soolein shook her head. "Uh uh. I want candy, *Rafi* Tam."

"This isn't what your mother would want," said Tam.

Little Soo gave him a crafty smile, one so very much like her mother. "I know," she said. "We just won't tell her."

Tam smiled and shook his head. There's nothing more innocent, he thought, more fascinating, than watching a child believing that they had just invented, entirely on their own, the concept of lying.

He felt some sense of pride, picking her up from school. The primary center where she took her morning lessons was one of the few remaining legacies from the People's Regime—a school for girls, for the poor. It had been a proud achievement, one of many started during those beautiful early years of the Regime.

Soolein was a pretty little girl, with dark hair and dark eyes like her mother's. And Tam expected she'd grow to become just as beautiful as her mother. He only hoped she would come to adulthood in much happier times and in much better circumstances.

They heard a loud boom and glanced over in the direction where many other people were looking. It was one Tam had heard many times before.

"I want to see!" Soo exclaimed, pulling him along.

"I'm coming as quickly as I can," said Tam, never letting go of her hand. He hurried along to see what it was that had gotten the child so excited and looked ahead and saw a familiar sight. Breaking through the rows of low buildings ahead was a column of steam and smoke rising into the air — another shuttle launch.

"Is that going into Space, *Rafi* Tam?" the child asked. He heard the emphasis in her voice. Space to her was a magical faraway place, populated by spirits, sorcerers, and *jinn*, and not by people just as strange and diverse as the ones in the Royal Bazaar.

"Yes, little one," said Tam. "It's probably from the mines. Ships are waiting up there to collect the cargo."

She then turned to him, beaming at him like he was her hero. "Have you been to Space, *Rafi* Tam?"

He laughed at her innocence. "No, dear. No one I know has. No one from our world, anyway. It costs way too much."

"What about the Kalif?" she asked. "He's got more money than anyone! Can he go to Space?"

Tam laughed again. "Well, he doesn't count, sweetie. He actually comes from Space."

"He *does*?" She looked rapt with fascination. Obviously, this was a subject in school her teachers did well to avoid.

"Oh yes," Tam said with a smile. "The Kalif wasn't born on Jiballah. He comes from a world in the Diaspora very far from here. After the war, the Squa—I mean, the Lyr, they made him our Kalif."

"Oh," Soolein shrugged her shoulders. Talk of war and politics were of no interest to a child. They held no magic for her. "One day, I want to go to Space. Do you think they'll let me, *Rafi* Tam? Even if I'm a girl?"

Tam looked at her with dismay, kneeling to look her in the eyes. "Why, that shouldn't matter at all, dear. Anyone should go if they want to, boy or girl, rich or poor. Maybe when you're all grown up, it will be different. Maybe we'll build our own spaceships, and we can go into space without help from the Lyr."

Soolein smiled proudly, hearing exactly the words she wanted to hear. "I'm gonna visit every world in the Diaspora! I wanna see Lyr and Aris and everything!"

Tam chuckled at her innocent conviction. "Well, it may be a while before we can build ships that can travel through the jump-knots. I hope you get to see it one day."

But that did not deter the child. "I'm even gonna go to Earth! And maybe you and Mama can come with me."

He shook his head gently and put his hand on her shoulder to steady her. "I think that's a bit too much make-believe, Soo. None of the jumpknots lead to Earth. None that still work, anyway."

"How come?"

Tam shrugged his shoulders. "No one knows. Not even the Society Worlds. Probably the *jinn* that still live there don't want us to visit."

Soolein then leaned in, her face looking more serious, as serious as a five-year-old could get, and whispered to him. "We're not supposed to call them that."

"I'm sorry?"

"Teacher says they're really called the Tran, the Transeedee—," she tried to speak as she struggled with the words.

"The Transcendants," he corrected her, repeating the term he'd heard the offworlders use so often. Machines built on Ancient Earth, ones that became smarter and more powerful than their creators. Whether they were humanity's companions or enslavers was a truth lost to history. What was known was that one day, over two millennia ago, they simply disappeared, leaving humanity scattered across more than a hundred worlds to rebuild and eventually reconnect.

"That's right," said the child. "Teacher says if we call them *jinn*, then offworlders will hear and think we're all stupid. 'Cause *jinn* are just made-up stuff to scare little kids."

"Right," said Tam, with mock seriousness. "You're quite right. I'll try to do better next time."

They smiled at each other, enjoying the moment. And for a

while, Tam imagined, just for a little bit, if he would ever be more than just the kindly *rafi* who would pick her up from school, tell her stories while Jaya was working, or sneak her candy so that she would know there was someone else in this city besides her mother who thought kindly of her.

But looking past her, between the crowds moving about the market's stalls, he saw three people standing, watching, and waiting. One of the group, a bearded male in a very fashionable green embroidered *gallabeya* with a red turban, stood at the lead. It took Tam a minute to look past the prosperous clothes, but he quickly recognized the man.

"Hakam?" Tam exclaimed, standing up but still holding Soolein's hand to keep her close. "Is that you?"

"Tam Ergun!" the man exclaimed, his arms extended and smiling broadly. "It's been what, nine years, at least? You'd think even in the city that old friends would see each other more than we have."

The two men came closer and embraced as friends. Soolein had let go of Tam's hand but hid behind the leg of his trousers, fearful of the new faces approaching. Tam looked over Hakam's shoulder to see the other two figures and realized both were women. Each was dressed in more neutral and conservative full-length *gallabeya*s and matching shawls covering their hair, contrasting the brighter colors and vibrant patterns worn by Hakam. Tam didn't know the woman on the left, but he soon recognized the face of the other.

"Oh my, Yarra," said Tam, as he stepped away from Hakam and nodded his head. "It's been so long."

"Yes, it has, Tam," said the woman. She was roughly his age, but her gray eyes and the lines on her face made her seem so much older. Life and circumstances seemed to have added to her years.

"I heard you are a widow now," he said. "I'm so very sorry."

Yarra nodded her head solemnly. "Thank you. Toma was a good man." She then gestured to the woman next to her, younger with a more rounded face. "You haven't met my cousin, Birri, have you? She would have been far too young to be with us in the old days." She turned to the younger woman. "Birri, this is Cadre Captain Tam Ergun of the People's Regime militia."

"*Nama*, Captain Ergun," the younger woman greeted him with the formal address in Tuka.

Tam blushed at the mention of his old rank. "That was a long time ago, Yarra."

"A long time for all of us," said Hakam.

Soolein tugged on Tam's trouser leg to get his attention. "*Rafi* Tam, are you *really* a captain? Do you have your own spaceship?"

The adults all laughed as Tam kneeled to face her. "I wasn't that kind of captain, sweetie. And it was a very different time." Tam then looked up at the adults gathered. "This is Soolein, the daughter of my very good friend."

"Well, aren't you just delightful," said Yarra.

"Mama says not to talk to strangers," said the girl.

"Well, what if I brought you a gift?" said Yarra, gently. "Some candied yams on a stick? Now we're not strangers anymore."

"That's right," said Birri. "Now we're all friends." The light in Soolein's eyes showed she agreed with the two women wholeheartedly.

"Tam, old friend," Hakam said. "There are urgent matters we need to discuss. Let the ladies watch over the child while we talk."

Tam stood up and shuffled uncomfortably. "Hakam, perhaps

if we met for *kafa* another time? I promised Little Soo's mother I'd get her lunch and bring her home. She's my responsibility."

"Tam, you know Yarra. And Birri is wonderful with children. They'll be right over there," he said, pointing at a bench near one of the food stalls. "You'll be able to watch them the whole time. I swear on the lives of my children that your little friend will be safe. But you and I must talk. *Now*."

Against his better judgment, Tam allowed Hakam to lead him off to the side of the Bazaar, but still close enough for him to see Little Soo and the two women together and appear quite happy together. He turned to face his old comrade. "So, Hakam, you seem to be doing well. You still have the shop in Jeweltown?"

"By the blessings of the Twelve Angels, I do well enough. There's much competition, but I've found a good market. My stones have become quite popular on Lyr lately, even with the export fees." Hakam's face then turned serious. "But that's not what I wanted to discuss. You know what's been happening in the city, don't you? Akka'haman himself is paying a visit."

Tam rolled his eyes. "It seems like that's the only thing people are talking about today."

Hakam nodded. "They tried to downplay it, but there's no way to keep that a secret, not in Tannapol. And did you think to ask why the big man himself has come all this way? To a place so distant and uncomfortable to his kind?"

"He has his investments," said Tam with a shrug. "I imagine he likes to be kept informed."

"Oh, he could have sent underlings for that if all he wanted were reports and numbers. It's something else entirely." Hakan then looked at Tam even more seriously. "Something is happening out in the Diaspora, something political. I don't know what exactly, but it's something that has the full attention of the Lords of Lyr. Akka'haman has come personally to demand from Pendrago an increase in the output of our mines. At least double, maybe triple."

Tam looked at him incredulously. "Triple the output? How? Are they bringing in machines from offworld?"

Hakam shook his head. "Hardly. Machines may be productive, but they bring their own set of problems. They'll put a lot of miners out of work, and the ones they keep will need to be trained and educated in how to use them. Unemployed laborers and educated managers is a combination that doesn't suit the plans of our Kalif or his Squat masters."

"So, how do they plan to meet the new quota?"

Hakam sighed as he went on. "Increasing the labor force. The plan is to expand the penalties for debt bondage. Fall too far behind in your debts, and your sentence is commuted to forced labor in the mines."

Tam's eyes widened in alarm. "You can't be *serious*! How does Pendrago think he can get away with that?"

Hakam laughed, but not with any trace of amusement. "He's doing it because he *can* get away with it. Or he thinks he can. Because the people just accept it the same way they've accepted *everything* these past twenty years!"

"And how do you know all this?" said Tam.

"Because there are some of us—" Hakam said before considering his words carefully. "Some of us make it a point to know. Just like I know you saw Akka'haman's visit with the Kalif in Greytown this morning."

Tam perked up upon hearing his old friend's words. "How did

you know that?"

Hakam looked at him squarely. "You remember Dimon, back from the cadres?"

"Dimon? Yes, of course, I remember him. It's been nearly as long as it's been since I last saw Yarra, but I remember him."

"Then it's fortunate that Dimon remembered you too. Because that's what saved the life of you and your friend this morning."

Tam blinked in surprise. "Dimon was there? He saw us?"

"He almost had to shoot those three troopers who stumbled across you. In a way, you did us a huge favor. You kept Dimon from doing something impulsive that would have ruined everything we planned. All of Greytown could have been locked down."

"Hakam," Tam said, leaning in closer and looking around nervously, fearing who might be listening in. "What are you talking about? You sound like this was something from the old days, when the Regime first—"

"Exactly," said Hakam with a smile. "Tam, we have an opportunity we may never get again. Akka'haman completes his visit and heads back to his ship in two days. And when that happens, we may never get a chance at him or Pendrago together, not for years." The man leaned in closer, speaking softly. "We're going to take them both out, Tam. The Squat and his puppet. Dead."

Tam said nothing, unsure of what he could say. The enormity of what he was hearing was like nothing he'd heard in nearly thirty years, not since the rise of the Regime.

#

After years of contact with off-world cultures, it became apparent to many, including a young Tam Ergun, that a better life was possible for the people of Jiballah. After a succession crisis between two royal cousins for control of the Satrapy, the movement that became the People's Regime took to the streets, forced the remaining Satraps into hiding, and declared themselves the new governing authority of Tannapol.

It had been heady days for those first two years when anything seemed possible. It wasn't just men fighting for a better future, but women fighting alongside them. The Regime built schools and hospitals for women and the poor. Separating the Church clergy from the governing process was enacted as law. *Every man a Satrap, every woman a Queen, and every child an Angel.* That was the Regime's slogan. But for the Regime Council, it wasn't enough. The real promise was in what they had witnessed in cultures like the Society Worlds, where money and inequality no longer existed. They welcomed the Society Worlds delegation with hopes for an agreement of protection, and technology to allow a complete transformation of their society.

They didn't get the answers they wanted.

The Societan delegates congratulated the new government and wished them well. But they could offer little more than that. For one, they had no army with which to protect Jiballah. What's more, rapid transformation to a new culture, they insisted, would be a disaster for their world. There were too many entrenched institutions on Jiballah, they said, too much history and culture, that the task of creating a society of abundance without scarcity would take at least a generation, maybe two. It had taken their homeworld of Aris centuries to become the heart of the Society Worlds. They urged patience and time and to do the best they could with what they had.

That was the beginning of the end for the Regime. Disappointment led to disagreements and then to factions. The unity and clarity of the early years were gone. Also gone was the love and goodwill of the city's people, who thought, for a brief moment, they might all live like kings and want for nothing.

And loyal partisans like Tam looked on with disbelief, wondering how everyone had become so stupid and shortsighted.

While the Regime dithered and disagreed and accomplished nothing, the ousted Satraps had taken refuge outside the city, each gathering supporters to reclaim what was theirs. And when the fighting started and the city streets were overrun with blood, while men like Tam fought and killed and watched comrades die for their revolution, the Lords of Lyr watched from space and saw their opportunity. With their army of mercenaries and the latest in military tech, they swooped down and put an end to the fighting. They quickly eliminated the Regime Council and any remaining Satraps, and resurrected the ancient title of Kalif. The Lyr Cartels and their new puppet ruler declared that peace had now arrived. And for a time, the people cheered the Lyr and the Kalif as their liberators, while surviving partisans like Tam went back to make whatever life they could under the new imposed peace.

That was over twenty years ago. Historians called it the Proxy War. Tam called it the Great Betrayal.

#

Tam snapped out of his reverie as he let Hakam's words sink in.

"You disapprove?" asked Hakam.

"I—" Tam looked squarely at Hakam. "Look, nobody would be happier than me to see Lord Squat and Pendrago gone forever. But—this plan—do you really think you can assassinate a Cartel Lord and the Lyr are just going to *allow* it to happen?"

"That's why it has to be *both* of them," said Hakam. "We have to cause chaos on the ground. Create an opening to declare a new Regime. We were the legitimate government of this city once, and we have every right to declare ourselves the successors once this . . . occupation is ousted. The people will see that and rise to support us."

Tam waved his arms frantically. "Rise? Look around you. These people are *beaten*. They didn't support the Regime the first time around. What makes you think they'll do it for a Second Regime?"

Hakam grabbed Tam by the shoulders and looked at him intently. "When they see that their oppressors have fallen, they'll stand with us. They're not beaten, Tam. They're afraid. Just like they were the last time."

"Yes," said Tam. "Afraid of the Lyr. And of Pendrago and his thugs."

"Not just that, Tam," said Hakam. "They were afraid of *us*, of all the changes we were bringing. That was the mistake we made the first time. We promised too much and expected the offworlders to deliver it for us. We won't make that same mistake again. We Jiballans have to solve our problems, at our own pace, with the tools and resources we have at hand. Otherwise, we're still slaves, whether it's to the Lyr or the Society."

Tam was still in a daze from everything he was hearing. He then eyed Hakam with suspicion. "This movement of yours, this Second Regime, how long has it been going on? And why is it you're only now just reaching out to me?"

Hakam sighed and looked at Tam awkwardly. "You know that I owe you, Tam. You saved my life all those years ago, so the last thing I'd ever do is judge you. But still—" He could see the distaste in his face, hear it in his voice. "That *place* where you work in the Red Ward. We just didn't think you still had anything to offer."

"I see," said Tam, folding his arms and eyeing him narrowly, "and tell me, old friend, this new Regime Council, are they all prosperous merchants from Jeweltown? As long as we're not judging each other."

"I've offended you," Hakam looked at him, shoulders dropped and sorrow creeping into his voice. "I'm sorry. That's the last thing I wanted to do. It's just...many of the old partisans fell on hard times since the Regime collapsed. Dimon was practically living on the street when I found him. But he still has a sharp eye and something to give for the cause."

"And what is it that *I* can give now?" asked Tam, not entirely sure of himself and still a bit stung because he hated to admit his old friend's judgment rang true.

"What happened this morning could have been a disaster," said Hakam. "We knew Akka'haman would have bodyguards with him close by. But he came with more people than we anticipated. Plus, our dear Kalif is trying to whip the PTs into acting like a *real* army for the duration of the tour. They don't have to be any good, but they're *everywhere*. It just takes one in the wrong place to spot one of our people—"

"One?" said Tam. "You mean, there's more than just Dimon?"

"Tam, we're leaving nothing to chance. We've got at least half a dozen snipers, explosive experts to cover their escape, holocam operators—"

"Holocams?"

"Oh yes," said Hakam. "Holocams from offworld, editing equipment, everything. We want this documented for everyone to see. Most people may not have sets in their homes, but they'll be able to watch somewhere. Let the people see that their oppressors are mortal and vulnerable after all."

It all sounded so reasonable the way Hakam said it to him, Tam found himself being drawn deeper into the telling. "So, what does this have to do with me?" he asked.

Hakam sighed as he continued. "Where you work, that... *brothel*. A lot of troopers like to go there. For the drinks and the women. We figure if someone's had a little too much, they might let something slip. Something, anything, that could be useful, so that we can plan around it."

"Hakam," Tam said, shaking his head. "That's a real long shot. Even if someone knows something and shows up tonight, they're not just going to offer it up."

"We're *desperate*, Tam," he said. "That's all we have. That, or we take our chances in the morning—"

"I can't promise anything," Tam sighed. "But we get some regulars. Most of the troopers usually show up around ten."

"That—" Hakam said with a smile, "that sounds very promising. Just keep your eyes and ears open. Find out what you can. Ten, you say? Fine. I'll have someone come by around midnight to make contact with you."

"Whoever you send," said Tam, "make sure they look like they fit in. Not like—" he gestured at Hakam's embroidered robes. "Like they belong."

"I'll make sure of it," said Hakam with a chuckle. They both then glanced over to see Yarra and Birri in the distance, playing games of magic with Little Soo.

"The child," said Hakam, "you're doing this for her, aren't

you?" Tam said nothing in response and just watched her laugh.

"Her mother, your very good friend," Hakam continued, "she works there, doesn't she?"

Tam nodded sadly.

"That's unfortunate," said Hakam, shaking his head. "A horrible shame. My youngest is about her age. Imagine having to grow up around all *that*."

Tam quickly glared at him. "Jaya keeps her away from that. As much as she can."

"Of course, she does. It's easier now the child's young. She doesn't understand. But she'll get older. She'll see it all soon enough. Understand it all. And may the Angels watch over her, she might end up a part of it."

"No," said Tam silently, barely noticing that Hakam had walked away. "I won't let that happen."

#

Big Sallah's was at capacity that night, as if all of Tannapol, the Red Ward in particular, could sense something had changed or was about to change, even if not everyone knew what that meant. Tam certainly knew, and that knowledge both excited and terrified him.

It was past ten, and Tam was behind the bar, as usual, pouring his drinks, all while keeping a watchful eye for anything of interest. Residents of the Estates dressed in fine robes mixed among the shabbier denizens of the Shallows and the Red Ward, all the varied economic classes united in their vices. Sallah kept the barroom dark and lit with old-fashioned oil lanterns, both to save on power and to hide the dinginess of the decor. The one modern indulgence was an array of holo-screens along the back wall, all running live feeds from the Battle Pits. The few customers not drinking, inhaling, or fondling the staff were fixating on the blood and gore projected from the screens in faded flickering pastels. Bets were being placed on the new boy, Karrou, to defeat all challengers. Sallah was at her table, the Twins by her side, counting the money and taking in the action. Tam wondered, should the Kalif get his way with the planned changes to the debt laws, how many residents of Tannapol would end up slaughtered in the Pits if they couldn't work the mines?

It had been a quarter to ten when the first of the Peace Troopers arrived, proudly strutting in their freshly polished armor plating and helmets. And leading the first squad was that fool, Merrek.

The first time Tam saw Merrek visit Big Sallah's as a grunt, before his promotion, he could tell he was a man uniquely suited as a Trooper, having that perfect combination of cruelty, greed, and stupidity. He was a bulky man, paler in complexion than most Tannapol residents. He'd been born with a lazy eye, pockmarked skin, and was prone to give out beatings to anyone who dared to stare at him or comment on his face. Another quality that made Merrek so well suited to service in the Kalif's Peace Troops. He, more than most, had something to prove.

As much as Tam wanted to monitor the room for something useful to report back to Hakam, his eyes would keep drifting back to Merrek. More specifically, to Jaya hanging on Merrek's arm and stroking his chestplate, laughing at his weak attempts at being witty and charming.

Jaya was painted heavily and dressed in a tight and clinging red gown slit open along both sides to reveal her bare thighs. She wore matching gloves, a translucent pink veil across her face and neck, and adorned with an elaborate display of jewelry that was obvious to anyone was fake. Perhaps, thought Tam, that was one reason Hakam thought so little of Big Sallah's establishment, him being a professional in the jewel trade. Of course, that wasn't the only reason.

Thinking of Hakam forced Tam to focus his mind, that he had a mission and couldn't let Jaya or his emotions distract him from whatever was needed from him tonight.

"Hey, Tam!" Merrek banged his glass on the bar. "You hearing me, you old fat fuck? More honeywine!"

"Of course, *sarjen*," said Tam, in his most subservient and flattering tone.

"And I mean the good stuff! Not that watered-down shit! And one for the lovely Miss Jaya. This is an important day, you know."

"Absolutely, *sarjen*," said Tam. "Nothing but the best for the Kalif's men." Tam tried not to smile or share a conspiratorial wink with Jaya. *All* of Sallah's drinks were watered down, and Jaya never drank real alcohol when she worked, preferring to keep her wits sharp. As weak as the drinks were, Merrek had already consumed enough to make him too intoxicated to tell the difference.

"That's right," said Merrek, barely listening to Tam as he focused on Jaya's face. "Your man's a big man in the Kalif's troops. And he's gonna get even bigger."

"I bet you already are, naughty boy," she giggled, and her hands started to wander lower. Tam pushed the drinks in their direction and quickly looked away.

"Damn right," he laughed. "But I'm talking about power, sweet thing. Power! Big, shiny, Angel-size shit is coming down the chute."

And with that, Tam turned his attention back to the bar.

"You know the Squats are here," Merrek went on. "Big Fat Lord

Squat himself is checking on things."

"Really?" said Jaya, fluttering her eyes and moving her gloved hands around his forearm. "The Lyr are visiting? That's so exciting!"

Tam tried not to roll his eyes. Leave it to a fool like Merrek to think he could impress a woman with news that everyone in Tannapol already knew by mid-morning.

"You know what it means, right?" Merrek said, unable to resist the opportunity to boast. "More money for the Kalif. And that means more for the troops."

"More money to spend?" Jaya leaned in, breathing heavily. Tam wished he'd thought to recruit Jaya himself, as she was far more the natural spy than he'd ever be, even if her agenda was entirely focused on how much money she could get out of Merrek's coin pouch.

"And more toys." Merrek grinned wickedly. "It's already started, sweet thing. Look at what they gave me today."

Tam was ready to dismiss anything Merrek thought he'd be receiving from the Lyr, until the flash of light at the corner of his eye got his attention. He turned to see that Merrek had slipped a gauntlet onto his right arm, something previously clipped to his belt. Merrek waved his left palm over the back of the right wrist, and the gauntlet projected a holographic field, a city grid with several dozen markers, all at a higher resolution than Sallah's cheap screens in the back.

"Offworld tech," Merrek said proudly. "Pretty, isn't it?" Merrek then noticed that Tam seemed far more interested in the gear than Jaya, but he reveled in the attention nonetheless. "Know what those are?" he said to Tam. "Troop positions. The circles are *my* people. Mine! I'm gonna have forty troopers reporting to me tomorrow while Lord Fattie Slug Face comes to count his money." He then turned back to Jaya. "Forty! See what a big deal your man is!"

"Forty troopers," said Jaya. "That's a *really* big deal."

"Damn right, sweet thing," he replied, his lazy eye drooping more as the honeywine hit him.

"Most impressive, *sarjen*," said Tam, careful not to irritate him while he seemed intent on Jaya's approval. "And that tech is fascinating—all those markers. I wonder, what are those small squares on the grid? And the diamond shapes?"

Merrek chuckled, unable to resist more bragging. "The diamonds are the Kalif and the Squat party. They'll be coming down from the Citadel, past the Gold Tower, along the Boulevard of Stones into Greytown. The squares are the fucking mercs, those Azrali freaks."

"Azrali," said Tam, staring intently at the holofield floating over Merrek's wrist. "There must be at least a dozen of them in formation. What a sight they must be—"

"Bunch of damn freaks," said Merrek, snatching his wrist away and disabling the projection field. "They ain't natural, not a damn one of them." He then turned back to Jaya. "You know they ain't really human, not like us. They don't have mothers. They grow 'em in tanks. That's why they always wear that armor, so they don't have to look at each other's faces, that's why. Azrali and the Squats. All of 'em, a bunch of freaks." He then laughed at a joke in his own mind and turned back to Tam. "Of course, that don't mean their money ain't no good."

"Yes," said Tam, forcing himself to join in the laughter. "Thank the Angels for offworlders and their money."

"Yeah," Merrek laughed, a bit too much. "Or none of us would get paid, right?" He then turned back to Jaya. "Ain't that right, sweet thing?"

"Of course, you're right," said Jaya, leaning into him. "You're always right."

Tam tuned out the rest of their conversation, trying to conceal his excitement. It was more than he had expected. He'd seen precisely where the troopers would be, along with Akka'haman's entourage and bodyguards. It was everything that Hakam could possibly need.

Another hour passed as the bar slowly turned over more customers. New faces came in as the staff was leading others into the back rooms for the main indulgences of the night. Jaya and Merrek were nowhere to be seen.

"Good evening, *sahi*," he heard a voice stirring him from his introspection. It was being addressed as '*sahi*' that got his attention more than anything. He was used to being called by name or some choice insult to remind him of his status. Respect wasn't something he encountered much in Big Sallah's House.

Tam looked up to see a woman, but not one of the staff. She was short, with a pleasant round face. She had short hair and wore a gold headband and a black gown with a low-cut neckline. Not the sort of thing a proper woman wore in the daytime in Tannapol, at least outside of the Red Ward.

But there was something about her eyes, her voice—

"Wait, I—" It then hit him. "*Birri?*" His voice lowered to a whisper as he said her name.

"I'm glad that you remembered, Captain. Hakam told me I

would fit right in."

Tam leaned in and whispered at her. "Don't call me that here. People might be listening."

"Of course," she said. Tam shook his head. It never occurred to him, especially given how conservatively she'd been dressed earlier in the day, just how young she was. Or that she could walk into a place like this as if it simply didn't matter.

"Order a drink," said Tam.

"Excuse me?" she asked.

"My boss and her thugs," he said. "They'll notice if we're talking and you're not ordering anything." He quickly poured her a glass of honeywine. "Hakam sent *you*?"

"Is there something wrong with me, Cap . . . I mean, Tam?"

Tam leaned in as he passed her the honeywine. "Our customers are usually men. We get some women, some even come alone. But that draws attention. I thought that was something Hakam wouldn't want."

"Women get underestimated in Tannapol," she said. "In a place like this, they'll look at the woman, and they don't care to listen to what she has to say."

"Still—" Tam said, still shaking his head in disbelief. "Couldn't Hakam have come himself? This is no place for, well, you know."

Birri laughed. "Hakam coming down to the Red Ward. What a thought! He's far too pious a man for that. He'd be mortified that someone might recognize him and assume the worst."

Tam looked past the young woman, only to see Jaya laughing with Merrek. They had moved off to a private alcove. She followed her standard approach with rougher customers like the squad leader, by plying him with enough liquor and inhalants to make him more passive and less dangerous, all before taking him to one of the upstairs rooms to conduct business.

"Is that her?"

Tam's attention turned back to Birri. "Excuse me?"

"The woman with the squaddie you can't seem to stop staring at," she said with a broad smirk. "That's Soo's mother?"

Tam sighed. "Yes, that's her."

"I can see why you're so protective of her," said Birri, grinning with the same appreciation he had seen among so many men. "She's quite . . . lovely."

"The Peace Trooper," said Tam. "You said you needed information. He has it." He went on to explain to her about Merrek and the offworld tech in his gauntlet, about the locations of the troops and the Azrali mercenaries, and when their enemies would be making their inspection.

"Cap. . . I mean, Tam," Birri exclaimed. "That's fantastic! It's exactly what we need. Did he show you anything else? Are the Azralis laying down any shield emitters or drone sensors? What about heavy weapon support?"

Tam shrugged. "He didn't say anything about that. He just mentioned the foot patrols and where the offworlders would be."

Birri shook her head. "We need more. The fool probably has access to more than he realizes. We need the gauntlet."

Tam looked around nervously and anxiously poured another drink. "Wait just a second there. Merrek's not just going to give it to us. He's not *that* drunk." He quickly handed Birri the filled glass to maintain the pretense of another bartender and patron conversation. "And if he reports in tomorrow morning without part of his uniform and a possible security breach, won't that put everyone on alert?"

Birri leaned in, her eyes practically gleaming. "We don't need to keep the gauntlet. If we can get our hands on it for just a minute or two, we might be able to pull the information we need."

Tam looked at her in surprise. "You can do that?"

The young woman playfully cocked her head. "We've got a few tools. Offworld tech. From the Society Worlds. It's not their best stuff, but then I don't think the Lyr gave us their best tech either. A few minutes might be all we need."

"But how do we get—?"

"Ask your friend," said Birri. "She looks more than ready to get that *sootra* out of uniform already."

Tam looked at her with total horror. "I can't ask her to—" He then glanced over his shoulder again, watching Jaya playfully laugh and tease the Peace Trooper. An angry brute he'd once personally seen stomp a man's head in, and here he was now, like molding clay in her palms.

"She can't be a part of this," he said, as much to himself as to Birri.

"All Jiballans will have to be a part of this," she said, "in one form or another." She then looked around cautiously and leaned up to the bar, gesturing to the coin purse on her belt. "I have money, if that's what it will take to get her with us. Hakam can cover anything we might—"

"I'll handle it," Tam said to her icily.

"Understood," she replied, chastened. She placed a few coins on the bar, enough to cover her drink. "I'll get the word out. Be in the alley around the corner in twenty minutes, the one with the red banner—"

"I know it," said Tam.

"Of course. With or without the gauntlet. Whatever you can do. We'll only need it for a few minutes. You can put it back when we're done. I'm sure you know, it's for the revolution."

"And a revolution is not a tea party," Tam finished the mantra, a favorite of the People's Regime, its exact origins dating somewhere back to Old Earth, the context long since forgotten.

He barely noticed Birri slip away as he arranged a flight of glasses on a wide platter. When he was certain no one was watching, he slipped an orange tablet into one of the glasses and made his way to the booth where Jaya entertained Merrek.

"More to celebrate your good fortune, *sarjen*," said Tam. "If I may borrow the lovely Miss Jaya for but a minute—"

Merrek might have been halfway drunk, but he was still sober enough not to be entirely agreeable. "Now just a damn—"

"This is my treat, *sarjen*," said Tam quickly, handing him the drink where he'd deposited the tablet. "To your continued rise and recognition, *sahi*."

The promise of free drink and Tam's submissiveness was enough to put Merrek at ease, and he reached for the glass and quickly downed a few quick gulps. Tam smiled broadly and led a very puzzled Jaya away. "I promise, *sarjen*. Just a minute. Then she will be yours again."

"Tam!" Jaya hissed at him once he pulled her back to the bar. "What are you doing? You know how he—"

"Do you trust me?"

"What?" Jaya blinked in surprise. "What kind of a—"

"Do you trust me?" Tam persisted. "After everything I have done, for you, for Soolein. Do you *trust* me?"

"I—" She shook her head. "I trust your intentions, Tam. I always have. Maybe not always your choices."

"Then trust me now. Please. And don't ask questions."

"But Merrek will—"

"I put a *sangello* tablet in his drink. He's probably already giddy as a schoolgirl."

"What?" Jaya did her best not to raise her voice, not that it could be overheard over the cheers in the room once the latest results from the Battle Pits were announced. "Do you know what the boss lady will do if she—"

"She won't know. You need to take Merrek upstairs *now*. He'll be easier to handle."

"Tam—"

"And once you're in the room with him, once he's out of his armor, you need to—" Tam sighed before continuing. "I mean, *I* need you to get that gauntlet, the one he showed us, to put it out in the hallway. I'll only need it for a short while. When I'm done, I'll knock on the door, and you'll know it's safe to get the gauntlet. Merrek will never know it's gone." He silenced her before she could say anything. "You said that you trust me. Please trust me now and don't ask any questions about it. You're safer if you don't know."

"Tam," she said breathlessly after what felt like an eternity. "I'll do it. I trust you."

He let out a sigh that felt to him like a mixture of relief, joy, and just plain exhaustion. "Thank you. You'll never know how much this means. I'm so sorry to involve you."

"I understand," she said, casting her eyes down and then glancing back to the table, where Merrek was already smiling and laughing at some joke playing in his head. "But please," she added, "don't tell me if you're part of something stupid."

Tam sighed and shrugged his shoulders. "By tomorrow, we'll know if I am or not."

#

It was another early morning at Breha's for Tam, sipping his honeywine, watching the Royal Bazaar come to life and the first stalls setting up, and hearing the call for the Dawn Prayer.

But everything, the energy of the city, felt different this morning. Part of it was his anxiety. It had been so close last night, so dangerous. But it all ended up coming together. It had to be the will of the Angels that assured their success.

It had pained Tam to ask, but Jaya came through for him. He'd waited a few minutes after Jaya had taken Merrek to the upstairs apartments, enough time to go on break. He'd gone upstairs, and sure enough, the gauntlet was in the hallway waiting for him. He'd managed to scoop the gauntlet up, wrap it in a towel, and make his way outside, all without Sallah or the Twins paying him any notice, and then deliver the gauntlet out to the alley where Birri and Yarra were waiting. He'd watched with fascination as their device, likely Societan tech from the way it changed its shape, extruded several probes into the gauntlet, and in less than four minutes, Yarra proudly announced that they had what they needed. Tam then delivered the gauntlet back outside the door where Jaya was entertaining. He softly knocked on the door and waited a minute and watched as she reached out and pulled the gauntlet back inside. Merrek had apparently slept through the entire experience and was none the wiser when he woke up and went on his way.

It would have killed him if Merrek had caught on and Jaya

ended up paying the price for it. But she and Tam had each done their part. Now it was up to the brave souls in Greytown to do the rest.

He stirred from his musings to notice, just like most mornings at Breha's, that Filo the Unshaven was approaching him. But it wasn't his regular genial sauntering. Instead, he was running toward Tam in great alarm.

"Oh, my friend!" Filo exclaimed. "Did you hear? It's everywhere. They tried to project it out on the public holos, but they keep shutting them down! I wasn't sure if you knew—"

"Hear what? What do you mean?" Tam tried to maintain his calm, showing no indication of any expectation. If all went well, Filo would tell him exactly what he imagined, or hoped, he would hear.

"In Greytown, not far from the very place we visited. Oh, my dear friend! Lord Squat himself. He's dead! Blasted into pieces. Oh, it was horrible. Not that I didn't wish such a fate on that creature, but even so, to see it—"

"Akka'haman is dead, you say?" said Tam nonchalantly.

"Oh yes, yes indeed," said Filo. "Less than twenty minutes ago. The terrorists *actually* recorded it all, made a hologram, and tried to send it out through the city projectors. The Kalif's people have been shutting it down every time—"

Tam jolted up in alarm. "Wait, you say the Kalif's men. The Kalif, wasn't he killed too? Is he still alive?"

"Regrettably, very much so," said Filo, "but I'll be making an extra prayer to all the Angels at dusk in hopes of rectifying that. The troopers are everywhere. They're starting to make arrests. Who can account for all this madness? I tell you—"

But Tam didn't let him finish. "Filo, do you know a shop in Jeweltown, run by a man named Hakam? He . . ."

"Oh yes," said Filo. "Most of the merchants there chase me away, but *Sahi* Hakam is a most pious and generous man. He gives tithes to the Church every—"

"We need to go there," said Tam. "Now!"

#

Tam paid for a pedicab to Jeweltown, even with the news of the assassination spreading through the city. Peace Troopers were out in force, marching in ragged formation and occasionally seen dragging beaten and battered prisoners behind them in restraints.

Naturally, the cabmen were all raising their rates as a result.

No sooner did he and Filo arrive in Jeweltown, with rows of crowded shops ranging from the elegant to the modest, that Tam paid the driver, and he and Filo dashed out. He saw one shop that fell between the two standards, neither elegant nor modest, the one owned and operated by Hakam. He urged Filo to stay out of sight of any authorities and wait for him.

He feared he'd arrive to see the shop burning or Hakam dragged out by the PTs, but nothing seemed out of the ordinary. There he could see Hakam, this time in a blue robe, but with no turban, exposing his smooth shaved head. And he was speaking with a customer as if today were just an ordinary day.

It was incredible. Even if Hakam hadn't heard the news, Tam thought the man would at least be expecting an announcement of the plan's success.

Seeing Tam at the window, Hakam looked alarmed and quickly wrapped up his business with the customer and sent him on his way. Nervously, he pulled Tam inside and rolled down the window shades.

"Tam? What are you doing here?"

"Hakam, it's all gone wrong!" Tam exclaimed. "I had to make sure you and your family were safe!"

"My children are at school, and my wife is with her mother. There's nothing for you to panic about."

"Nothing?" said Tam. "Akka'haman is dead, but the Kalif is still alive! I heard all about it. What happened? How did it all go wrong?"

"Tam, please be quiet! You're babbling like a maniac. You can't be talking about this out loud, or someone might hear. I've been seeing Peace Troopers strutting around for the last half hour, and we can't do *anything* to get their attention, do you understand?"

"Yes, but—" Tam breathed heavily, trying his best to make sense of it all. "What happens now? Does the Regime make an announcement, take credit? What about the people in Greytown? What happens to them? Or us?"

"Tam," Hakam sighed, motioning with his hands to urge calm. "There's no cause to worry. No one knows your name, no one except me, Yarra, and Birri. And the only other one who knows is Dimon. The women are both safe. But *we* won't be if you keep shouting and put us all at risk."

"Yes, but if they capture Dimon—"

"They won't. Dimon is dead."

Tam went silent and looked up at him. "How do you know that?"

Hakam said nothing, turning away. "You're safe, Tam. That's what matters. You should go home and forget about this. The less you know, the better. Whatever has happened, it's because of me, not you."

Tam's eyes widened with shock as everything all came together for him. "There was never going to be an announcement about a new Regime, was there?"

Hakam let the accusation hang in the air for just a few seconds of silence before turning to face Tam. "No," he said. "I'm sorry. It never existed."

"The plan didn't go wrong at all, did it?" said Tam, anger and accusation rising in his voice, "because the plan went *exactly* the way it was supposed to."

"Tam," said Hakam, "don't ask questions you don't want to know the answers to."

"How many?" said Tam, with tears welling up in his eyes. *"How many people did I just help kill today?"*

"It isn't like that—"

"What's it like then, eh, old friend?" Tam shouted at him. "That you sold out the ideals of the Regime, that you were the Kalif's man all along?"

"Be quiet!" Hakam desperately pulled Tam away from the window. "Don't you say that, Tam! Don't you *dare* say that out loud! I am *not* the Kalif's man! I never was. That was *never* what this was about. You start shouting things like that, and someone hears it, then we're both dead, do you hear me? Pendrago doesn't know my name. He can *never* know my name!"

"What are you saying? How can he . . .?" Tam tried to make sense of it all. "Why would he want to kill his benefactor? He'd have no reason—" He then looked up at Hakam. "He's not part of this at all, is he? He never was."

"No, he's not," said Hakam. "Those shots came too close to his head. Pendrago would never volunteer for that."

"There's someone else, isn't there?" Tam looked at him squarely. "Someone else out there who wants to pull Pendrago's leash, is that it? Who is it? Who's behind all this?"

Hakam sighed, his shoulders sagged, his eyes deflated. "Abba'aleh, Akka'haman's niece back home. It was her plan. It always was. Kill her uncle back home, and all suspicion falls on her. But if he dies out here, at the hands of Jiballan savages, well, now she has deniability."

"I can't believe it," said Tam. "You're working for a *Squat*?! How? How would they even know you?"

"I told you, my stones are very popular on Lyr. Abba'aleh is one of my most valued customers."

"But . . . *why*? What's the reason for it all?"

"The same reason the Lyr do anything, Tam," he replied with a shrug. "For money. That and power. You have no idea what they're like, really like, up close. They're vicious. Everything is a competition with them. And they live a long, long time, almost as long as the Societans. Akka'haman ruled over Cartel Bountiful for over forty years! And he could have gone on for another sixty or more before age finally slowed him down. Abba'aleh just couldn't wait that long to get what was hers."

"So, she approached you?"

Hakam stood a bit straighter, almost with a sense of pride now. "I'm the most influential person she knows in Tannapol, outside of Pendrago's circle. Her agents reached out to me about three months ago, told me what they had planned, and what they needed from me, and what I would receive for going along."

"And what exactly do you get, old friend?"

"About what you'd expect. Fortunes. And a lowering of the export tax for all my goods going to Lyr."

"Which you gladly accepted."

Hakam leaned forward, almost angry in his response. "You don't get it, do you, Tam? When someone like Abba'aleh makes a proposition to you like this, you go along. You don't have the option to say no or walk away."

"And Pendrago? I don't understand. Why kill her uncle and spare him?"

"Believe me, Tam, I wasn't happy about that part either." Hakam then started to pace anxiously, showing his frustration. "But her people made it *very* clear. They didn't want chaos in Tannapol or competing factions trying to seize power. They wanted to keep things *exactly* as they are, only with Abba'aleh and her people reaping the benefits. Right now, Pendrago is probably soiling his trousers, wondering what all this means or if he's going to lose his power. That's why he'll start cracking down hard for the next few days and why *you* need to keep quiet."

Tam was now standing like a statue, his tone low and even, the only way he could convey just how appalled he was by now. "Because Pendrago will be hunting for the guilty parties to please the Lyr, to make them happy, because he's worried they'll blame him, is that it?"

"Something like that," said Hakam. "He'll put on a good show to prove that he's hunting down the guilty. In a few days, an emissary from Lyr will arrive to inform Pendrago of the change in cartel leadership and that he gets to enjoy staying on as Kalif." Hakam then looked at Tam with greater intensity. "Eventually, he'll figure out what happened, why he's reporting to a new benefactor. And it won't matter to him one bit. As long as he keeps putting on a good show."

"Punishing the guilty," said Tam coldly. "Or at least getting the names of all the guilty parties he can find."

Hakam then laughed bitterly. "You still don't understand at all what's about to happen, do you? This has happened before with the Satraps. *Guilty* doesn't matter. *Names* don't matter. All that matters is having warm bodies to offer up. All for the show. And the public will be more than happy to supply more bodies if the PTs can't arrest enough on their own." He then looked at Tam nervously. "You understand now why Pendrago can never know about this or who I am. If he knew there was someone else in Tannapol with a connection with the new Lord of the Cartel, he'd panic at the thought she might replace him down the line."

Tam almost laughed out loud at the idea of it. "*You*? As Kalif? A jeweler born in the Shallows?"

Hakam's eyes narrowed at him coldly. "Pendrago was an offworlder, a mercenary, not even a full commander. Don't you think he'd be worried that the people might prefer someone who was actually born and raised in Tannapol?" He then snorted as he walked away. "I have no desire to be Kalif, believe me. I'd rather remain anonymous. I'm more than happy with what I'm getting out of this. It's enough." He then looked directly at Tam and folded his arms. "So now you know my secret."

"And you know mine," said Tam with a cold reply.

"Yes," said Hakam. "In the Diaspora, this is what they call mutual assurance. Now we have balance. Now there can be trust."

"Trust," Tam almost spat the word. It sounded like poison from the man's lips. "So nothing is going to change at all," he said, now with a sadder tone to his voice. "What you told me before, about the mines and the quotas—"

"Unfortunately, that part is completely true. I'm sorry."

"And the debt bondage penalties—"

"That will almost certainly still happen," Hakam said sadly. "They might delay it a month or two while Pendrago and Abba'aleh get used to the new arrangement, but the need for more mine labor, that's unavoidable. There's just too much money involved, especially while the new Lord is consolidating her position. She won't say no to that. And honestly, she cares about as little for the welfare of the people of Jiballah as her uncle did."

"Yeah," said Tam, "but you did pretty well for yourself, didn't you?"

"I deserve that," said Hakam. "I did what I had to, Tam, for my family, for me. It's just the way things are, the times we live in. I tried the best I could. I at least kept your name out of it. I owed you that much."

"A pity you couldn't have done the same for Dimon. And what about Yarra and Birri?"

"They're safe. I took care of them. They're family, after all."

"And what happens now?"

"Now," Hakam sighed, looking about his shop, at the jewels and ornaments in their glass displays. "My family and I move out of our apartment above the shop. We get a nice home in the Estates. My son goes to the university, and my daughters will be married off to husbands from fine families." He then looked at Tam, "and you go back to your life and find whatever happiness you can find."

Tam stood silent, letting the moment hang in the air before replying. "You said we have balance, Hakam. Trust. So tell me honestly, why did you *really* not let me go out there to Greytown or give up my name? Was it because you felt you still owed me?"

"No, old friend," Hakam said, eyes filled with sorrow. "Because I saw you with that little girl the other day, the one that you loved. Dimon and the others had *nothing* in their lives, only memories of a past no one else cared for anymore. You at least have something to live for."

Tam shook his head and laughed bitterly. "You know the one funny thing about all of this, Hakam? I think that in your mind, you *really* believe that you're the victim here, and by saving me, you're some kind of decent human being. But we both know that isn't true at all, is it?" Tam walked towards the door. "We managed to go nine years without seeing each other. I think we should stick to that arrangement. Our lives are not the same anymore."

"I think that would be for the best," said Hakam. "It's safer that way. *Ayluna hafess*, Tam. May the Twelve Angels protect you."

As soon as he was out the door, Tam spoke softly so no one else could hear. "And may the Angels have mercy on your soul, you fucking *kahlet* bastard."

#

Tam found Filo waiting for him around the corner, waving him on. "Come, let's get out of this neighborhood, old friend. I have bad feelings about this place. Everyone looks like they're ready to pop!"

"You're probably right," said Tam. "We're in for a rough couple of days. It might be a good idea for you to stay off the street, at least until things settle down."

"You are indeed a wise man, my friend. Wise indeed."

Tam had hoped to hail another pedicab, but none were forthcoming. It seemed clear that word of the assassination had spread throughout the city, as the Peace Troopers were now out on full display. While he and Filo made their way along the twisting passages of the city neighborhoods and left Jeweltown behind, he witnessed random people dragged out of their homes and shops, troopers gleefully beating and kicking whomever they could catch. Hakam's earlier words seemed painfully prophetic now, he thought. Guilt and innocence didn't matter. Old grudges, false reports, even blind panic and prejudices, all would be revealed in the days to come. Pendrago had let his troops off their leash, free to brutalize and terrorize whoever they wanted, all to maintain the illusion of control. But it was clear to Tam that the unfolding chaos had a calculated logic behind it, to lay a groundwork of fear and intimidation over the city until the meaning of Akka'haman's death was made clear. The Kalif was terrified, so his strategy was to make sure everyone in Tannapol was even more terrified than him.

And how many would suffer, Tam wondered, until Pendrago no longer felt afraid?

It took longer to get back to the Red Ward than Tam would have liked, but he and Filo had to skirt through multiple back alleys and passageways to avoid the patrols. Dressed as they were, they both would have stood out in any merchant wards or more respectable neighborhoods. And today was not a good day to draw attention.

"Oh my," said Filo, struggling to keep up with Tam, "this is the worst I've seen the city in a long, long time, not since the Regime fell. The streets stink of fear."

Tam said nothing, but he nodded in agreement, navigating his way through one of the stone-paved alleys, past the smell of uncollected garbage and fetid pools of water. They were closer to the Royal Bazaar, but that and any other open courtyards would be an excellent place to avoid right now, a more likely chance of crossing paths with any Peace Troopers looking to inflict damage for the fun of it.

He knew a pathway that would take him close to Big Sallah's, so there at least, he could take refuge inside. Whether or not Filo could find safety anywhere was another matter.

His heart stopped as he rounded the corner and saw the crowd milling around Big Sallah's, including what looked like more than twenty PTs and one of the new three-wheeled electric troop wagons parked in front. They smashed the windows and posted signs in front, and at least ten of the assembled troopers were leading a towering figure out of the building, entangled in stick binding as a restraint. It was Sallah herself, her expression one of abject humiliation. For all her years of pushing and fighting her way past obstacles, Tam could see on her face her realization that she had finally hit a barrier she could not punch her way past.

It seemed so hard for him to believe it. Last night, she seemed as solid and unshakable as the Great Plateau itself. Now she was, for lack of a better word, smaller. Just as broken as everyone else in Tannapol.

He looked past the gathered crowd at the wagon, and saw someone in the back seat, bound, bloodied, and beaten. It was one of the Twins. Tam couldn't tell if it was Rami or Zuro or where the other one was. Given the look of despair on the man's face, he suspected the state of the other twin could not have been a good one.

Could it be he was actually feeling pity for Big Sallah and the Twins? Or was it guilt, that he had played a very small part in what was certain to be a most unpleasant fate?

Tam came closer to the crowd and scanned it for familiar faces. But a voice he recognized called out to him first.

"*Rafi* Tam!" He recognized Little Soo's elevated voice from the crowd, and he turned to see her waving her arms at him. She'd have run over to him, but Jaya stood behind her and held her protectively in place. Tam made his way through the crowd where the mother and child were standing, overcoming any anxiety he felt regarding proximity to the Peace Troopers.

"Tam," exclaimed Jaya as she came closer to him, still keeping a firm grip on her daughter. "I was worried. I thought maybe one of the patrols—" She then carefully eyed the gathered troopers. "You heard what happened, right? In Greytown?"

"I heard," he replied, too hesitant to say the words '*assassination*' out loud for fear of the attention it might bring. "What happened here?"

But the expression of concern on Jaya's face changed to one of complete joy and elation. "Oh, Tam! It's wonderful! They're taking Sallah away. They tied her into the plot. She's *done*, Tam! *Gone!*"

Tam looked at her with confusion. "Tied her in—?" He then looked at her with alarm. "Jaya, what exactly are they saying?"

But Jaya smiled broadly and put one hand on Tam's arm to help steady him. "They got a call. They figured out someone learned about the troop positions. The plotters only could have got it from a squad leader. And Sallah would sell her own mother for fifty bira if she could."

Tam's eyes widened with alarm. "Jaya, if you're talking about, you know what, what if they tie it back to—"

"Oh, Tam," Jaya laughed, stroking his arm. "You don't have to worry. I took care of it. They have someone to blame now. And its not as if Sallah hasn't slipped *sangello* to a customer before to help them part with their money."

Tam looked in anguish as he saw one of the troopers emerge from the building in full gear. Even with the helmet on, he recognized the sallow skin and lazy left eye. Merrek smiled at Jaya, and she pursed her lips and gestured a kiss towards him. He wanted to come closer, but Soolein immediately hid behind her mother. Jaya silently motioned to Merrek that now was not a good time. At least Tam took comfort in knowing that Little Soo had the sense to recognize Merrek for what he was.

"Just like I told you," said Jaya. "One day, friendship with someone like Merrek would pay off."

So, Tam thought, this is what 'not terrible' looks like.

As the wagon with Sallah and the one Twin pulled away, Tam took a look at the building with the posters indicating confiscation by the city. "So we're out of work now?"

"It's just for a little while," said Jaya. "It's a formality, Merrek told me. The property will go to auction next week. But there's already a buyer lined up."

Tam didn't notice at first but then realized Jaya was still looking at him with delight. A new employer should have been a reason for even greater anxiety until he realized she had no reason to be worried at all.

"Wait—" he looked incredulously. "You already know who will—?" And then it hit him. "What you were saying the other morning. *You*?"

Jaya grinned ear to ear. "I didn't want to say anything until I had all my investors lined up. And I couldn't dare risk Big Sallah finding out. I had to wait until just the right moment came along to take her down. But after you asked me to help last night, I knew I had my moment. And after what went down in Greytown, it all fell into place. It couldn't have gone more perfect!"

"But . . . *how*?" Tam was incredulous, appalled, and even a little bit heartbroken, all rolled into one. "How long were you planning this?"

"Oh, at least two years," she said proudly. "It's like I've been telling you. The opportunity was there, right in front of Sallah. But she was just too blind and stupid. All these so-called respectable and pious types coming down to the Red Ward, all wanting to live dirty for just a night, but not too dirty. How many opportunities were we missing out on because we just weren't classy enough? All we had to do was meet them just halfway." She saw the confusion on Tam's face, and she went on to explain. "*Gambling!* A casino! Something with just enough class and respectability but just a little bit of adventure to lure them down into the Shallows. And Sallah just couldn't see it!"

"And you could?" said Tam. He had to contain himself not to storm off. "How could you even begin to afford this?"

"I told you," she smiled at him. Even in a housecoat, she made a sultry pose and gesture with her hips, standing with her little girl. "I have investors. Friends who want to see my idea succeed—"

"Friends like Merrek?"

"Not just him," she said, her tone now a bit sharper. "I've got some interest from Chikki—"

"Chikki?" Tam almost spat out the name. "You're doing business with that . . . that *maggot*?"

"Oh, Tam," she rolled her eyes. "He's not—"

"Please," he said, raising his hand dismissively. "Please don't tell me he's 'not terrible'."

Now her voice was a lot harsher, almost angry. "I was going to say, not that bright. He's thinking he's getting one over on me, that I'm just a dumb whore who'll be working for him inside of a year. He hasn't seen my business plan. Inside of two years, I'll be the one buying him out."

"But—" Tam's anger had dissipated, now replaced with sorrow and regret. "I thought you'd want to be away from this place. This life. The Red Ward. At least for Little Soo's sake, if not your own."

"No, Tam," she said. "I tried to tell you, but now it's you who isn't listening. It's Sallah I wanted to get away from. But leave the Red Ward? Where would I go? Waiting tables in some cafe, or cleaning homes in the Estates? This is my world, Tam. That's the reality of it. What matters now is whether I end up working for someone worse, or I take control and make the rules of this world work for *me*! Not some future promise delivered by offworlders, but here and now, something I can control. That's how someone like me makes a better life, for me and my little girl. That's how I get Soolein out of the Red Ward and into the Estates! My little girl's mama isn't going to be someone else's *whore*! Her mama is going to be a *boss*!"

Tam said nothing. There was nothing he could say. It was a painful realization that the woman he had hoped to save had never needed him to save her. All this time, she had a better grasp of the world they lived in than he ever did.

"You're upset with me," she said, her hand now back on his forearm.

"No," he said. "Not upset. Just a little sad, that's all."

"Oh," she said, now being playful once again. "I'll be fine. I always was. I wanted to be sure none of this touched you. But I'll always love you for caring about us." It stung him, just a little bit, the ways she used the word 'love.' He realized just how casual the word was to her, as casual as the word 'trust', but that too was the reality of the world she lived in. That they all lived in.

"And don't you worry," she said. "Once I've got the place locked down, there will be a place for you. I *need* you, Tam. I need someone I trust, someone I know will always be on my side, mine and Soolein's. There will always be a place for you."

"Of course," he said, trying to fake some kind of enthusiasm. He really couldn't, though.

"Oh, just you see," said Jaya. "This will be a quality establishment, with a real bar, music, entertainment. It'll be the kind of place you'd be proud to be seen in."

"I'm sure it will be," he said.

"Oh, Tam," she said, now stroking his arm. "Please be happy for me. Be happy for Little Soo. I couldn't see myself doing this without you."

He nodded, still with sorrow but now with a bit more acceptance. "I am happy for you, Jaya. Really. If this is your world, then I at least want you to be safe and doing well in it."

She practically giggled like a child, even though he knew she did it more for his benefit than her own need for approval. The fierce woman who called herself a boss, who had strategized and planned for this moment, that was the real Jaya, not the one stroking his arm and looking at him all wide-eyed. In a way, she was molding him just as easily as she did Merrek the other night.

#

Tam found Filo cowering in the nearest alleyway, looking about to make sure it was safe to come out.

"You're a braver man than I," said Filo. "Standing so close to the troopers amid all this madness. But as I've told you, you're also a far more respectable man than I am."

"I appreciate that," said Tam.

"The lovely Miss Jaya and her daughter," said Filo. "They are safe?"

"Oh, you don't have to worry about Jaya," he replied. "She'll come out of this just fine."

"As I expected," said Filo. "She is a survivor, that one."

"So I'm learning," said Tam. "Just so you know, it's not going to be safe on the streets for the next few days. You have somewhere to sleep?"

"I will . . . make arrangements," said Filo, "but it is ever so kind of you to be concerned for me—"

"Yes," said Tam with a resigned laugh. "You can sleep on the floor at my place, so you don't have to flatter me or beg. At least until things calm down. I can't promise much, though. It looks like I'll be out of work for a little while."

"Oh, I am indeed blessed by the Angels to have a friend like you, especially in this time of madness." The beggar then looked about the neighborhood and could hear the din of public announcements, of sirens in the distance. And of more green-helmeted troopers marching chaotically through the streets. "Change is in the air, not a good thing at all."

"Really?" said Tam as the two of them walked in the direction of his apartment. "And why is that? Why is it I keep hearing about everyone being so afraid to change things? Especially when things are so terrible the way they are?"

"Oh, my idealistic friend," said Filo. "Did you learn nothing from the final days of the Regime? People are terrified when things change. Because as bad as things get, they know it can always get worse."

Tam rolled his eyes. "I can't let myself believe that, Filo. Not if I want to get up in the morning."

"And that is why the lovely Miss Jaya and her delightful daughter are so fortunate to have you in their lives. I only hope they one day come to realize it before it is too late."

Tam then stopped for a minute and held out his arm to stop Filo. "Wait a second there, old friend. I have a question. And for the sake of our friendship, I'd like you to answer it honestly."

Filo would normally have given a flowery response but this time kept quiet in anticipation of the question.

"That morning, when you dragged me off to Greytown, what prompted you to do that? Or was it someone else's idea?"

Filo cast his head down and gave a sad, humiliated sigh. "Forgive me, my friend. A man, one I do not know, gave me fifty *bira* and said, come and see, Lord Squat himself is in the city, and wouldn't it be a wonderful thing to show it to your friend Tam at the cafe." Filo then looked up at him. "That is all I was told, I swear it. I did not think you would come to any harm. Have I done a terrible thing? Have I betrayed our friendship? Will you cast me out now?"

Tam chuckled softly. "No, Filo. You didn't betray me. And my offer still stands. I already ended one friendship today. I have no desire to end another."

"Aye," said Filo. "By the will of the Angels, or the *jinn*, or the Transcendants, whatever they choose to call themselves, I am blessed to know a gentleman of your quality, my friend. I pray only that the lovely Miss Jaya will see it as well one day."

As Tam and Filo walked down the alley to his apartment, it occurred to him that for all their differences, Filo, Jaya and Hakam were not all that different in one respect. Despite all they had all done and said, it somehow mattered to each of them that Tam thought well of them, that he was someone who would still think of them as good people. A merchant rising in wealth and power, an ambitious prostitute from the Red Ward who wanted better for her daughter, and a beggar who considered a twenty *bira* coin a great victory. Oh, he would never think of Jaya as treacherous as his former friend. And Filo could no more help being who he was any more Tam could help being who he was. But regardless of what they each deemed necessary, or the consequences of their choices, the acceptance and forgiveness of someone like Tam Ergun still mattered to them.

Of course, perhaps he was just inflating his importance once again, he thought wryly. But maybe what it also meant was that people all wanted to be the heroes of their epic fables. The truly wicked were the ones who stopped caring what others thought of them. And in corrupt times, Tam sighed, people wanting to be heroic was the best you could hope for them.

And Tam understood that that was how every great change or revolution began, with hope.

About the Authors

Caitlin Demaris McKenna is a science fiction writer and freelance editor. She currently lives, works and writes in Vancouver, British Columbia. When not writing, she enjoys reading, watching video game Let's Plays, and entomology. She grew up in the Minnesota woods, where on clear winter nights, she would look up at the stars and wonder.

Jennifer Graham was born and raised in Brooklyn NY, but has travelled to Barbados, the UK, Canada and throughout the East Coast. Her first published story, "Intelligence", appeared in the anthology *Beacons of Tomorrow*. Her story "Burden of Proof" appeared in *Nights of Blood 2* in 2009. Her stories have appeared in previous *Infinite Dimensions* anthologies. She also writes Sci-Fi Romance under the name Jacqueline Zest. Her sci-fi romance adventure novella "Star-filled Wishes", set in the *Future Jinn* universe, was published in 2011. *Rouge Desire* is the first full length novel of the Future Jinn scheduled for release soon. Previous jobs include: a chemist, a programmer, a data processor in a financial firm and an administrative assistant. More of her writing can be found at jennjettmedia.wordpress.com.

Mackenzie Reide graduated with an Honors Degree in Mechanical Engineering and a minor in Aerospace. While she was born and raised in Canada, she loves to travel and has worked at the German

Aerospace Center and the University of Stuttgart in Germany. When not staring into space, wishing she was traveling in Dr. Who's TARDIS, she writes mystery-adventure and science fiction with strong female characters for both kids and adults. Her novels include *The Mystery of Troll Creek*, *The Mask of the Troll* and *The Mine Caper*, and short stories in the anthologies *Altered States of the Union*, *Infinite Dimensions*, and *Brave New Girls*. You can find out more about Mackenzie at www.mackenziereide.com.

Paul Smith is UK born and bred, an energy healer with designs on releasing and teaching his own system, developed from years of practice and study. When he's not healing people and their pets energetically — he's a genuine wizard in training!

Paul has loved fantasy and science fiction since he was a child and hopes his writing will bring a touch of the real. He lives in a quiet part of the United Kingdom with his son, his partner of 26 years and has two step daughters, twin girls who have both blessed this earth with grandchildren.

Michelle A. Belgrave is a former Brooklynite who now lives with her family in Huntsville, Alabama. In the past she has worked as a programmer and web developer. She enjoys reading and writing about technology, science, science fiction and current events. Her sci-fi romance novel, *Princess and the Emperor*, was written under the name Mechelle Downes.

New York City native **Steven L. Rosenhaus** is a bit of a polymath: composer, arranger, conductor, lyricist, dramaturge; educator; occasional actor; and author of both non-fiction (*Writing*

Musical Theater with Allen Cohen, Palgrave; *The Concertgoer's Guide to the Symphony Orchestra*, The Music Gifts Company) and speculative fiction short stories. His first published fiction, "You Are Music" is featured in JennJett Media's anthology *Infinite Dimensions: Memory*. Another story, "The Nitty Gritty," is included in Peter David's anthology *The Fans Are Buried Tales* (Crazy 8 Press).

Michael Ben-Zvi has had a long-standing love of science fiction and fantasy adventure ever since his first time watching Star Wars as an impressionable youth. He has participated in several New York-based writing groups and critique sessions over the years, gradually honing his ability to put into words where his mind has always chosen to wander. Residing in Manhattan, but a refugee from suburban New Jersey, Michael is a graphic designer and desktop publisher with a history in the corporate world, and is now seeking to explore ever more strange new worlds.

In addition to his work with *Infinite Dimensions*, he is developing his own collection of speculative short stories and a series of novels set in the same Diaspora universe as his previous contributions to *Infinite Dimensions: Crossroads* and here in *Infinite Dimensions: Powershift*.

Also from Infinite Dimensions

Crossroads (2017)

Challenging times require difficult choices — not only in the here and now, but on other worlds, in times long past or futures yet to come. We present a collection of five tales of characters each facing their own personal crossroad, a critical choice that could change not only their own lives, but the future of their societies, in ways they can't begin to foresee.

Memory (2019)

In all its forms, memories shape our past, present and future. Memory exists in both minds and machines. If information stored is lost, it can be found; or that which exists can be taken away. Two people may share the same experience, but can remember it very differently. Whether saved for eternity or slowly eroded over time, memory remains an essential part of our lives.